lovely,
dark
and
deep

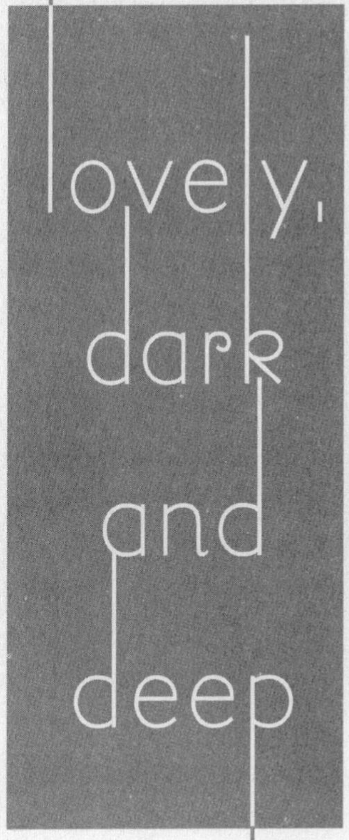

amy mcnamara

SIMON & SCHUSTER BFYR

new york
london
toronto
sydney
new delhi

SIMON & SCHUSTER BFYR
An imprint of Simon & Schuster Children's Publishing Division
1230 Avenue of the Americas, New York, New York 10020

For information about special discounts for bulk purchases, please contact Simon & Schuster Special Sales at 1-866-506-1949 or business@simonandschuster.com.
The Simon & Schuster Speakers Bureau can bring authors to your live event. For more information or to book an event, contact the Simon & Schuster Speakers Bureau at 1-866-248-3049 or visit our website at www.simonspeakers.com.
Also available in a SIMON & SCHUSTER BFYR hardcover edition
Book design by Lizzy Bromley
Cover photographs copyright © 2012 by Lissy Laricchia
The text for this book is set in Elegant Garamond.
Manufactured in the United States of America
First SIMON & SCHUSTER BFYR paperback edition November 2013
10 9 8 7 6 5 4 3 2 1
The Library of Congress has cataloged the hardcover edition as follows:
McNamara, Amy.
Lovely, dark and deep / Amy McNamara.
p. cm.
Summary: In the aftermath of a car accident that kills her boyfriend and throws her carefully planned future into complete upheaval, high school senior Wren retreats to the deep woods of Maine to live with the artist father she barely knows and meets a boy who threatens to pull her from her safe, hard-won exile.
ISBN 978-1-4424-3435-6 (hc)
[1. Depression, Mental—Fiction. 2. Grief—Fiction.] I. Title.
PZ7.M4787928686Lo 2012
[Fic]—dc23
2012008258
ISBN 978-1-4424-3437-0 (pbk)
ISBN 978-1-4424-3438-7 (eBook)

for

rynn

john wells' daughter

BE CAREFUL WHAT YOU WISH FOR.

I had things I didn't want, and then I lost them. One minute I was breaking up with my boyfriend, Patrick, the next I was the only one left standing. Empty-handed. A ghost of who I'd been. Broken in a way you can't see when you meet me.

My name is Mamie, but my dad calls me Wren. My parents never agreed on anything when they were married, so I answer to both names. I like having a spare. Especially now. Besides, it drives my mother nuts. She thinks my dad calls me Wren to bug her. She says she named me Mamie because it means "wished-for child" and she had to try so hard to have me. Like she conjured me out of sheer will. Which she probably did. That's the kind of person she is. But I looked it up, and it also means "bitter." Either way, Mamie died on the side of a road somewhere back in my old life, and I moved away. Now I'm Wren full time, in a house on the Edge of the Known World, upper East Coast, with my dad, who spends his days in his studio. Perfect for us both.

I came here because it's pine-dark and the ocean is wild. The kind of quiet-noise you need when there's too much going on in your head. Like the water and the woods are doing all the feeling, and I can hang out, quiet as a headstone, in a between place. A blank I can bear. I wake up in the morning, get into clothes and out on my bike before I can think about anything. It's a place that could swallow me if I need it to.

So that's what I'm doing, music on full blast, trying to think about nothing, crunching over brittle twigs and sticks in the woods along a road I never see anyone use, when a Jeep comes flying around a bend, right at me. Before I can think, I swerve off the road and into a huge tree. My front tire crumples when I hit. Dust and pine needles lift into a cloud as the car skids to a stop.

The driver door whips open and a guy gets out. A couple years older than me.

"Are you all right?"

He looks totally rattled, and maybe even a little annoyed, like I'm the one who messed up somehow.

I sit up, untangle myself from the bike, and wipe sticky needles from my palms. The fall knocked the wind out of me. Takes me a second before I can make air come in and out again normally. The front wheel of my bike is bent like an angry giant grabbed it and gave it a twist. For a second

I think it looks kind of beautiful. Like something my dad might like. Something that used to make me wish I had my camera. I stare at the ruined rim.

"Are you all right? Can you talk?"

He's looking at me wildly, like he thinks I might be really hurt or something.

I can breathe again, but I've kept quiet for so long, I'm out of practice—I can't think of a single thing to say.

He turns away and I hear the engine clunk off. Grabs his phone.

"Wait," I say, finding my voice. "I'm fine. See?" I stand. "I was just shocked."

He tosses his cell back onto the passenger seat and runs a shaking hand through his hair. After a deep breath, he says, "I didn't see you. There's never anyone along this road."

I'm trying to think if I've seen him around. The town's pretty small, but I haven't exactly been hanging out anywhere. And he doesn't look small-town. Charcoal-gray shirt; thick, dark hair falling into his eyes; long, straight nose. Something faraway inside me rings like a little wake-up bell in a long-abandoned cavern.

He's still kind of scanning me, a slightly frantic up-and-down, like he might spot something broken, like I'm a miracle for not being flattened into the ground.

"God. I could have killed you." His eyes go to the bent tire. "I wrecked your bike."

I can't find anything to say. When you've been quiet as long as I have, words leave you.

"I'm fine," I manage, again. "I had my music on loud. I

didn't hear your car." I reach up to my hair and pull some leaves and sticky needles out of it.

"Did you hit your head?"

"No, it's just tree stuff, in my hair." I blush.

He stares at me for a second. I look at the sky. Like maybe I could somehow slip out of this situation. Fly up and away.

"Are you John Wells' daughter?" He's starting to sound relieved. Runs another shaking hand through his hair. "I thought I heard you'd come up here."

I nod. God knows what he's heard. I'm sure I made the news last May. The *Telegraph* doesn't miss a chance to print stories on my dad. Their adopted famous son. Never mind that his work leaves them scratching their heads and laughing at what people will pay good money for and call "art."

I look at my hands. Both palms are torn up and pitch-sticky. I pick a small piece of rock out of one. The knee of my jeans is torn. Like I'm an eight-year-old and just wiped out on my bike in the park.

His eyes follow mine. "You're hurt." He winces. "Let me take you into town. Dr. Williams can check you out, clean you up."

"No, no. That's okay. I'm okay." I don't want to go anywhere, see anyone. Certainly not to the clinic. Or anywhere remotely like a hospital.

"I'm fine," I say more assertively. "Really, I'll just go home and wash up. It's no big deal."

"Let me give you a ride home, at least," he says, getting in the car, reaching across the front seat, and pushing open the passenger door.

I start to pick up my bike but my palms are a wreck. I

stop a second, wipe them a little on my thighs.

"Leave it," he says, watching me. "Please. You're bleeding. I'll come back for it later."

I lift the frame a little more, lean it against the tree. A bird is loud overhead. A hawk maybe, hunting. That strange raspy screeching sound.

I wasn't even close to the end of my ride. I need to be out, alone. But he's not going to let me walk home, that's obvious. I kick around in the needles to find my iPhone, buy myself another few seconds to get it together, calm down a little. I look at my bike one last time and walk around to the waiting car door.

A pair of metal crutches lean against the passenger seat. He moves them over a bit and I slide in. He watches me look at them.

"Break an ankle?" I ask. I always say the right thing.

His turn to blush. Shakes his head. "I'm sick." Looks away. "Buckle up."

I'm thrumming from adrenaline. Takes me a minute to get the buckle in the right place.

He backs the car into the woods a bit, whips a U-turn, heads for my dad's.

i won't start now

"I KNOW YOUR HOUSE," he says. "My father was the architect."

I keep my eyes on the trees whipping past my window. I can't look at him. Not without my heart doing a little flutter. And I don't want to feel anything for anyone, that's the whole point of coming to this godforsaken place. But he has this sure, quiet air to him. Apparently I still react to things like that. I wonder for a second what he meant about being sick. Then I push it away. I don't want to know.

We pull out of the woods and onto paved road. The pines are replaced by a sudden emptiness that feels like a deep breath. A crazy wide-open sky over the ocean. It's a coast road, a stunning route, the kind you could accidentally drive off because you're staring at the view.

When I was little I imagined I was an arrow above it, shot from the city, speeding and twirling up the coast, flying high and free. The few times I came up to visit my dad after he left, this part of the drive was the best. It meant I was close to running wild for a day or two. No rules.

It's definitely the right place for my dad. Freedom-wise. No distractions. I guess we were a distraction. When he's not traveling, showing his work, he's in his studio all day, every day. At least that's what I think he's doing. I don't know much about his life. I was little when he left, and I only really saw him when he was in the city for an opening or something. We would have awkward dinners. Mom, Dad, and me. Little fractured trinity.

My mom hates it up here. When I was ten, I wandered into the woods, away from one of his parties, and she stopped letting me come up after that. I'm kind of hazy on the details, but I guess another kid at the party and I sampled from a few forgotten wineglasses. Then we explored the cliffs and woods. After dark. An impromptu search party was involved, and that was the end of summers at my dad's. Probably she was trying to punish him or something. At the time I thought she was punishing me. Dad didn't push back too hard, so I stopped coming.

I think it kills her now that I want to be here. The cliffs scare her—she doesn't like heights. My dad's place sits on one. Overlooks the water. Behind the house the woods are thick to the road. It's a great place, if a little man-cave-ish. Very quiet, private, which is ironic because anytime anyone interviews my dad, they send a photographer to get shots of it.

Our driveway winds off the highway through fifty-foot red spruce and white pines. The house is a wide V shape—arms flung open to the ocean. Tucked in the trees behind the house is the giant outbuilding my dad uses for his studio. More like a galvanized steel barn with concrete floors, skylights, and a roll-away wall that makes a space in front for showing work to visitors.

As soon as we pull up, I throw open my door. My knee's stiff, and my palms sting.

"Wait," he says, touching my arm. "Are you sure you're all right? I don't want to just drop you off if you need someone to look at you."

"No. That's okay."

I want to get away from him, out of the car. Don't want to keep looking at his face.

"I should talk to your father, tell him what happened."

"My dad's working today. He hates being interrupted. He's got people from RISD up here."

"If you're sure . . ." he says.

"I'm fine. Really. I'll just go in and wash up. It's no big deal."

I'm shivering, out of nowhere, like I've caught a sudden chill, like I'm excited or terrified or both. He hears it in my voice. Gives me this look like he can see into me or something. His hand is warm on my arm. To my horror I think I might cry. I haven't cried since May, since the world flipped upside down. I'm not going to start now.

I pull my arm away. I have to get out of his car, into the house. The place on my arm where he touched me feels like it might keep its heat the rest of the day.

He's unconvinced. "Well, then here." He opens the glove box and pulls out a pen and a scrap of paper. Writes on it. "Take my number. Please. Call if you need anything."

"I'm fine," I say again, getting out of the car.

"And when you're ready, pick any bike in town, I'll buy it, or anywhere, buy it online, any bike you want. And I'll get your wrecked one . . . I should have today. I'm . . ." he glances at the crutches and looks pained.

"Oh, it's okay," I say fast. "Really. It's fine. I'm not worried about the bike. Thanks for the ride." I sound like such an idiot. I give the car door a little shove before he can say anything else.

I'm at my door and in the house in seconds. Lean against the entry wall a few minutes to try to control the shivering.

After I get the dirt out of my palms and knee, I look at the scrap of paper. No name. Just as well. I'm not going to think about him another second. That's something Mamie would have done, wandered around the rest of the day imagining things about this guy. Not me. Not now. Not anymore. My heart's shut tight, if I still have one. No complications. It's how I keep it together. I toss his number in the recycling.

And my dad isn't working in the studio. He's not even in town. Flew out the day before to meet with a new gallery in Berlin. Like I said, I moved up here for quiet.

the woods

MORNING, NIGHT, then morning, then night. Sunlight flashes its SOS on the water all afternoon, then slips down, lets dark roll in. It's reliable. I move through time because I have to. Watch the light. Wake up. Breathe. Eat some things. Take a sleeping pill, sleep, and wake again. It's all I can handle.

When Dad's gone, other than endless calls from my mother, I have little contact with anyone. Mary, one of Dad's grad students, pops in and out of the house during the day. I find her in the kitchen from time to time washing dishes, which is supposed to be my job, but Dad's a charmer. People do anything for him. She's started coming into the house before I wake up, and I find fresh coffee and usually fruit or some baked good waiting for me on the table. Dad probably asked her to keep an eye.

I'd skip Mom's calls if I didn't know that would make her jump right in her car and head up here. She wants me to get past what happened. Move on. Like we planned. Think of it as a "clean slate."

Clean slate. Empty plate. Whatever. My mother's a planner. She's a hospital administrator. Solo unit since my dad left, not one to show a lot of feeling, but I'm pretty sure he broke her heart. When he left, she washed her hands of the art world and their friends in it. It was like watching workers collapse a circus tent, Mom went back to work, and our house got very quiet. So junior year, when I mentioned I might want to go to art school instead of one of the schools on our list, she told me if I was still interested, I could *pursue art* in grad school. End of discussion. Any conflict between what I wanted and what she thought was best, she won, hands down. But if I hit her marks, toed the line, she pretty much left me alone. It worked for both of us. According to Meredith, I should be glad I have a mother who actually cares what I do. Her parents pay no attention to her or her brother but act like they care when it makes them look good. I hated it when she said that, made me feel bad for complaining, but she's right. I do have a mom who cares, a little controlling, but she cares. Even so, I was ready to get out of there. Move on to the next thing. It was a matter of weeks between me and freedom, starting fresh on my own. I didn't even care too much about the art-school debate, just as long as come September I was waking up somewhere new.

Got that wish.

But I missed my graduation. Didn't leave for Amherst. Meredith and I didn't go shopping for matching duvets and mini-fridges. We didn't map out the travel time between Vermont and Massachusetts. The plan changed.

I'm lying across my bed trying not to think about it when the phone rings. According to the clock, it's nearly five. The day's gone, and I haven't showered. It rings again. My mother. She calls and calls. She's the only one who still bothers. The phone's ringing and vibrating a little now, like it's learned the language of her constant need to check in, rattling noisily on the shelf where I dropped it the last time she called. Third time today. I never have anything new to say. She talks at me, saying this or that about one of my friends. People I no longer want to see. Mostly I listen to her voice, not the words, the music of it. Sometimes it's soothing.

Any more buzzing, and the thing's going to work its way right off the shelf.

I answer without looking at it.

"Yes?"

I don't even try not to sound annoyed.

"Mamie?"

His voice.

My heart picks up a few beats. I switch the phone to my other ear.

"Yes—well, no."

"Oh, sorry . . ." He sounds surprised.

"No, I mean, it is Mamie—was—I don't go by that name anymore, well, here, my dad calls me Wren." I talk too fast.

Sound like a first grader. *My dad calls me Wren*. Who says that?

"Wren?"

"Yeah, like the bird." Deep breath.

"Okay, Wren." He laughs. A nice sound.

My body tenses and I sit up. To clear my head. I'm not going to get interested in this guy.

"It's Cal Owen."

Cal Owen.

"With the car, the other day, in the woods?" He clears his throat. "I'm calling because I hadn't heard from you or your father, and when I try to reach him I don't get voice mail."

"Yeah," I say. My voice cracks a bit, scratchy from disuse. "He doesn't do voice mail. You either get one of his assistants or no one. No distractions."

"I felt like I should tell him what happened. Apologize—to you both."

Silence.

He pauses a second.

"I just wanted to see if you were all right. I thought I might hear from Lenore down at the bike shop by now. Or from your dad's lawyer, or something." Another laugh.

"I'm fine." I emphasize the word a bit, try to sound busy, or distracted, like I need to hang up and get back to whatever fascinating thing I might have been doing. "My bike took the hit worse than I did."

If he only knew. That little wreck in the woods was nothing, miniscule, a small stand-in for the kind of thing that can really happen. Does happen, all the time. The kind of thing I'm trying to forget. I look at my scabby palms.

"I'm fine," I say again in a clearer voice.

Long pause.

My heart's pounding so hard I can hear it. Worry for a second that maybe he can too. I should say something else, I just can't think of what. It occurs to me that I could just hang up.

"I asked around," he says finally, voice low, cautious. "I heard your dad's out of the country."

Aha.

"Yeah, so?"

"So, I thought maybe . . ."

I cut him off. "I'm an adult."

Excellent. Heat creeps up my cheeks.

"Of course," he says. "I don't mean to bother you, I just wanted to be sure you were all right, alone over there—if you needed anything."

"I don't." I try to sound crisp, my mother's daughter. Regain control.

"I couldn't stop thinking, what if you'd hit your head when you fell or something, and you—I just wanted to hear your voice."

Hear my voice? Did he just say that? My heart picks up, even faster. Defies me.

"It was just my hands, when I fell. And my knee. And they're fine now. Everything's all right." My throat catches.

Nothing's all right.

It's a joke to say that, ever, to anyone. Tears rise up inside me like a rebel army. A flood after a drought. I am not going to cry.

He hears everything. "You don't sound fine. I don't mean to pry, but you don't sound fine. And I know most of your dad's assistants left town when he did. This is a small place; people might leave you in peace, but they know everyone's business."

"I have to go," I say.

I hang up and kick the pillow away from me. Now I wish I had that damn bike. I'm lost in the center of my bedroom for a second. Can't figure out what I should do. One thing is clear, I can't stay inside another minute. I grab my phone, earbuds, and pull on some running clothes. My hands shake so badly I can hardly tie my shoes. I don't lock the door. I'm out of the house, across the main road and into the woods before I notice it's nearly dark.

no-person

I RUN UNTIL I CAN'T.

No music. Just the sound of my breath and the few tall weeds and low branches whipping lightly at me as I pass through. My skinned knee is bleeding again, sticking to the inside of my sweats. The little light left from the dropping sun is mostly hidden by the boughs overhead. I am a no-person in the woods. The last person in the world. I try to let out a loud shout. A triumphant "Ha!" But it comes out strangled and small. And suddenly it doesn't matter that the woods are huge around me. I can't get lost in them. Can't lose myself. I won't ever be free of what happened.

I sink inside. As low as ever. Lower. There is no escape.

It'll always be part of me. The car crunching and collapsing around us while we flipped and rolled. So loud, so fast, then so quiet, so long. The before and after. All of it. The stopped moments where time's an airless, endless slide show.

My throat aches, it's been so long since I've cried. I am not going to cry. Won't. Can't. I haven't, not once, not since Patrick and I started that last fight. A sob chokes up. Another on top of it. I bend over, press my palms hard against my thighs, and pant. The way I've pieced myself together since then feels like it's breaking apart, and I might not get it together again.

I turn around and run back toward the house. I feel like I might run off the edge of the world. Like I might need to. I trip a few times. Slip on the sweet-smelling wet leaf rot on the forest floor. Down on my torn knee, scraped hands. Snot runs down my face and tears streak hot against my temples. My eyes burn.

I run faster, harder. Like I can outpace the dark. When I fall, I get back up again almost between strides. The pain's good. Feels like a solution to something.

The trees thin near the house, the shore. It's working. I'll outrun it. This time. Leave the black feeling in the woods. Box myself up again.

I'm nearly at the front door when I notice his car. If I'd been paying attention, looking, I could have hidden, waited him out. I stop short. But he sees me. He's at the door, about to knock, leaning on crutches. I wipe my face, fast. The snot. Tears.

"Hi, I . . ." He stops, taking in the full picture. A worried look comes over his face.

"I was jogging." I try to sound casual, which considering how I look probably just makes me seem demented.

I shrug like everything's normal. He just looks at me.

"Sorry I hung up like that. I needed to get out for a run."

I wave my hand vaguely toward the sky, like it explains everything. "It was getting dark."

Try to breeze past him to my door.

He grabs me by the elbow. Firm.

"Wait a second," he says in a low, calm voice. "You're upset."

He's so close I can smell him. He smells good. Soap, maybe. Laundry detergent. His eyes, dark with concern. My stupid heart climbs in my chest again.

I try to toss my hair, look casual, like he's got it wrong.

"No, I'm fine."

He doesn't buy it. Shakes his head.

"I don't think you should be alone right now."

"So, come in a minute, then." I yank my arm free.

He follows me in.

"I need to clean up," I say, leaving him standing in the entry. I go back to my room. It's a pit. My clothes are all on the floor. Haven't kept up on laundry. I dig through a pile for a T-shirt, a hoodie, a pair of jeans. Give them a quick sniff. Nothing smells too bad. I go into the bathroom and face the mirror. Dirt streaks run down my cheeks from crying and my hair looks like I've been camping a few weeks.

Cold water on my face makes my eyes reappear, but my hair's hopeless. Whatever. It's not like I care. Maybe this will put him off. Make him leave me alone. I finger-comb it into a ponytail.

When I come back out, he's still standing by the front door, leaning against it, looking polite but concerned. God, how many times have I seen that look on people's faces in the last few months? I wonder if I scare him. The idea almost makes me laugh. Maybe he thinks I'm crazy. Maybe I am.

"Oh, sorry, I didn't mean to leave you standing there. Come in."

I motion to the living room. My dad has a lot of art, pieces he's collected over the years, stuff from friends, but other than that, the place looks like a man lives in it. Alone. Battered couch and an old red velvet overstuffed armchair. Stacks of books like outcrops on the floor. At least a month's worth of old newspapers. I step over a pile of them near the windows. Honestly, it's a relief after the careful elegance of my mother's town house. No cleaning crew here.

Cal crosses the living room on those crutches. Looks out the wall of windows to the Atlantic. Black night outside, but the house is dark and you can kind of see out onto the water, the waxing moon starting to mirror its slivered self on the sea.

"I forgot how great this little place is," he says. "I was a kid the last time I was in here." He walks back across the room, sits on the sagging couch, and lays the crutches near him on the floor.

"I loved it as soon as I saw it," I say. Look out the

window, anywhere but at him. Pretend I wasn't just staring. Wondering why he uses crutches when it looks like he walks just fine.

All the things the old me would have said drift and float around me, twinkly and insignificant as tinsel. She trails me, frivolous, unaware. She's busy thinking about what she can tell him about herself to seem interesting. And what she should hold back.

"I don't remember you here when your dad moved in," he says, probably hoping I'll say something, at least try to have a conversation. "He had a little party. Our family came. I remember running around the place with my brother."

"They split up—I was little. My dad left her—us—to come up here and work."

I try to seem casual. Sound normal. So he'll see I'm okay and leave. Forget what I looked like at the door. Not that I really even care what he thinks. I don't. Won't.

I click on a small lamp and our view of the water disappears into black. Now the window's a picture of us. I turn away from it. Sit on the wide arm of the chair next to the couch.

"Our house is basically an earlier design of this," he says, playing along, like he didn't just find me in the driveway looking crazy. "My father's work got simpler over the years. Every project a little better, a scaling back of the last."

Dead silence. That ghost girl's gone. I can't make small talk. I look around the room.

His eyes follow mine. Doesn't seem uncomfortable with the quiet—unlike most people. He takes in the pitched ceiling and the dinged-up bleached wide plank floor.

"And he let your dad have his say on a lot of the details in here, this has a wilder, more organic feel to it than most of his houses. They collaborated on this one, I think."

"Wild and organic," I say. "That's my dad. A force of nature." But he doesn't mess with how other people live, like my mother does. Never tries to make me do things or change who I am.

Cal keeps his eyes on me in this calm, still way that makes me shift on the chair, talk more than I mean to.

"Do you live with him? Your father?" I ask. It's a stupid question, he's obviously older than I am. There's no way he still lives with his parents.

One corner of his mouth lifts, makes me feel appraised and found to be young. "No. My dad's in Montreal. He's semiretired. Still does an occasional house."

"And your mom?"

"Dead."

I can't win. I shouldn't even try.

"Oh. I'm sorry," I say. "About your mother."

The words are clunky in my mouth. Inadequate.

He shrugs. "It was a long time ago."

I nod slowly. Try to seem less nervous and idiotic than I feel, like I'm not counting the seconds until I can go hide in my room.

"My dad remarried. They moved to Montreal. Sent us to boarding school. My little brother and me. The place up here's kind of a family house, for holidays and vacations."

We sit in silence. I'm getting good at that. His eyes are slate blue, the color of his shirt. He looks at me like he can see right into me. Like he might slip a hand in and unlock everything.

I have to look away.

My neck tightens, throat aches. Patrick looked at me like that when we first went out. I swallow, hard.

"I-I'm fine." I say for the thousandth time, even though he didn't ask. It's his eyes, searching my face. Makes me feel like I'm supposed to say something.

"I was upset before. But I'm fine now. And I wasn't upset because of your car or my bike or anything like that. I'm not hurt. You didn't hurt me."

My words fly out in a rush. He listens like I'm saying something interesting, like he has all night.

"How are you sick?" I ask.

Curveball. I'll do anything to get the focus off me.

He's surprised. His posture shifts. Hardens. He gives the crutches a dark glance.

"I have MS."

A look of such pure anger flashes across his face it's like lightning.

I blink. Silence. I don't know what to say.

He looks at the ceiling, then back at me. Pushes his hair back with one hand, shrugs. "I probably shouldn't have been driving that day. I was going too fast. Blowing off steam."

"Oh, it's fine," I say, embarrassed. Stupid, stupid.

He looks around the room for a second, then back at me, pained.

"You have no idea how bad I feel. I had to check on you.

And then you sounded so awful on the phone. I knew you were alone. That your dad was in Europe."

Caught. I shrug. What does he want me to say? That I needed him to check on me? That all I really need is a new friend and everything will be okay? Or maybe I should stick to the truth. Tell him I want him out of here, that I just want everyone to leave me the hell alone?

"I heard rumors about why you came to live here. I couldn't not come by."

Of course. Rumors. He's heard rumors.

I stand. Maybe he'll get the hint, leave.

He doesn't. I'm uncomfortable standing there. Not sure what to do with my arms.

"Can I get you something to drink?" I ask, finally. "My dad has a few beers in the fridge, or seltzer? Soda? Or tea? I could make tea?"

I need water, something. I go over to our little kitchen. At this point, if Dad had vodka in the house I'd pour a glass of that and drink it down. The liquor's all in the studio.

"Sure," he says. "Seltzer's great." He's smiling at me again. A half smile, like he knows something about me, like we've known each other awhile.

I get myself a huge glass of the weird, iron-tasting well water that comes out of our tap. Drink it down. I don't remember the last time I was so thirsty.

He puts his hand on my arm when I pass him the seltzer. Looks right into my eyes.

"Sit."

He pulls me down on the couch next to him. I can smell

his skin, maybe his shampoo, something great. The heat of our bodies crosses the small space between us. For a second I think he's going to kiss me. He doesn't. Just sits next to me, quiet. I look away again.

"What have you heard?" I ask, chewing my bottom lip. I move away slightly, draw my knees up against my chest, and lock my arms around them. I'm a fortress. "You said you'd heard rumors . . ."

"Your dad told someone you were in an accident but that you weren't hurt. That you were coming here awhile, before college."

Silence again.

Like he's waiting for me to say something. Spill. Not a chance. The thought of it makes me sick.

"Not many secrets in a small town, are there?" I offer, finally.

He looks at me, apologetic.

My hands and arms start to shake a bit and lose their heat. Loosen their grip around my knees. I look at them, surprised.

His eyes follow mine, and he lifts one of my clammy palms, traces lightly over the gouged-up spots with his finger.

"God, your poor hands."

I try to keep breathing normally. Pull my hand away.

"That's not just from you . . . our . . . the bike and the car. You didn't . . ."

I can't get enough air again. I hate this feeling. I try to relax a second.

"I fell tonight, while I was running. I . . ."

My breath catches. I look up at the ceiling to keep a hot tear in at the edge of my eye. It rolls down my cheek anyway. Stupid tear. I have to move away from him.

"I don't really want to do this," I say, standing up, stepping away from the couch. "I came here to be quiet and not do this. I don't want to do this anymore."

"Do what?" He looks at me like he's trying to understand. More and more people talk to me in the voice you use when you talk to a disturbed person.

I back away a bit more, move closer to the windows. I can't be near him. The ocean pounds the rocks behind me like a giant heart.

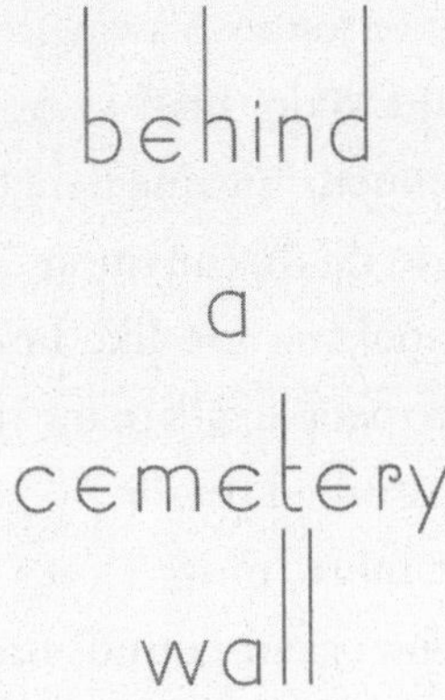

I LOOK AT Cal's face like it's far away. A trick that came to me in the hospital. Everything's distant. Out there.

My heart eases up a little. A few seconds like that and I'm almost calm. Head back to my safe perch on the arm of the chair. From there I look at the air just above his head so I don't have to see his eyes.

I can play it in my head anytime. In full color. The last six months of my old life. Can't stop it, really.

Our senior prank. Posting an ad in the *New York Times* Real Estate section with Patrick, listing the school as a home for sale by owner. Tennis courts, darkroom, roof deck. The Headmistress's phone ringing off the hook. It was lame, but we thought we were funny. Retro, even, for being so lame. I was confident, sure of myself, of the unfurling of my glorious future. Then I wrecked it. Us. Everything. Upside down in the car, Patrick dead next to me. Crushed window glass sprinkled over us like dewdrops on grass. The frogs singing their endless night song.

"Whatever my dad said is right," I say, finally, picking at a bit of the tattered and matted velvet beneath me.

He's waiting to hear something. If I tell, maybe he'll leave. An unfair transaction.

"You probably know everything there is to know, anyway." I'm trying to sound casual. "I was in a wreck with my boyfriend, and he died. But I'm fine. Now. I mean I was—I am."

I straighten my spine a little and try to imagine my eyes are turning to stone so I can't really see the look on his face. Another hospital trick. I wish he'd quit looking at me like that.

In my head, I'm running through the rules of normal social interaction, asking him in my mother's overbright voice, "So, what brings you up here?" Tit for tat. We'll play conversational ping-pong. The little trading of details; this about me, that about you. All those stories you swap so you can pretend you actually know each other. Only what's the point? There is no point.

I swallow and it feels like I'm going to choke. I cough a little and take a sip of water. Breathe.

Cal sits silent, leans forward a little, forearms on his knees, holding his water, looking at me. Waiting, like he's ready to hear more, like I'm going to tell him everything.

I rub my clammy hands on my legs. My scraped knee's stuck to my jeans. The part of me that thought I might be able to ask him questions, have a conversation, is long gone. I don't really care why he's up here. I just want him to go away. Leave me alone.

Then, thank God, even though my heart's a runaway pony in my chest, my trick finally works. I harden. Calm. Cool. Like I slipped behind a cemetery wall. I feel it happen. I'm a cold, carved thing. A person who keeps it together.

"That's all," I say. As in, *that's all, folks*. The end. Because it is. Just me, left.

He keeps looking at me, like he thinks he might hold me or something, reach into me somehow, but I see him through an impossibly long tunnel. The tiny end of a spyglass. He's far away. Insignificant. It's almost funny, how sincere he looks.

I'm calm, a stone girl.

He lets out a long breath. "Wren, I'm so sorry."

Whatever. Words. Just words. Mean nothing.

Cal's eyes stay on me, like he's worried I'll startle if he moves.

For a second he rushes forward in my focus, and I see his open face. Full and kind and beautiful. Like a person who still wants things.

I push him away again.

"Thanks for checking on me. I'm fine."

I climb off the arm of the chair and leave the room.

After a little while, I hear the door close and his car pull away.

IF YOU SLIP FAR ENOUGH out of your life, time picks up. Passes in waves instead of notches. One month rolling by, then another.

Winter sets in. The trees sag with snow. Icicles dangle from eaves and boughs.

The phone wakes me. My daily alarm. Either that or tears pooled and cooling in my ears. Apparently some kind of floodgate's open now or something, and they just keep coming. Even in my sleep.

"Mamie," my mother is saying as I try to wake up. "I can't make the drive this weekend. Not with this nor'easter. Too much snow on the roads."

I yawn and try to sound disappointed.

"It's okay, Mom. Dad canceled his London trip, so he'll be here this weekend."

That would have been cozy. The three of us. Snowed in.

We get together when we have to, but Mom's frosty, Dad looks pained, and we sit there, miserable. I can only take it a few minutes before I want to divorce them both. It was worse right after the accident when I quit talking. I would kill to have a sibling, someone else to take the heat.

"So, I was thinking you could take the train to the city," she says.

No way.

"Mom, I can't. It's fine. It's not like you don't talk to me every day. You can come up in the spring or something."

I hold my breath a second. She'll be hurt that I pushed the visit so far out. Or maybe she'll take the hint instead. Skip it altogether.

"I see," she says, her voice formal.

Feelings hurt.

This is the kind of daughter I am. Now.

"Well, Wren, I've been talking to your dad, and we think . . ."

I cut her off. "You've been talking to Dad?" Impossible. "On the phone?"

She sighs.

"Well, no. We e-mail. About you, of course."

My mother didn't remarry. There was a guy, when I was in eighth grade, but she never even invited him to the house. Didn't last long. She claims she doesn't need another man in her life. She has her work and she has me.

"Your dad tells me you're living like a recluse."

Here we go.

"He says you're not working on anything." She's gentle with me. "That you spend most of your time jogging in the woods. That you're not even trying to make friends up there."

Silence.

She sighs.

"Look, honey, I let you go because I thought a change of scene might be good, but Wren, you've had a while now. The longer you wait to start school, the harder it will get. We agreed . . ."

We agreed on nothing. I made a choice.

"Mom—"

She cuts me off. "I've been on the phone with the admissions people at Amherst and they are still amenable to letting you join them at the end of January."

"Mom," I say again, somewhat forcefully, "I decided to come up here. Me. It was my decision. We agreed not to fight about it. I'm not going to school. Not yet. I can't."

I can hear her breathing. I've been doing a lot of that since May. Listening to people breathe while they wait for me to say something.

She tries again. Her voice is carefully cheerful. Like altering her tone could maybe make anything different, better.

"That editor from *Focal Point* called to say she'd be happy to let you finish your internship if you were to come back to the city before you start school."

Focal Point. I almost laugh. At Bly, my school, we did

this project called Senior Endeavor. If you had the grades, you did early exams and then proposed some kind of internship for the month of May. The internships were meant to be a way for us to reach beyond the bubble of school toward the larger world before they packed us all off to the next bubble. I told Meredith I wanted to do a project I'd call "*Anonymous Lunch*." I would put an ad on Craigslist for strangers to come have lunch with me. My treat. The only requirement was that they let me set up the tripod and take a photograph while we ate. I thought it would be cool. I liked the idea of how uncomfortable it might be, lunching with a stranger and catching that look on their face. Meredith said I was a weirdo.

My actual Endeavor was to intern at *Focal Point*, a fine arts magazine in one of those cast-iron buildings in SoHo. The office was in a massive, high-ceilinged room at the top of the building. The rickety elevator bounced a little at every floor, and I worked at a desk near a window that overlooked an internal courtyard. If you let your eyes go soft focus, and didn't look down, it was just this white-washy light from the sky spilling down into a vast private interior. I loved it.

I interned in the design department and worked with one of their editors. The work was more technical than I'd expected, mostly learning layout, but I spent my days looking at incredible photographs. It was a great compromise for my mom and me. She felt I was learning something practical about how the world works, and I got to spend all my time looking at art.

That was then.

"I'm not going back to *Focal Point*, Mom," I say. My

Endeavor seems like it was a thousand years ago.

"Mamie, really, what are you doing up there?" she asks, weary of the same question over and over again.

I'm in a nowhere place.

"Honey, the best cure for melancholy is industry." Her soft voice. No perma-cheer.

Family rule: If things fall to pieces, don't drop the ball. And if, God forbid, you do, pick it up and toss it in the air again like nothing happened.

I can't think of anything to say.

So I say nothing.

That's how it started, before. My not speaking. It was like a heavy blanket I pulled over myself. All those moving mouths asking me could I hear them, telling me I was okay, telling me Patrick was dead, then my mother's cool hand, smoothing my hair from my face, whispering, whispering, almost a lullaby in my ear. I dropped down into my own silence like an anchor to the dark sea floor. Silt silent and all that heavy water above. Words are mostly pointless. I let go of the thread between my mind and my mouth, and it went from chaotic to peaceful.

My silence makes her nervous. I feel bad for making her worry, but I'm empty. I don't have anything else to offer.

"Mamie?" she says, "Please don't—are you there?"

"Yeah, Mom," I say quietly. "Only it's Wren now, okay? Please don't call me Mamie."

Another big sigh from her.

"Oh yes, well, I'm sorry, Wren. It's hard. I named you, you'll recall. I'll try."

I roll over. The sheets stink a little. I've let everything slip. I'll have to get on that. Today. Laundry.

She pauses a second, then, "Meredith called. She's coming home for the holidays. She wants to know if she'll see you."

"No. No way."

I answer that one fast. I can't see her. Talk to her. How could I see Meredith? Like everything hasn't changed? Been ruined? She's too close. She'll pull me back. The thought makes me sick.

"Well, she's asking again for your father's address. She wants to send you letters," Mom says.

Letters. Our letters. Summer after tenth grade Meredith's parents broke with tradition and sent her to Italy for the summer. Then Mom seized the opportunity and made me do a program in the city on economics and social policy. Right up my alley. Nerds in khakis and polos prepping for future desks in D.C. Total nightmare.

Meredith read somewhere about these old-guy poets who'd written to each other once a week, their whole lives. We figured if they could do it, so could we. The letters saved me. Once a week, mailed on Wednesday.

We kept it up when she got home. Even though we saw each other all the time. It was kind of like writing in a journal, but one that talked back, saw you more truly than you saw yourself. Every Wednesday, no matter what, no matter how busy we were.

We went through phases with them. We gave ourselves assignments, calligraphy only, or cut and pasted like a ransom note. We competed to see who could make the coolest envelope. Mostly we just wrote them on our laptops. But they had to go via U.S. Post. That was part of it. Printed and mailed. Old-school. No possibility of forwarding them to anyone else.

They were our secret, confidences we held for each other, from the rest of the world. Sometimes we argued about things on the page that we wouldn't dare talk about face to face.

". . . I really hate telling her no," Mom's saying. "It seems like a perfectly reasonable request."

I'm quiet. Go back there in my mind. Back to the city, back to my little room. In our house. On my bed with a letter from Mer. Writing mine back.

I can't think of any of it now without knowing what happened. What it came to. I pull my knees up to my chin. Curl into a ball.

"Mamie?"

"Mom," I say. "Don't give her the address, please." I'm tired. Beaten down. The last thing I need are Meredith's letters streaming in, making me feel worse about everything. "No," I plead. "Please don't give her the address. Say sorry—I'm sorry. But no. Please, Mom, please."

Big sigh.

"Mamie," she says, after a minute. "I'm concerned. Moping in your father's empty house in that little backwater isn't the best thing for you right now. For your future. You're going to lose your momentum."

Momentum. She's got to be kidding.

I can hear her tapping her desk with her finger. She makes little sounds like that when she's upset.

"Mom, I'm hanging up now," I say. And I do.

It gets easier all the time. She might call several times a day, but I can end the conversation.

I roll over to the cooler edge of the bed and look outside. The trees are soft with snow. And I like how it falls and falls into the gray ocean—back to where it came from. Oblivion.

A knock on my door startles me.

"Wren?" Mary's voice. My dad's assistant.

"Come in." I sit up. Pull on a sweatshirt I threw off in the night.

Mary. My mother would have a field day with her. Appraise her with one of those tight smiles she has for people she finds foolish or impossible to understand.

It took me a few weeks to realize Mary was even around, working in the studio, coming and going from the house. I didn't look up much when I first got here. I can't keep all my dad's people straight.

Mary's in her usual bright something-or-other. Today it's a cherry-red scarf gypsy-wrapped around her head, with her nearly white-blond hair sticking out of the top of the fabric in a crazy twist. Huge hand-tatted white lace earrings drift from her ears like she has snow under her command. Stained overalls and boots. She's like an ice cream sundae in work clothes.

"You're here early," I say, taking the mug of hot coffee she's offering. She even knows how much milk I like.

She looks at the clock and laughs. "It's nearly eleven."

Sits on the bed next to me, a painful little intimacy. "Were you up late?"

Mary does this. Pops into my room. Asks little questions. I say nothing. It's eleven and I'm still under the covers.

"Do you think you're sleeping too much?" she asks. Her eyes dart like birds between my face and the clock. It's overly personal and annoying, and knowing my dad, something he asked her to do. Check on me. The great delegator. Even up here, I can't catch a break.

"What do you need, Mary?" I avoid her eyes, look around for my running clothes.

She leans back on her elbows.

"Two things—I was going nuts with the quiet when I first got up here—you know, I like to be around people—so I started this Secret Cinema Club in the back room at Gallagher's Bar. Every Tuesday. All ages. A decent group shows up. Do you want to come?"

I don't answer and for a second she looks the tiniest bit nervous or something. One hand flutters up near her ear. Fiddles with a snowflake. She takes it off and inspects it, her short neon-orange fingernails teasing out a loose thread, finally lifting it to her mouth and snipping the stray bit off with her teeth.

"Sorry," she says. "I just learned how to make these, and that thread's been driving me nuts. Tickles the side of my neck. Anyhow," she draws the word out with a grin. "Secret Cinema—the theme this month is kind of dark—dead under thirty."

She gives a sudden, high laugh, like she just realized

how inappropriate this invitation might be. I love her a little for it.

She forges ahead anyway. "This one wasn't my idea"—another bright laugh—"Anyway, last week was *My Own Private Idaho*, River Phoenix, of course, and this week I have *10 Things I Hate About You* with Heath Ledger. Have you seen it?"

I shake my head and set the mug of coffee down on the floor next to the bed. "The second thing?"

"Oh yeah, sorry, the second thing is that your dad wants to have lunch with you in the studio. Check in. But come to Gallagher's? You'll like it, I promise."

I lie on my side. Lunch in the studio. Great. He's definitely been talking to Mom. This is a first. An invite to the studio during the day. I let out a huge sigh.

"Thanks for the invite," I say, without committing to anything. "What time does he want me? My dad?"

"Around one." She bends to peer at me. "And you're supposed to bring lunch."

I groan.

Mary laughs and leaves the room.

"I'm on it," I call after her. Check in. More like checking up on me. I can't blow it.

My running clothes stink. Worse than the sheets. I keep meaning to wash them, but then I don't. Nothing's clean. My room's a disaster. I never really settled in. I'm sleeping on the twin bed Dad bought when I was little. He offered to get me a new one, update the room, but I don't really care. The closet's so full of his stuff, I just left my suitcases on the floor in front of it. A small shelf by the bed holds a reading lamp and my cell phone charger. The rest of my stuff, my iPhone, laptop and camera are all on the floor.

My camera.

My old eyes. I look at it for a second. Try to remember what it felt like, heavy in my hand. Why I was sure it was so important.

My clothes are rank. So, no run. I still have a few standards. I'm pretty sure clean clothes are kind of a bare-minimum marker of mental health. Don't want to wave the red flag of poor hygiene. I scoop up everything and carry it to the little, dark utility room where my dad has the washer and dryer. Throw it all in the machine on a short cycle.

Make lunch. I said I'd do that. The fridge is empty. A few bottles of wine, some old cream, part of a dried sausage-looking thing, and a waxy rind of cheese. I'll have to shop. Something I've mostly avoided. A trip into town. My heart does a little lurch. Stupid lunch in the studio. Dad's truck keys are on the hook by the door. I open the drawer near the sink. He leaves an envelope of cash in there, in case I need it. Which I haven't. Until now. Sitting around is totally free. I pull it out.

I sit and make a grocery list until I can move my stuff into the dryer. Then I go back to my room and flop on the bed to wait.

Most of my friends fell away. A few came to see me after the crash, but the not-talking thing kind of spooked people, I guess. Social death. When you decide to stop speaking, people hang on to you a little while. Try to figure out what's been shaken loose. I missed the funeral, thank God. Meredith delivered the blow-by-blow, as if that might snap me out of it. Stalked into my room after it ended and recounted the whole thing to my silent face, dragged me to it in words. Emma's shaky voice up at the podium reading a letter to her big brother, Patrick's mom sinking to her knees on the rain-soaked ground at the edge of the open grave.

Emma. That Snow White coloring like her brother, a surrogate younger sister. She and Patrick were a package deal, nothing like Meredith and her little brother Jay. Mer and I kind of adopted Emma, especially at Bly. When she was crushed at the prospect of wearing her braces for an extra year, we took her back to my house after school for an image upgrade. Meredith's idea. She does stuff like that. Takes up the cause. She redid Emma, head to toe. When they were done, I took pictures. Cute ones she could post when she felt bad about the mouth full of metal. I can still see them, her bright eyes under those dark brows, turned up like morning glories to the sun.

Her letter to Patrick would have killed me.

My cell chirps. Sounds like a text. No one texts me anymore. I pull a pillow over my face. It trills again like a wicked little alarm, a reminder of exactly how selfish I am. I didn't say a word to any of them. Patrick's parents. Emma. Didn't call. Not once. I couldn't. Can't. Even Meredith gave up on me, but not before she came by one last time to tell me how terrible I was, for not speaking, for shutting down. "You weren't even hurt," she hurled at me. "You're being selfish. And now you're making us lose you, too."

There were no good-byes when she left for school.

My phone beeps louder. I stretch across the bed and reach for it. It *is* a text. From my mother. LOVE AND KISSES! Excited like that, so not her. It's probably the only non-work-related text she's ever sent.

I have this image of all the people around me, contorting themselves to help me, grotesque. I should probably ditch my phone, too.

The dryer buzzes and I dump a mountain of clean clothes on my bed. Hot jeans on a snowy day. Simple things. I pull on boots and one of my dad's huge jackets and head into town alone for the first time since I got here.

a small town is a small town is a

I KNOW I'm supposed to be over it. I wasn't the one driving that night. I've been in cars since. But this is a first—driving alone. I sit in Dad's truck and try to relax. Rest my head on the steering wheel a minute. Deep breaths. Then I start it up and back out of the shed. The snow's no match for this ancient miracle of American engineering, and I slip and fishtail my way through the drifts and curves up to the main road.

We're only a few miles out of town, but as you head down in, the landscape changes. Trees and cliffs give way kind of suddenly to scrubby little rock-front beach cottages and campy fifties-era "Holiday Havens." Everything sags a little, like it's resigned to a future outside the action. I could love it for that.

Main Street has the usual places meant to charm summer visitors. A lobster shack, a coffee shop with checked curtains, Uncle Kippy's Old-Timey Candy Shoppe that sells ice cream sodas in the summer, a little wharf where visitors can book a schooner cruise, an old and rare books shop, Lenore's Bike, Board 'n' Skate, The Ski Outfit, a "general store" that sells scented candles and postcards, and three restaurants.

At the end of Main, further inland, past some townies' houses, you find the real artery of town, the strip where they hide fast food joints, gas stations, the boat shop, a liquor store, and a chain grocery. I pull in there, next to the Tire Depot, and go in.

Like a normal person. I'm a normal person today.

A small town is a small town is a small town. You might be able to find organic greens now, and people might not outwardly stare, but walk into any small-town grocery and expect to be inspected. I catch one of the stock guys hightailing it around to the front of the store to let the checkout girls know I've come in. Whatever. I push the rattly little cart up and down the aisles. Fill it high enough to restock us awhile.

When I pay, the same guy bags my stuff. Looks average. My age, maybe. A regular guy. Probably has a very normal life.

Finally he says, "Carry these out to your car for you, Miss Wells?"

Miss Wells.

He and the cashier exchange a glance. They're on to me. Want me to know. It makes me want to do something really weird. Give them something to talk about. Maintain the family name. God knows what my dad's given them to go on over the years.

"Nah, that's okay," I say as he reaches for his parka. "I've got it."

He looks disappointed but shrugs, and I go back out the automatic doors to where my dad's truck is already nearly buried in fresh snow. Their eyes are on me the entire time I clear the snow off the windows. I'm a sideshow. I won't be back here anytime soon. The place is deserted. Everyone in for the storm. Either that, or this town really is just that empty.

Back on the road. Past the gas station. Past the Movie Nook. Fishtail a little at a stop sign. More calming breaths. Past the diner with the truckers parked on the side. Past Gummer's Pie Place with the giant rotating whoopie pie sign. At the light, a car pulls up close behind me, taps the horn.

That Jeep.

Nearly stops my heart. It's Cal Owen, striped scarf, dark hair, framed in my rearview mirror, hand raised in a relaxed hello.

At green, I step on it. Back out to the wilder parts, the good, upward geometry of trees and the punching-rock coast. My foot's heavy on the gas. Can't get distance between us fast enough.

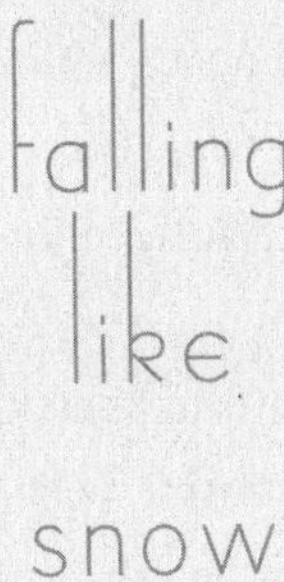

falling like snow

BY THE TIME I'm back at the house it's nearly one. I shove aside last night's dinner dishes I was supposed to wash and get to work. Some tests you can't fail. A simple lunch. Salad niçoise. Dad's standard. Only minus the niçoise. The grocery store didn't have any of those little bitter-brined olives, and I don't have time or energy to do the beans or boil eggs. So it's more like tuna and tomatoes on lettuce with vinegar and oil. Whatever. It's the best I've got on short notice. I tear a few chunks off what passes for a baguette up here, pile lunch on a big teak tray thing that may or may not be a piece of sculpture, and head out.

"Wren—" Dad sounds happy to see me when I shoulder

open the door. He takes the tray and sets it on the small table he uses for working meals.

An enormous bronze something-or-other dominates the space. It's curved in a way that makes me want to curl myself into it, surrender to a cool metal cradle. He watches me while I look. I say nothing. I've learned that much over the years.

Then he pulls me into an unexpected hug. My dad's a big man, but you don't notice because he's gentle. My face is crushed against the soft front of his shirt. I hug him back. We don't usually do this. Something's up. I look at him when he lets me go. It's on his face, like scaffolding. Mom's worry. He's been listening to her. Listening. God. They're united. He looks at me like he's seeing me in some new way. Like he did in the hospital, and when I first got here, before we settled into our routine of mostly ignoring each other, doing our own thing.

"What?" I say.

Before he can answer, a woman—Zara, I think—and Mary come out of the back room.

"Zara—" Mary's traipsing after her, wiping blackened hands on a rag hanging from her belt. "If you're coming back here later, can I catch a ride with you now to Mercy House? Then I can leave my car here. I'm kind of low on gas—" She stops when she spots me standing awkwardly next to Dad.

"Oops! Sorry!" she says, making an apologetic face toward him. "I didn't know you guys were already lunching."

Before my dad can reply, Zara swings an arm around

Mary's shoulders, and while looking right at my dad, says somewhat assertively, "Yes, I'm coming back. John, we need to work on those models a little more. Something's not right yet, and you need to work with Mary to figure it out."

Some other kind of look passes between them. Zara reaches for a work jacket on one of the hooks next to my dad's and slips it on, lifting the heavy golden rope of a braid she wears pulled to the side. Mary flashes another apologetic smile our way, like she thinks she's interrupted us, and slips into an electric-blue-and-purple toggle-button coat.

The studio is momentarily filled with cool air, as if it had sucked in a huge breath, before the heavy door swings shut behind them.

Dad looks at the space where they were for a second, then turns back to me, sits, and motions for me to do the same. He uncorks a bottle of wine and fills two slightly cloudy-looking glasses with the burgundy liquid.

"You'll have a little?"

He's sending me back to the city for sure. Has to be. My mind begins a frantic racket. I won't go. Not yet. I'll figure something else out. Have to.

He pushes the glass toward me before I can say yes or no. Pointing out that I'm not legal or that it's early in the day is pointless. We're in the studio. Dad's fiefdom. He's the law.

"Your mother's been calling me, e-mailing," he starts.

"My condolences." I'm sarcastic.

"Don't be snide. You know what I think of false feeling."

There's nothing false about my feelings, but I don't point that out.

"I have never asked you to be anything more than you are," he starts.

My heart sinks. Here it is.

"I know what happened in May, all of it, was terrible for you. I know you wanted time—to come sort yourself out. And you're welcome here, you know that."

I force down a few bites of salad and a small sip of the wine. Tastes dusty. Strong.

He says nothing for a minute, samples the salad. Dad knows how to keep an audience. I watch snow hit the skylights above us. I can't eat. Not now, not until I know where this is going. Another sip of wine. It moves through me like a calm kind of heat.

He clears his throat and sighs. "If you tell me . . ." Sets down the fork. Wipes his mouth.

"If you tell me you're okay, but you just need a little more time to sort yourself out, I'll tell her to back off."

Folds his napkin. Lays it next to his plate like he's enacting some kind of serious ritual. A rite of improvement.

"But she's worried." Studies me a second. "*We're* worried. She's got it in her head that you're not doing better up here—that you're heading in a—wrong direction."

Sighs. Looks at me like he might stare a new truth out of me.

"Your mother is afraid you're too isolated—that you could, might, get hurt—hurt yourself." He pauses. "Of course I know that's not the case, and I told her that, but—"

This is what I love about my dad. He cuts to the chase. No warming a person into an idea. The wine flushes up like a mossy wall between me and what he's saying.

"What do I need to do, Dad?" I ask. Ignore what he said. "I'm not going to school. Not yet and probably not to Amherst. And I don't even know if I want to go to art school anymore. Or what I want."

"We're not asking you to start school."

"Am I bothering you?" I say. "Being here? Is it too hard for you to work with me around?"

His face looks sad for a second. He leans back noisily in his chair and runs a hand through his shock of white hair. It stands up when he pulls his hand away. Like a swan's wing. He looks at the back of his hand.

"I hardly notice you're around," he says softly. "You're so quiet. And I respect your privacy. God knows I hate people telling me how to live. I trust you, that's why I said you could come here."

"But . . . what?"

"But I think she's right. You need to do something. I don't think you should go on spending your days sleeping and jogging in the woods. It's not enough—"

"But if I were working on some art project, it would be okay, right? If I said I was making notes for something, writing, or taking pictures . . . ?" I'm defensive. "You don't want to tell me how to live, but you're uncomfortable that I'm not living how you want me to all the same."

He doesn't respond. I'm right, and he knows it. He unfolds his napkin and finishes his salad.

I stare at my plate. Force a bite into my mouth so he can't accuse me of not eating.

"Dad, I don't know what you're saying. What do I have to do?"

I keep my voice cool, but a panic rushes over me, makes me want to get out of here. I'd leave if I had somewhere to go. I hate being the cause of their concern. When I quit talking, they put me through a few sessions with a shrink. Made me take antidepressants. I've listened to everything everyone had to say on the subject of loss and bereavement. Survivors' guilt. None of it mattered. Matters. They're just words. Falling like snow. But I have to listen to them. Because I'm not free. My parents are still in charge, and apparently now frighteningly united. Another weight on my chest. I want to get away from weights. From the possibility that people need me not to disappoint them. But where else can I go? I have nowhere else.

"I thought coming here would be different." My voice wavers. "I'd be in charge of myself. Could deal with it my own way. Until I felt right again. Or didn't. Now you're saying I have to do something if I want to stay?"

"Look," he begins again. "You're right. I'm telling you how to live. But I'm not asking much, Wren. Just do *something*."

"Like what?" I look at my lap. Stunned. This has to be the first time in my entire life he's asked me to do something. It's like he's breaking a secret agreement between him and Mom. He's the troublemaker, she's the taskmaster. Not the other way around.

"Lucy Shepherd—at the library. She's a friend of mine and Zara's. She says she can use you in there with her. A light job. Mornings. A few hours a day."

He drops his napkin on his plate and stretches back in his chair again. The weathered wood creaks.

I put my face in my hands. The library. I'll have to interact with people. This Lucy woman.

He clears his throat. Looks at me a second, then off to the right, like he's composing his thoughts.

"A young man called a few times looking for you, the son of my architect. Says you met? Mary talked to him." He coughs, takes another sip of wine. "He could use a hand from time to time at his house—says he'd hire you."

Cal. No way. I die inside.

"Meet with him. Help him out. Give me something I can tell your mother so she'll get off both our backs about this, okay?"

I drop my hands and look up through the skylight again. Still snowing. So quiet, the snow. I'll run away. Thumb it out on the highway. Canada, maybe.

He reaches across the table and pushes my chin down so I have to look into his face. "I'm not asking for much, kiddo," he says.

I look away from him again. He has no idea.

"Just throw us a line? Some kind of signal so we know you're all right. Do it and I'll find a way to call her off."

Tears again, a seriously annoying development. I blink them away. Make myself hard inside. I'm hot with shame. My parents are managing me. I'm pathetic.

I try to breathe through my nose, not gulp at air like a fish on land. I'll do what they want. Adjust. No choice. I'll make my heart go solid stone again; work my little job, then come home and lie in bed, watch the treetops sway.

My father leans across the table and puts his scratchy hands on my cheeks. He looks at me like he's been watching my thoughts on a screen. "Wren," he says, "I'm sorry."

nearer

now

I HATE EUPHEMISM. Passed on. At peace. Try dead. It's winter, and everything's more dead than not, and it looks like it's going to stay that way. Everlasting snowfall. Spring's impossible. Dad's plow service digs us out day after day.

Cal's number goes up on the fridge along with a little pink "While You Were Out" note from Mary, saying he called. Again. While I was out. I like that. I am out. I look at it in the morning while I stand at the sink eating the toast and egg or whatever Mary's left for me. Then I put on my winter running gear and head out on the trails. The only human footprints out there are mine. Snowshoes would help.

Finally I wake up one morning and the note with Cal's

number's taped to my bathroom mirror. Along with another note. This one in my dad's scrawl. *Library. Today.* I lean against the sink a minute and imagine I can do this. Will. Time to get my act together. I run, shower, dress, and drive in to meet Lucy Shepherd. Start my job.

The library's a little one-story brick building on a small wedge of land in the middle of town. It's flanked by big old trees and has tall windows on all sides, rounded at the top. Looks like a quaint small-town library right off a movie set. We all have roles to play, I guess.

Ms. Shepherd says almost nothing. I like her. She welcomes me in a quiet voice and says I should have a look around for today. Like she knows a look around is pretty much all I can take on my first day. The place is deserted. Fine by me. I walk around the stacks, feeling stupid, like she's watching me, but when I glance at her, she's not. She's working at her desk and looks like she's actually focused on something. Other than me.

I spend about an hour staring at a *Guide to Northeastern Conifers*, but then I find an old, raggedy collection of poems by Philip Larkin. I loved poetry in school. Drove Meredith mad. If I read one out loud, she'd roll her eyes, call me Emo Girl, then go right back to her Bio homework or whatever other no-nonsense class she was acing.

I flip through the worn pages of the slim book. There are so many good ones. Lines lift themselves off the page, exactly the kind of talk I need right now. The poems are conversational but resigned like when you and a friend sigh at the same time.

Ms. Shepherd—"Lucy, call me Lucy"—tells me Larkin was one of the great English poets of the twentieth century. She puts her hand on my shoulder for a minute while she talks. Shows me his poem "High Windows," which I read because she's standing right next to me. All adults think kids will like that one because there's swearing and sex in it. I don't tell her I read it in junior English seminar.

When Lucy walks away, I flip through the book, not really focusing on any one poem in particular until I spot "Aubade."

I read it twice.

Then again.

Finally someone who tells it straight. No smiles and lies. Debates with despair. What I now know about sleepless nights, hours moving us toward what's never not there. How scarce it matters to be scared or brave. Dawn lifting itself to the window all the same.

I lean back in the chair a little. Feel my shoulders fall. A surge of relief. Larkin gets it, got it, the lies we live just to tread through time. Too bad he's dead.

So, at the end of my no-work shift, I give in, ask Lucy for a library card, and check the book out. I agree to come back in a week and start a regular schedule. She smiles at me so kindly when I push open the heavy doors, I almost throw the book back in at her. I'm not going to last long in this little fake job if she gets all touchy-feely. I don't need pity. Just some space to breathe.

a good house

Another damn day.

Only on this one I'm going to call Cal. Because I have to. Make a friend, because I have to. Get my parents off my back. The urge to go back to bed is overpowering. Instead I dress and sit at the table with my juice, a yogurt, his number, and the phone. Like a normal person.

I can't stare at my phone all morning. Now or never. Do or die. Ha.

He answers on the fourth ring.

"It's Wren Wells . . ." I say, ". . . calling." Stellar debut.

"Wren." I swear I can hear him smile. "Great to hear from you. You must have talked to your dad?"

"Yep," I say, playing with my spoon. I'm a small-talk artist.

He doesn't seem to notice.

"How are you?"

"Look," I say, "I'm calling because my dad said you had some work you wanted done. He wants me to do some work. So I'm calling you. About the work."

God, kill me now. A new low. At this rate I'm going to have to hire a coach if I plan to reenter the world and actually interact with other humans.

He takes a breath. "Yeah . . ." he says. "Work, yeah, well, maybe you could come over and we can talk about it? I'll be around later today."

Shit. Shit. Later today.

"Okay."

I guess I sound unenthusiastic, because he laughs again. "I have to go out this morning, but I could meet you here around three?"

"I don't know where you live, but sure, three's fine. I can be there then." I wonder for a second if my dad needs the truck. Maybe I could jog over there.

He reads my mind.

"Or I can pick you up on my way back?"

If he picks me up, I'll have no way out. I'll be stuck at his house. My palms are clammy. I remind myself I can always run home, if I need to.

"Where's your place?" I ask, like I know where anything is around here other than the main drag.

"That road, the one you were on the day I—we met? The one just past Carver Cove? It comes up to the house if you follow it to the end."

That road. I can find it on foot through the woods.

"We're on the water, like you guys. You'll recognize the place, it looks like yours."

"I, um, I'm not sure I know how to get to that road in the car," I say. "I found it after riding trails through the woods."

My bike. I'm an idiot. I never went back for it. Or replaced it. Once I started running, I forgot about it.

"Then it's settled. I'll swing by for you on my way back," he says. "Around 2:45?"

"See you then," I say and hang up, fast.

What am I doing making plans with a guy?

I'm ambushed by memory. Patrick's face, the way his eyes looked when I told him I wanted to break up. Total disbelief. Hurt. He didn't see it coming. How could he have? I didn't involve him in the decision. I was doing it for me, because I was ready to be done, not because there was something wrong with him.

I squeeze my eyes against the memory, but he's crystal clear. I can almost hear him saying my name. My hands are icy. I go into my room, strip out of my jeans, and put on my running clothes. I'm out the door.

I close my eyes off and on while I run. It's tricky. Easy to fall, but the light on my eyelids is kind of mesmerizing. Like the end of an old film on a projector or something. Flickering, flashing. Something about it puts me back in photo studio at school. Junior year. The day Miss Hennessy, my photo teacher, asked to see me after class. I sat there, nervous, while she flipped open all the shades. Dark to light. Sun flooded the room. I could hardly see her face for a minute or two.

"Mamie," she said, sounding grave, "I have some questions and concerns about the work you've done so far this year."

My heart sunk. I felt caught out. Like I was a fraud, trying to make photographs that were good, interesting even, but totally failing at it. I slid down in my chair, locked my eyes on the way the light angled in through the windows.

"And," she said, "instead of reshooting the work this weekend, you need to go to Around the World with Patrick." A huge smile crossed her face.

It took me a minute. Then I laughed. Of course. Around the World. The Nellie Bly School's idea of a fall dance. Meredith kept telling me that Patrick liked me. Miss Hennessy smiled, happy to be in on the stunt, and nodded toward the now-open door, where Patrick stood leaning against the door frame, looking kind of nervous and pretty cute.

His face. The way that late-day light slanted against it. My heart drops. *You are running*, I tell myself. *Here*. I start to count my footsteps. Out loud. It works sometimes. I'll do anything to empty my head.

I run until I can't, then head home. My muscles are wrung out. I'm too tired to think. Heaven. After reheating in the shower, I find some college radio podcast where they're reading Larkin poems. I lie on my bed to listen, for just a minute.

I wake up to the sound of a car crunching up to the house over ice-packed snow in the driveway. My right arm's asleep, I'm still in my towel, and my hair's dried into a matted tangle. I hear my dad. The car must've pulled him out of his studio. He's talking extra loud like he's giving me a signal, buying me time or something. I rush around, pulling on jeans and a shirt I used to think I looked good in, back when I still paid attention to how I looked. I pull my fingers through my hair. It's long and sort of wavy, so maybe the slept-on look will seem intentional. I brush my teeth so fast I poke myself in the gums with the toothbrush, and I'm still checking for blood with my tongue when I run out the door. My dad's leaning in the driver's window of Cal's car. A different car, silver. Looks new, expensive. Reminds me of Patrick's. I shudder, hope it passes for a shiver.

My dad pats Cal on the shoulder and moves away from the driver's window. "Good to see you again." He shoots me a fast glance. One that says *Do this right*. I nod to him and get in the car.

Cal turns toward me, a huge smile on his face. It makes him even better looking. Why on earth is he so happy to see me?

"Hi," I say. Try not to notice his eyes. I blush. Or maybe my face is still red from sleeping. I lift my hand to my face to check for pillow lines. I usually wake up with those. I'm fuzzy-headed. My heart's a drum.

"Hi, yourself," Cal says, still grinning at me.

He waits for me to buckle up, then we pull away from the house. My dad's watching, trying to look like he isn't.

"It's good to see you," Cal says.

Say something back. Say something back. How hard is it? I'm starting to feel like someone just let out of The

Home, unfamiliar with "normal human ways." It makes me laugh.

God. The Home. Meredith invented it to torment Andy whenever she spotted him trying to talk to a girl. Meredith is like that. Smells weakness on people. She'd remind him in a really loud voice not to miss the short bus back to The Home. Poor Andy. The worst part was that he was in love with her.

I have to swallow in order to not laugh again. My dry throat is loud. I can't remember the last time I felt like this. Must be nerves.

Cal looks at me, an eyebrow raised.

Say something.

"I'm—yeah—I was sleeping," I say. Like he'd care. It's rough for those of us just out of The Home, not much news to report.

"I mean, I fell asleep, and now I'm awake."

God. I have to stop. Before I make it worse. More blushing. I look out my window. Lean my head against it. He laughs at me. Probably thinks I'm insane. I sneak a peek out of the corner of my eye. He's still smiling.

My stomach growls loudly enough we both hear it.

He laughs again.

I haven't eaten anything. "Missed lunch," I say. Eyes back on the scenery.

"There's food at the house. We'll find you something."

He turns on music so I don't have to try to say anything for the rest of the drive.

His house is like ours only bigger. Double or maybe

even triple the size. We pull up and I can see that it's all landscaped. Even looks good under the snow. Huge burlap-covered planters. Stone steps going down around the front of the house. None of the random-size rocks or insane-looking scrap-metal collections my dad has clumped around our place. An attached garage, immaculate. The Jeep's parked off to the side. Cal grimaces a little when he sees me look at it.

"The garage was a sore point for my father. He's against that kind of thing, garages on houses, but when he built this place, we were up here full time, and my mother was still home with us. She needed to get into the house with as little trouble as possible, so he put it in the design."

He stops the car and gets out. One crutch. I get out too. He hauls a heavy-looking messenger bag out of the back-seat and leans against the car while he slings it across his body. The garage door sinks down quietly behind us as he unlocks the door to the house.

It was a kindness for him to say our houses are alike. His place is like something out of *Architectural Digest*. Pale, shining floors, soft white furniture, lots of comfortable-looking places to sit. Tasteful and simple. My mother would approve. A length of paneled wall near us reveals a closet. Cal sits on a bench near the door and takes off his coat and boots. I feel like a hobo in my dad's ratty work jacket. I slip out of it and hang it on one of the many hooks.

"This," he says, pointing to the overfull messenger bag next to him on the bench, "is part of the problem, one of the things I might want help with." He sighs and closes the closet. Walks slowly over to the dining table. I try not to watch him. Seems like I shouldn't. I stay by the door. Not sure what to do.

"C'mon in." He waves me over. "And bring the bag, would you?"

I pick it up and join him. My heart's galloping, making a racket in my chest. The light in the place—it's not as tree-hidden as ours and the window span's nearly double. At the far end of the living room there's a step down to a workroom and more windows. Papers everywhere, a long table, stacks of books, a few chairs. On one wall, a huge photograph of Cal and someone who has to be his brother—they look alike—windsurfing. The room ends in a wall of shelves, and behind that, if it's like our place, a hall leading to bedrooms.

Cal watches me take it in. I look at him. He's smiling. "It's a good house," he says. I nod at the understatement. "Dad wanted to do something other than the standard sea-bleached clapboard cottage you see around here. He thought if you're going to live in such an intense landscape, you should build a place that doesn't separate you from it," he says. "I wish it were mine."

"Isn't it?" I'm confused.

"I'm doing architecture. Was. At Cornell. I mean I wish I designed it. This place. It's so simple—such a great use of this site."

He looks out at the water.

He's right. Where our house sits, assertive, right on the edge of the bluff, his is set back. You can still see the water, but there's space before the edge, a wide bluestone terrace, then the cliff, then the drop.

"Sit, will you?" he says. I'm standing next to the table, like I'm frozen or something, holding his bag. He pulls out a chair for me. I set the bag down.

We sit. Close. I can feel the warmth of his body. I focus on the windows.

"So," he says, finally, "I ran into your dad in town, at the garage, and he told me you were looking for something to do, to fill your time?"

This gets my attention.

"My dad asked you for work for me?"

An ice wave rushes over me. Then heat to my cheeks. The room feels small. I could die. Did Cal even call for me, or did my dad just flat-out lie? I clench my teeth.

"Not exactly. I ran into him when I was having the car winterized. I told him I'd met you—*how* I'd met you. I never felt right that I hadn't talked to him."

Unbelievable. Dad neglected to mention seeing Cal. The opposite, in fact. He acted like Mary had been taking Cal's calls. I feel ill.

"He asked me how I was, then talked about you a bit, said he was worried you didn't have enough to do. He said it was the perfect opportunity for us both. I'm doing an internship with an old colleague of my dad's. It's a drive from here. About forty-five minutes." His jaw tightens. "I might need a ride sometimes, if I'm going to keep doing the internship." He clears his throat. "Once in awhile—when I maybe shouldn't drive."

I'm pissed at my dad. He's so transparent. He thinks he sees a problem and guns for it.

"Hire a driver." I'm furious with my dad for playing me. "You can afford it, and it's not like internships last forever."

Cal shoots me a look. Surprised. We're quiet a second. I swear I can hear my blood charging through my body.

"This one's open-ended," he says, voice tense. "I'm taking a break. From school. Not sure if I'm going back or not. This is kind of a trial thing—to see—"

He cuts himself off.

I try to back away from the angry edge I'm on. "So architecture's not what you want to do?"

He looks away from me. Ignores my question.

"Forget it," he says, shaking his head. "I was just trying to—it was just going to be a ride once in a while, or sometimes help hauling that thing." He points to the bag. Looks angry a second. "My balance sucks. The bag, the snow—"

"I don't have a car," I say, like I might do it, like my mouth isn't attached to the racket inside me.

"I'd give you the keys to the Jeep."

I nod slowly. But the room gets smaller. Work for Cal. On call. It's a little hard to breathe.

"Can you drive a manual . . . ?" He looks at me, leans closer. "Are you okay?"

My limbs are weirdly heavy. Like they turned to stone without me. Without my head. Too many people are expecting me to do things. I don't want to meet anyone's expectations. Be expected. I just want to—*be*. No explanations necessary. Me. Quiet. Anything more is too risky. I clasp my hands together, they're icy. My arms weigh a ton. I try to blink away the feeling. Come back to the room.

"Sorry," I say, taking a deep breath, filling my lungs against the lethargic weight of memory.

On our third time out together, Patrick drove me to Long Island and taught me how to drive a stick. He showed up at my house, tapping the horn lightly under my window, in his dad's tight little two-door coupe, and we flew out of the city, feeling older than we were and lucky. After mall security made its loop through the far end of the lot, Patrick coached me through stall after stall, showing me how to listen to the engine, feel it, give it just enough gas while easing up on the clutch.

Cal's staring at me, waiting. I shift in my chair. "Yes, I can. Drive a manual."

He inspects me another minute, then leans back a little.

"Good. You could keep it at your place so you'll have it when you need it. Feel free to use it whenever you want."

I nod. I should say something, show some interest, gratitude, or whatever this messed up situation calls for, but it's all I can do to breathe normally. Between this and the library—

He's still talking. I try to focus on what he's saying.

"Not like a volunteer or anything." He looks uncomfortable. "I'd pay you."

I almost laugh at that. Can he pay me by leaving me the hell alone? Can he get my parents off my case? Buy me a few months to get it together again? I seriously doubt he can pay me whatever I want.

I look at his hands. Bigger than mine. The skin perfect, smooth. Calm on the table before him. How can he be so calm?

My hands are like cold birds in my lap, fluttering around. I pull on my fingers. Try to sit still. Try to slow down the freak-out in my head, surrender to the heavy blur overtaking me. I'm slipping away. Then I'm underwater, sinking, pulled down by all that weight, in that place where nothing comes in clear.

Only for the first time, it's no relief. Feeling follows me and the mute place stretches out in all directions, heavy, indistinct, like another kind of nightmare, one where I'm an endless witness.

I look up. His eyes are on me.

Not Patrick's, Cal's. Here. Waiting.

I shake my head. Look out the window. The world around me expands a little. Some of the heaviness leaves my arms and legs. Just a bit. I drop my shoulders into a more relaxed position. Shake my head again. There aren't words for it. To explain myself.

"I'm sorry—" I start.

His face falls like he thinks I'm going to say no.

"It was a stupid thing to say, the driver thing. I'm sorry. I'm—"

There's no out. Maybe I should do something. For someone. Doing something might get me away from the edge of whatever it is I'm on the edge of.

"I'm just—"

"I think I know," he says quietly, nudging my knee with his. "Me too."

We look out at the snow and the failing light. Night comes faster every day.

"I'm out of practice, being around people."

He laughs.

"It sounds dumb, but it's true. I've been kind of enjoying some, ah, solitude." I glance up at him.

He's looking at me with that look I could fall into. Am falling into.

"I know," he says. "I'm figuring that out. It won't be much, I promise. Little stuff. Here and there. So it's a yes?"

I try not to think of what it will mean to have to do something when someone asks me. I've been running on my own time for so many months. I'll have to pretend I'm a normal person.

He pushes away from the table.

"Why don't I show you around the house, give you the alarm code, and then, if you're up for it, I could take you out for an early dinner? There's a little place on the edge of town that's not half bad . . ."

nothing
happens
anywhere

RECLUSE TO DINNER DATE in a few short hours. I don't even bother to check my face in the bathroom before we leave. It's not like I can pull better clothes out of nowhere or find lip gloss in my empty jeans pockets. Mamie would have died before she'd go out looking like this. I wasn't obsessed with fashion, that's more Meredith's thing, but years of being my mother's daughter and Meredith's best friend taught me to at least do something with my hair and wear a little color on my lips.

Now I regret not taking at least a quick glance in a mirror. There's a splotch of paint or something on the thigh of my jeans. I pick at it with my fingernail. It's not going anywhere. My sneakers are ragged and my socks don't match.

Cal drives us fast along the curving road to town. I try not to notice how the trees whip past my window. Tell myself the car is solid around me, it's got a good grip on the road. Cal looks comfortable driving, casual, in control. Not at all like someone who needs a ride. I close my eyes. I'm not sure, but I think he slows down a bit.

We pull into a lot behind a weathered, whitewashed cottage. A place called Stone's Harbor. A small deck wraps around the front, facing the water. Looks like it's probably a nice place to sit in the summer. We walk into the warmth of the restaurant and the not-so-subtle stares of other diners. It rattles me. A celebrity can walk down the street in New York and people will pretend not to notice. These people could use a lesson in the illusion of privacy. A dark wood bar dotted with little white candles runs the length of the room.

"Nice to see you again, Cal." A woman greets us. She looks like she's around his age. Happy to see him. Maybe a little flirty.

"Sarah." Cal acknowledges her. "Snow doesn't seem to be keeping people away." He nods to the semifull dining room.

"Nope," she says with a smile and a quick glance at me. "People need to eat and we have good food." She gestures toward a table in the corner just past the edge of the window. "Want to sit near the window, or over there, in a quieter spot?"

Cal looks at me, and I eye the corner. If they're going to stare, at least I can have a wall behind me. I wonder for a second how long it would take me to jog home from here. Deep breath.

"Corner's great," he says.

He puts a warm hand at the small of my back and guides me through the narrow alley of tables.

The server follows us, another woman who knows Cal and wants to chit-chat. He's polite with her but keeps his answers short. She gets the hint and slips off to get us water.

The menu's full of local, seasonal food. I would have been impressed a few months ago. Now I have a hard time figuring out what to get. I can read the words, but somehow they don't translate into food I can imagine eating. Cal orders winter diver scallops. I give up and choose a salad. Beets and greens, at least that's what I think it is, the description on the menu reads like an article.

"A salad for a rabbit," Cal says, when she leaves.

It takes me a second to register what he's said.

"Did you just call me a rabbit?"

He smiles a half smile that makes me feel light-headed.

"I did. It fits. You're skittish and always running quietly through the woods. Also, you seem like the littlest thing might scare you to death."

"Very funny."

A rabbit. My face flushes.

He fiddles with his fork, but doesn't take his eyes off me. Smiles at me. I feel like hiding under the table. The silence is heavy between us. For me. He seems happy enough.

"Did you grow up around here?" I ask. I'll say anything to get him to stop looking at me like that. Like he knows me well or something.

He laughs. Apparently I'm funny.

"I mean, did you go to high school up here?" I try again, wishing myself away.

He laughs again, "High school . . ."

Runs a hand through his hair. Another smile.

It dawns on me. "You told me already, didn't you?"

Terrific. I'm repeating myself. I probably remind him of his grandparents.

"No, seriously, it's okay. Auden. They shipped us off, my brother and me."

I nod. I knew people who went to Auden. From the city. Small world. Too small.

"And you?" he asks.

I unfold my napkin and put it on my lap. Pay extra attention to it. Like spreading it out is interesting or difficult. My heart's lurching around in my chest like a weepy drunk.

"Nellie Bly. In the city."

He nods. Smiles again. "Oh, you went to Bly," he teases. "We used to look for Bly parties when we came back on break. It was generally held that people at Bly were less . . . uptight."

Our parties. We were good at those. Pile into Patrick's or Meredith's car, roll down the windows, open the roof, and sing at the top of our lungs while we wove through traffic out to Meredith's parents' beach house. They were never around. Meredith and her brother are, as she puts it, "raised by committee." Nannies, tutors, lessons. An unspoken contract that Meredith and Jay never broke: They're good kids. Until my disaster, anyway. No, Meredith made the grades, and we partied on the beach. She and I ran the house on those weekends like it was ours, like we were so mature, in control. I would give anything to feel free, sure like that again, pulling up, throwing our bags in the house. The salt smell, the wet air, racing Patrick on hard-packed sand, getting thrown into the water regardless of the season, hanging out with people I'd known most of my life.

But I was ready to move on. *Focal Point* gave me a taste of everything else, the messy glory of the world that Bly hid from us. After a few days at my internship, I couldn't wait to be done with high school. I was so close, so ready to fly into my awesome future.

So close.

The food comes blessedly fast.

"Anything else I can get for you?"

Our server's chipper. All her sentences end up, like she's asking a happy question. She looks at Cal like she'd trade places with me in a heartbeat. I should let her. Get up and leave.

"We're good, thanks," Cal says. Then he smiles at her.

She acts like it's an invitation. Leans against the back of an empty chair next to our table.

"So, what brought you back? Last I heard you were in Ithaca?"

She looks at Cal like he's going to say the most fascinating thing ever. And she's spent some time in front of the mirror.

I press my palms onto the tops of my thighs and force a smile in her direction. Like I'm civilized and can stand this inane conversation. But I might scream at her if she doesn't go away soon.

"Weren't you at Cornell?"

It's my turn to watch Cal blush. He takes a minute to answer.

"Change of plans. I'm taking a . . . break." His tone changes, he's less friendly. "Came back in August. I have an internship at a design firm." Looks at her with cool eyes.

She deflates.

"Well, everyone's happy when you and your brother come around." Nods to me. "Enjoy your meal."

"So," I say, after she's out of earshot, "you came in August? That's just before I did."

A thousand emotions whip across his face. He leans away from the table a bit.

"Yeah," he starts. He stops a second and looks me right in the eyes. "I—things changed in my life pretty fast last year. Everything—"

I wait for him to say more.

He doesn't.

"Is that when you got sick?" I ask, after I push my food around a bit. I have to force the words out. My stomach's tight with fear. I don't want to know more terrible stuff.

"When I found out," he says, after a minute. "I'd kind of known awhile, I guess, I just didn't want to deal with it."

I work on eating beets. Infinitely easier than saying anything.

"My mother had MS too." He says it fast.

His dead mother.

I keep eating, but my throat's so tight I can hardly swallow. I force myself to look at him.

He stares at me a second, chin up slightly, like he's daring me to look away. Runs a hand through his hair. He wins. I drop my eyes to his plate where the scallops steam, buttery, untouched.

"Then I got really sick, and everything went to hell. I broke up with Susanna—my girlfriend—left school, and came up here. My dad arranged this internship while I figure it out—change directions."

He looks around the restaurant like it's the last place he wants to be.

I feel for him all of a sudden. I don't want him to have that look on his face. Sad. Angry.

"So, you're not the only one who left a life behind," he says quietly.

I look at my food. Not sure if I can eat anything else.

"I know that look." He laughs, bitter.

I raise my eyebrows at him, try to pull myself together.

"What look?" I ask in a voice that sounds as bright and false as it feels.

His face falls.

"Susanna had it, the face people make when you talk about being sick."

"It's just . . ."

I don't know what to say. I won't lie.

"Your mother died of it?"

Never could beat around the bush.

"Sort of." He exhales like he's been holding his breath.

I close my eyes. I don't want to know about it. Any of it. The sudden heaviness of knowing what it means to die.

Seeing Patrick there in the car, next to me, but not there at all.

I'm trapped. Eyes open, Cal. Closed, Patrick. I don't want to know another person who might die.

"My mom got sick after my little brother was born. When I was in second grade, my dad moved her to a nursing home. She died when I was nine—pneumonia. It was a huge relief, which made it worse. For everyone. For my father."

This needs to stop. I can't hear any more. No more ugly words, terrible details. I know my face has a look on it now. I don't try to hide it. Can't. I hate the world. All the fragile people in it. Every one of us. I was so sheltered. I see that now I've been expelled. Released into the real world. The true one.

"MS isn't the same for everybody," he says. Looks at me. Almost a challenge. Then away.

I trace a figure eight with my finger in the condensation on my glass. Over and over. I want to get out of here. I feel like I'm being hazed. Life's hazing me. Seeing what I can take. How much. I'm an idiot for coming out. This was a giant mistake. If I didn't think it would be the meanest thing ever, I'd bolt. Run home.

Long silence.

He clears his throat.

"Mine's different. Comes and goes. I feel bad, they put me on drugs, and it gets better, sort of, mostly. I don't know. It's weird."

He shakes his head like he can clear the air that way.

"God, this got so depressing. Sorry." Tries to sound casual again. Forks a scallop.

I push food around on my plate. Can't think of a thing to say. This is an endless dinner. I can't look at him.

"I wanted to see you. Get you out of the woods and into some light." He waves a hand toward the dim little candle between us.

I could throw up. I pick up my fork and force myself to eat, instead. The food sticks in my throat. I close my eyes a second. Try to figure out how this is my life. It's like last May I stepped on the wrong stone and slipped into this rotten otherworld. A place where the stakes are higher than you ever knew they could be and people deal with these kinds of things. Accidents. Illness. Death. Loss. Weights I can scarcely carry. I bite the inside of my cheek to toughen up.

"My turn," he says, "for questions."

I make myself look up at him again. He's trying to shake off the gloom that's settled on the table between us. I force a small smile. His hair won't stay out of his eyes. I like that. The way it falls forward.

"So, are you an artist, too?"

I shrug, nod, shrug again. "I used to make pictures, photographs."

Then he hits me with it.

"You know, you don't have to let what happened to you end your life," he says. Casual. It's a tactic my mother would use. Keep it light. Turn the tables. Go for the gut.

The night's over. Either he takes me home now, or I'll go on my own.

"That's not even a question." I'm furious.

The anger in my voice surprises him. He opens his mouth like he's going to say something, but I go on. "I don't need you to play shrink. I've got my mother for that."

"Wren . . ."

"Save it. All the tired condolences. If I hear another person say *it is what it is*—"

I'm sarcastic. Caustic. I get angry when I'm scared.

"I—" he tries again.

I cut him off.

"Believe me, I've heard it all since May."

I'm overreacting, I can feel it, but I can't stop.

"Does it work for you? The bullshit talk about how it's all okay? How you need to get over yourself and move on? Because it's not. It's not okay at all. You of all people should know that."

I'm not fit to be in public. For a second the room does a dizzying spin.

Then it's over. Something falls inside me. Sinks down deep. I look at my lap. A terrible leaden loneliness. Try to breathe under the weight of it.

"You're right. I'm sorry," he says once he thinks I'm done.

I am. Done.

"I didn't mean to make you mad." He reaches across the table to touch my wrist.

I pull away. The restaurant's too quiet. I look around to see if I was as loud as I felt. A few people are looking at us.

"I would like to go now," I whisper. I can't look at him. If he won't take me, I'll run home.

"Come on, don't take it like that. I'm sorry. It was a stupid thing to say."

I shake my head.

"This was a mistake. For me, I mean. To come out. It's not you."

I need to go. I have to get out of here. This town is too small.

He looks at me, really sad for a second.

"Please." I beg. I can hardly make my voice work. I really don't want to walk out on him, but I will if he doesn't get us out of here.

He sees it on my face. Signals the server. After quick reassurances that the food was great, he leaves money on the table, and we're out.

I'm so relieved. Even to be in the car. The frigid silence after my door clunks shut. I lean back into my seat. Keep my eyes on the windshield. I'll never be able to look at him again.

"I'm sorry . . ." I say when he gets in.

He lifts a hand. "No, it was me. Really. I was stupid. You were pretty clear about things."

He drives the car fast along the snowy roads. We cut a silent path through the muffled landscape. Trees whip by in a dark staccato. The sky is deep and teeming.

We come to our road in no time.

"Here's fine," I say, starting to get out while we're still pulling into the driveway.

"I'll take you to your door," he says, surprised.

I shake my head. "Here's fine."

I can't explain it, that I have to get out of his car, now, before I start screaming. There's no air in here. There is something seriously wrong with me. I can't figure anything out. I'm too out of control. My heart does something when I'm near him. And it's messing everything up. He's too close. Familiar or something. I'm not getting tangled up in anything again. With anyone. Not like this. Especially not because my parents planned it.

He barely stops the car before I'm out.

"Thanks for dinner," I call out over my shoulder as I walk down the rest of our curved drive, away from him, as fast as I can in the snow, as quickly as I can get out of sight.

LIGHTS ON in the studio. Dad laughing inside. I throw open the door. It's heavy, but I shove it so hard it bangs back against the wall. He's with a small group of assistants and Mary. I startle them all.

"You asked him to hire me!" I say, trying, and failing, to control my volume. I lose it. Shout at the top of my lungs across the cavernous studio into his surprised face. "You. Asked. Him. To. Hire. Me!"

He crosses the room with a little backward wave of his hand toward his people. They scatter. Zara sticks around a few more minutes, putting away tools. She shoots me a sympathetic glance.

"Wren," he says. "What happened?"

He eyes me anxiously like maybe I've been hurt by Cal or something. Instead of by him. His humiliating betrayal.

"You set the whole thing up," I say. "You lied to me." I'm shaking with fury and something else.

I feel like I could take a tire iron and clear through this space. Smash all the work. Work. What a joke. It's so pointless. This group of earnest people in here day after day working on stuff, and for what? Small flames against a huge dark. Where's the meaning in that? If we're the ones who make it?

"I came here," my voice shakes, "I came here because you never judged me. Never. Those times I visited you, growing up, were like free time for me. I was happy here. Felt great about myself." I'm blind with tears. Snot. "Because you always liked me just as I was. You never asked me to be anything else." I feel impossibly sad.

He tries to put his arms around me. I shrug him off. He steps back and takes me by the elbow, pulls me over to his little sitting area. Pushes me down into a chair. Waits it out.

"Dad," I say, when I can speak again, "I feel like I have to get out of here. Go somewhere else. I can't do this. I thought your place was somewhere I could just *be* awhile."

"Why?" His voice is soft. "Wren, why do you think it's going to be better anywhere else? Different?"

Zara passes by us on her way out. Hands my dad a bottle of scotch and a shot glass. Sets a mug of herbal tea in front of me. Touches me lightly on the shoulder when she leaves. Dad pours himself a shot. Pushes my mug toward me. I shake my head, but he lifts it. "Drink. Something warm."

I take the scalding, honeyed tea down my throat. It burns through me like a tentacled thing, then steals my energy, and I sink back into the chair.

"I'm sorry you're so upset."

He's rubbing one of his permanently stained hands over the worn arm of his chair.

"I don't want you to leave. It was underhanded, I see that now, for me to set that up. I just wanted to you have someone. Someone your age. Someone to talk to."

"But that's the point, Dad," I say. "I don't want to. Talk."

"I think, if she'd made it up here for a visit"—he sighs—"but you know, Wren—your mother—she's far away, and she worries. She's planning to come up to convince you to leave with her, go somewhere else."

I groan and press my fingers against my swollen eyes a second.

"I don't want that for you, or for me. I'm glad you came. I wanted to buy you more time to do whatever it is you're doing up here."

He leans back in his seat, and for a second he looks old. Even his hands, which normally seem large and capable, are two sad dogs on his lap.

"I want this to be a place where you can be yourself. I've made mistakes. I know. I should have been around more. Don't leave now. Not like this."

There are points in time when you grow older than your parents. Or come up on them at least. I look at my father, who's shrinking before my eyes, and realize no one will save me. No one *can* save me.

"I'm sorry I interfered," he says, running his hand over his face. "You don't have to work for Cal if you don't want to. I'll lie to your mother. Put her off awhile longer. She—*we* really wanted you to make a friend." He looks at me. "Just don't go rushing off somewhere, okay?"

There's nowhere else for me to go. And being here isn't it either. I'm a stupid girl who screwed up a perfectly decent life, wished it away, who had a boyfriend and wished him away. And then I got my wishes.

Dad pours himself another shot. We sit in silence awhile. Snow falls lightly on the skylight.

I shake my head. Then, thank God, even though my heart's been battering my chest, I harden. I'm still. Cool. A grave angel. Gazing skyward.

The deep quiet I found after the accident slips up around me. My dad looks far away on his chair, the distance great between us. I wipe my face, the tears stop. I stand and leave the room.

"Wren?" he calls after me. "You're okay? You're going into the house now?"

I say nothing. There's nothing to say.

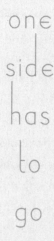

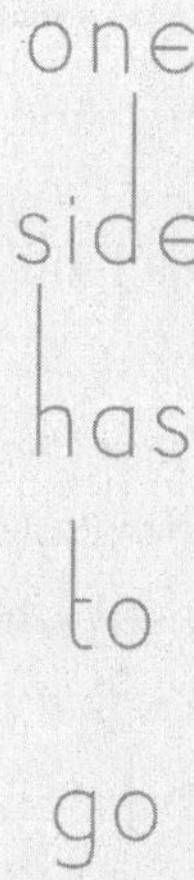

THE NEXT AFTERNOON, when I head out to run, Cal's Jeep is there, parked in front of our house, keys in it.

It takes my dad a few hours to notice I've quit talking again. I avoid him as long as I can but he keeps an eye, pokes around the house more than usual. Finally we're shoulder to shoulder in the small kitchen. His questions to me fall on the floor between us like crumbs. I feel him sag a little when I don't respond. Watch him shrink some more. I make dinner, and we eat together, quiet in the dark. I am empty, calm. The waves are loud.

A week later there's a note on my pillow when I wake up. "It's fine," it says in my dad's scrawl, "I understand. I'll deal with your mother. You still have to work in the library."

I stretch, then lie there awhile. My cell phone is gone. Where it had been, in place of the charger, is a little twist of metal, a small bird, like the ones he made for me when I was little.

Mary comes into the house around lunch. She's wearing a wild, flowered garden party kind of dress probably made by some housewife in the sixties. She has it belted over a pair of purple skinny jeans. Giant plastic daisy clip-on earrings complete the look. I can almost smell lilacs on her. She's a dream from another season. Another world. In her hand, a note for me. And the Jeep keys.

"Cal called," she says, poking her bright face into the air before mine. "He needs to know if you're free to help him or not." She jingles the keys in her fingers. "He needs a ride somewhere, or something? I guess I really don't know what he wants—I was doing forty other things when he called. Anyhow, I wrote down the security code to his house."

I look away from her. The thing about being quiet is that you get really far out, in your head. Forgetful, hazy, like you're not all the way here.

I'm reading Larkin. "Aubade" again. I put my finger there, on his lines, like I can record them somehow, let his words fill me until I can bear to be back inside myself again. Words, kisses, chances taken, or missed, none of it matters. Noise beneath an empty sky.

Larkin knew this nowhere place. Lived in it, too, managed to make a life anyway, for a while, at least.

"Wren?" Mary's voice cuts through the blank. I look up at her again, a little disoriented.

"Do you want me to call him, tell him to find someone else?" She jingles the keys again. Tilts her head at me sideways, like she thinks I might not be in there. No one home.

I look at the note in her hand. Stand and stretch. Walk over to her, give her an empty look, and take the keys. I'm flat. Far away. Insulated. I'll do this. What the hell.

When I pull up at Cal's, the sun's high and bright. It blinded me most of the way here, snow melt flashing off the road like a strobe. Maybe it's being at his house, but I start to feel weird. Like I'm waking up or something. What am I doing? I don't want to see him again. He can hire someone else to help him out.

The new snow's high around the door. Undisturbed. No one's come or gone in a few days. I spot the garage remote on the dash. I push it and the door pulls up and back, a modern guard. I gun it through piles of white and slide the Jeep in alongside the silver car.

My heart starts to flop around inside me like a dying fish, the calm of the last several days evaporated. I could go in, leave the keys on the table, and walk home. Run, even. My quiet is slipping away from me, too fast, my mind starts to race. What am I doing here? Am I going to go in, see what he wants? Face him? Mary's been talking to him? Are they friends? She's been chattering at me nonstop all week. Bright noise like a gabby squirrel. Totally in cahoots with my dad. She probably called Cal, set this up, not the other way around.

I put my head on the steering wheel. My heart might

explode if it doesn't slow down. That would be a fitting end to everything. Just kick it here in this Jeep, my weak heart flown apart inside me. Breathe. In. Out. In again. I'm not sure I can get out of the car.

My mute week. So easy. Peaceful. Once the words go away, they go away inside, too. No unceasing mental clamor. I'm nowhere.

Makes me wonder why more people don't just shut the hell up. My dad's been running interference with my mother, I think, taking her calls. Has to be, or she'd be up here by now. Even at the library, Lucy seems to know not to ask me anything. She shows me my tasks, and I do them. Every few days Zara comes by for coffee and they talk and laugh together, ignore me. It's good again. So what am I doing sitting here in Cal's garage?

I catch sight of myself in the rearview. I look insane. Well, maybe I am, so at least I'm consistent. I shower, but I've kind of let the mirror go the way of words. I pull my fingers through my hair. Not that it helps much. My clothes are pretty sorry, too. I've been lounging around in an old, holey moss-green cashmere V-neck of my dad's and some torn jeans. I forgot to grab a coat. That was a bit of a jolt. It's below freezing. Maybe I do need to see someone. Go away awhile. To The Home.

I bang my forehead against the steering wheel. The Home. Meredith. Normal Meredith Away at College. If she were here with me, she'd be lifting a golden eyebrow, part criticism, part concern.

I'm lost again, inside myself. Somewhere that's not nowhere.

Disoriented. I've let everything go. I think I have to go in. To Cal's house. See what he wants.

I get out of the car and try the door. It's locked. Relief for a second, until I remember the security code on the note shoved in my pocket. I beep-beep the numbers into the pad and the green light comes on. Go. I push open the heavy door and let it shut behind me with a loud clunk.

"Wren?" Cal's voice.

I look around the perfect house. No Cal.

"Back here," he calls.

One of the bedrooms. His. I cross the bright living room and walk back to the narrow hall. His door's open. The afternoon light is bright on his bed, a lit quilt of color.

Cal's on a long gray couch near the window, with a pile of books and his laptop. Pale. Dark circles around his eyes, like maybe he hasn't slept in a while. Sweatpants. A worn Auden Prep T-shirt. Papers on the floor all around him. A small collection of plates and mugs near his ankle.

"Sorry about the mess," he says, looking around. "I'm . . . I've been a little . . ."

Our eyes meet and for a weird second I think maybe I love him. Could. The feeling zips through my middle. Cuts through me. Opens me right up. Then that choking feeling in my throat. I swallow it away. Hard.

"I know you're not talking," he says. "Mary told me."

I just look at him. I don't think I could say anything even if I wanted to.

"That's fine. I just need a ride out of here. Into town. See Dr. Williams." He glances at the wall. "The closet's over there.

Will you grab me a pair of jeans and some socks?"

I go over to his closet. Touch an edge of the panel and the door pops open, soundlessly. His shirts hang in a row, neatly organized. Everything else on shelves. It smells like him. Fresh. I grab a pair of socks, jeans, a clean tee, and a sweater. Set them next to him on the couch. For a second my arm reaches out on its own, like I'm going to touch his face or something. Without thinking. Like he's mine to touch. I back away.

"Thanks," he says. Avoids my eyes. "I'm good. I'll be out in a minute."

I leave the room. My heart's racing like a bird heart. Fluttering, skipping beats, smaller than normal. My reckless heart. It's probably shot. Will always be small and far away.

He comes into the living room a few minutes later, one hand on the wall like it's some kind of anchor, using a crutch. I'm not sure what I'm supposed to do. I go over to him. Wrap my arm around his waist. He leans against me a little and we go out to the car.

The last I see of him is in the waiting room at Dr. Williams' clinic. A little while later, a woman in floral scrubs comes out to tell me I can leave. Gives me a professional smile. They must teach that one in nursing school. I sit there a minute in the ugly teal waiting room, not sure what to do.

"It's okay," she says, turning to me again, just before she goes back into the office. "He said to tell you to go. He'll find a ride. We're keeping him awhile."

So I drive away alone. The house is empty when I get there. Same for the studio. For once I'm disappointed. I wonder if I should have called someone. Call someone now. His family. I toss Cal's keys into the basket on the counter and grab my running clothes. If I stay inside I'll never figure anything out.

The sky's lower now, reddish. Frigid air smacks me in the face, burns my lungs. I set out slow, try to let my body carry me, quiet, simple, but I can't even get the run right. My mind's awake, words flying around in me like a vortex of bright snow spiraling up from the road in cold wind. Should I go back to town, to Cal? Do I tell my dad? Call someone? My muscles are tight. Nothing feels right. Or maybe I should go home, read Larkin, fall asleep.

I force myself to keep going. Silently count my steps. Circle the house until I hit my stride. Even though I haven't said a word, the quiet feeling's gone, and I can't pull it back over me. For the first time in months I wish I could call Meredith. Tell her everything. She'd know what to say, do. She'd take charge, or laugh at me, make everything seem not so big, not so bad. But I can't. Won't. I don't think you can go back again after something's torn open that wide.

I run the trails to Cal's road. Jog in my tire ruts until I get to the house. It's snow silent. Empty. I wish I'd said something to him. One kind word. Sucked it up, or least called Dad's plow service to deal with the mountainous drifts in the driveway. Hadn't he left the house all week? Meredith's right. I'm selfish. Small-hearted.

I turn back, take the road. Pass my bent bike leaning against a tree.

Stop. Back up.

How could I have left it there so long? He must feel horrible every time he passes it. I trek over to it. The glassy snow crust crackles and gives way with a hollow burp each step. Scrapes skin off my ankles. But I have to do something with it. Get that bike out of here. Now.

I grab the handlebars and pull it away from the tree's frozen hug. Drag it down the road behind me. I know what I'm going to do. I can see it before me, bright, clear. The bike's crusted with ice and weighs a ton, keeps catching my heel, my calf, smashing itself against the back of my legs. My arms burn. None of it matters. A small price for what I've done, who I am. Once I get to Cal's, I head around to the cliff side, that stupid bike clanking down each step behind me.

The ocean stretches before me, sequined in the sun. I'm spent, panting, a dog before it. I lie down in the snow near the edge for a second to catch my breath. Without thinking, I make a snow angel. The things the body remembers. I haven't thought of snow angels in . . . forever. I make it with the concentration of an eight-year-old, until my heart slows and I stop panting from dragging the bike.

Something has to be beautiful.

Cold sets in through my wet clothes. I stand as carefully as I can to protect my angel, step away from her, grab my bike, and drag it to the edge.

I recite Larkin's "Aubade." I need to hear the ending out loud. One of us has to go.

I take a deep breath, and with all my strength, I run toward the edge, yelling as loudly as I can, and hurl that wrecked bike over. My voice is weird. A banshee. The bike falls and crashes and falls. Yellow against the grey. For a minute the waves lift it and smash it against the rocks, and then I can't see it anymore.

thank you, mary

I OPEN THE LIBRARY AT NINE. It's early and I feel grim. I think they invented this job just to get me out of bed. Lucy comes in an hour later. Sometimes brings coffee. We're easy together. If she has opinions about me, she doesn't show it. There's no pressure to talk. I reshelve books and check things out for the rare patron. We fill special-delivery orders. Not part of the library's regular service, something Lucy does for the people who can't get in. Mostly old people. An occasional mother overrun with kids. Lucy's her own bookmobile. Says she hired me so she doesn't have to close the library while she's gone. Not that anyone would notice, but I guess, on principle, staying open is the goal.

When Lucy's out I read. One morning I find a book about Carthusian nuns on the table where I usually sit. It's not lost on me that they're an order that takes a vow of silence. Before I put it away, I lift the cover, spot their motto. My Latin was never strong, but it's something like *Steady while the world orbits*.

I'm still not talking, but it doesn't give me the calm, faraway feeling I had before. And I don't call Cal. I'm a coward. I want to know how he is but I can't make myself pick up the phone.

Dad's off to Berlin again to have an opening at his new gallery. He asks Mary to move in with me while he's gone. A babysitter. Nice. He says I have to ride with them to the airport. Keep Mary company on the drive home. I almost laugh at that one, I make such good company. He's so obvious.

Mary's banged-up car takes forever to heat. The air is so cold and sharp it makes me cough. I pull my parka up around my face and fall asleep in the backseat almost immediately. The drive goes fast. When I wake up, we're passing the squat little buildings that skulk around the airport like poor cousins. Depressing. I let my dad hug me good-bye extra long. He's afraid to leave, I can tell. Makes me feel guilty. He even hugs Mary.

On the way home, she's quiet. Puts music on. I'm relieved. Even my nap didn't feel like enough of a boost to handle a working-over by Mary. By the time we pull in to the shed I'm feeling almost cheerful. It's a foreign feeling. It was good to have a change of scene, even if it meant hours in the car. She grabs my hand before I get out.

"I went to see Cal this week," she says, avoiding my eyes. "He missed Secret Cinema, which he's never done before—so I thought I'd check on him. I just wanted you to know."

I pull my hand away and my heart skips a few beats. Jealous.

"He's okay," she says, surprised.

I'm shocked at my sudden jealousy. I look out the window. Some windstorm at some point bent the weather vane my dad made off its axis and it looks like the winds are prevailing skyward.

"You know, in case you were wondering. His dad was there a few days. Cal's home. Sleeping a ton, but he's supposed to. Anyhow"—she takes a breath, lets the words out in a rush, like she's not sure if she should say it—"I'm telling you because I'm sure he'd love to see you—if you felt like going over there."

She looks at me now. Part hopeful and part like she's trying to figure me out.

"Not to pressure you," she tries again, "but I don't think he's going to keep calling. You kind of seem like you don't want him to—I mean, if you want to keep him as a friend, or whatever, you could . . ."

It's dark out. The sky is crazy, more stars than dark. So many more than I can ever remember seeing. Far more than we ever see in the city. I look back at Mary. Those moon eyes, her wide-open face.

"I guess I'm trying to say it's up to you," she finishes.

I get out of her car and head into the house.

When I finally wake up the next morning, Mary's been busy. She's unearthed Dad's juicer, and next to a hearty glass of fuchsia brilliant beet-and-ginger juice, five orange tulips lean out of a jelly jar. I grab the bread knife, free a hunk of sourdough, butter it, and lean against the sink, chewing the bread and sipping juice. It's nice having her here, even if it means my phone's on the counter, charged, a scrap of paper tucked under it. Cal's number.

I step out the door a second. Music's blasting in the studio. Mary's working. The sun's high and huge in the sky. Its own triumph. Good for the sun. I test the mood waters. Feel strangely normal. No pink pill last night. I just slept. Blessed be the blank.

It's definitely easier to wake up when I don't take them. Instead of the ever-looping mental reel of disaster, Cal was there, filling my mind until I drifted off. I didn't try to push him away. Maybe I should call him today. Talk. Maybe I can act like a normal person.

I go back inside. The tulips look hopeful. I finish my juice—thank you, Mary—throw on clean, fresh-smelling running clothes and head out into the shimmering morning. I need to figure out what I'm doing. What I'm going to do.

There are two messages on my cell when I get back. Both from my mother. Dad's out of town. She thinks I'm alone. He must not have told her he asked Mary to stay. *Just checking in*, she says. *Hope all is well*—a desperate singsong—*tell me all is well*. I call back but dial right to voice mail, find my voice, leave a small *hey Mom, call you later* message.

Then, before I can think about it another minute, I try Cal. It was never a problem for me before, calling guys. My hands shake when I dial.

Voice mail. A letdown. I hang up. Just as well. My voice is kind of scratchy, unreliable. I toss the phone onto the couch. Time for a shower and loud music.

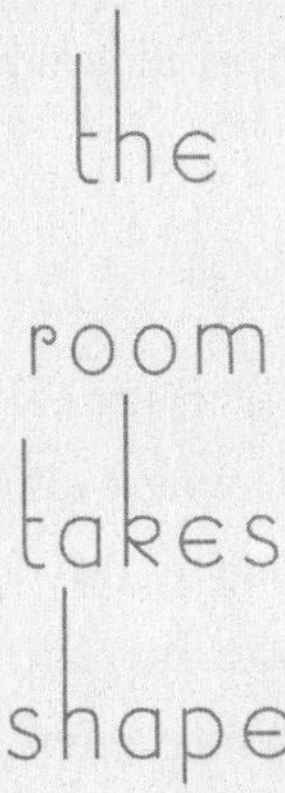

the room takes shape

HE DOESN'T CALL BACK. Time seems to have taken up with me again and the afternoon's endless. Don't know what to do with myself. So I go over there. Sudden bravery.

No answer at the door. I tried out my voice again in the car on the way over. It sounds weird, like I have laryngitis, but it's there. From the garage I try his cell one more time. Voice mail. I climb back into the Jeep to find wherever I'd shoved the paper with his security code on it. It's on the floor between the seats. I let myself in. The house is silent.

"Cal?" I call out in my crackly voice.

No answer.

Technically, I'm breaking and entering. Okay. Well, not

breaking, but definitely entering. Uninvited. It's starting to seem insane, coming here. Mary and her wild ideas. She's worse than Meredith. I sit on the bench a minute, try to catch my breath. I have no idea what I'm doing anymore. Ever.

"Hello?" I say again.

Nothing.

From the bench I look around. The place is a mess. And it shows, unlike my dad's where chaos is an everyday thing. Cal's jacket is on the floor by the door, and I can see dirty dishes on the coffee table. In fact, there are dishes everywhere. Like he hasn't washed anything in days.

I hang my coat and his, slip out of my boots. *He's probably out with someone*, I tell myself. But what if he isn't? Alarming images begin to form. What if he's here, sick? Needs help? My stomach's tight. I walk through the house. Look for him.

"Cal?"

The workroom's a mess too. Books all over the place, some open on the table, architectural drawings spread out. No Cal.

I go back to his room. The door's open a crack. I knock lightly. No answer. Give it a little push. Step in. I can't look. My heart's in my ears. I don't think MS causes sudden death but I'm not really sure. *Please don't be dead*, I say, a little prayer.

I look. He's there. Facedown on the bed. A pillow over his head. I'm frozen in place. Watch him so closely to see if he's breathing it makes my eyes hurt. Then he moves slightly, shifts. My knees almost buckle. Of course he's sleeping. What's wrong with me? That's what Mary said. He needs sleep. I back out of the room as quietly as I can, my socks silent on the wood floor. I pull the door closed and nearly run back to the living room. I'm so relieved I feel elated. It's strange. I'm going to clean up. He'll wake up to a neat house.

Why is it so easy to clean someplace beautiful? The surfaces in the kitchen shine in seconds. The dishes are heavy and warm in my hands in the soapy water. They fit themselves into each other on the shelf with satisfying clunks. I can see why my mother loves order so much. It's comforting. Even if it is a lie.

The workroom isn't as bad as it looks, either. I slip sticky notes on the open pages of every book and stack them near his computer. One set of drawings is titled "Structures on landscapes of fantastic seclusion." Something for school. Or one of his intern projects. I'm careful with the drawings, neaten them into a pile.

I step into my boots and hike out to empty the mailbox. It's full. I bring the pile into the dining room table and separate it into stacks of magazines, bills, junk. There's one personal letter, a small envelope from Spain, "S. Braun" in the corner. I try to remember what he said his girlfriend's name was. Can't. Maybe this is from her. I leave it on top.

There's nothing left to do. I stand in front of the huge windows. My snow angel's filled with some fresh snow, but she's still there. At least one of us is. And the drag marks from my bike. And a few of my footsteps. I turn away and survey his house. I should leave. I've made it nice in here again. Probably the best thing I have to offer him.

I spot a collection of softball-size rocks on a side table. I pick a whitish-gray one and go to the couch. It's heavy and fits my palm like it was made for me to hold.

A normal person would go, satisfied with having helped. But normal's so far behind me and it took a lot to get myself over here. I'll wait a bit. See if he wakes up. I warm the rock with my hands. It'll outlast me. Already has done. I pull a creamy cashmere throw off the arm of the couch and wrap up in it. Hold the rock and look at the water awhile.

looking up

"THE RABBIT CAME BACK . . ."

A quiet voice near my head wakes me.

I sit up, disoriented. It's dark. Outside. In the house. My side's sore from lying on something hard and my hand's asleep. Cal's next to me on the couch. He looks good. Bare feet, an old T-shirt, jeans. Those dark lashes, slate-blue eyes looking at me, a little smile in them.

"Oh," I say in my scratchy voice. Clear it. Try to come to. I run my fingers through my hair. His thigh is warm against mine. Crutches on the floor at our feet.

"And she speaks," he says cheerfully. "Things are definitely looking up."

"You're awake," I say, totally alert now myself. Embarrassed.

Start to get up. "I'm sorry, I know I shouldn't have let myself in, but I hadn't heard from you—I tried to call a few times and I—"

He grabs my hand and pulls me back down on the couch next to him.

"I'm glad you're here. I woke up and thought the house had been cleaned by magic elves. Then I saw you on the couch. I didn't mean to startle you, but it's nearly eight, and it kind of seemed like you might be asleep for the night."

I rub my hands over my face. "Aren't all elves magic? By definition?"

He laughs. A great sound.

"Long run this afternoon," I say, to explain the nap. Like it's a regular thing to run yourself silly, go to someone's house uninvited and nap on their couch. I'm nervous. I glance down at the crutches.

"Are you better? Feeling better?"

He leans back. He's so close. We're shoulder to shoulder. I'm light-headed. The air between us prickling with some current. My heart's in my throat. He moves his hand over, slightly, so it brushes mine.

I look at his fingers. They're cared for, not dry and overlooked, lotion having revealed itself to be another neglected item on my checklist of daily maintenance.

He leans his head closer, touches my cheek. My heart is going to stop.

"I'd really like to kiss you," he says. Looks at me.

I couldn't say no if I tried. I lean toward him. I have nothing left to lose.

He runs his fingers across my lips. Puts a warm hand on either side of my face and pulls me closer. I close my eyes. His mouth is on mine.

"You're talking again," he says, after a while.

We're entwined on the couch. My lips feel full and slightly bruised.

"I am." I wince a little, meet his eyes. "Sorry . . . about that."

"Don't be," he says. "You've got a lot going on. I thought I might not see you again."

I look down, ashamed. I wasn't sure either.

After I said yes to Around the World with Patrick, he followed me into the darkroom. Leaned me against the stop bath. Our first kiss.

No more first kisses for him. It's like a huge stone in my center. Presses me down.

"I don't know what's going on between us, but I've wanted to kiss you since I knocked you off your bike."

Cal. Talking to me. Here. Not there.

"I—" I say, try to pull myself back to him.

"But I'm sick, and you're young."

"I'm not that young," I say, sounding exactly that young.

He puts his hand on my breast, over my heart.

This is it. I know. This is where you're supposed to lean into it. Live a little. I hope I can.

"You just finished high school, and you're going through your own thing—no pressure."

I lean against him.

He lifts my hands to his mouth, kisses my palms, laughs. "I'm so glad something cured our mute."

I whack him on the arm.

"Very funny."

"Seriously. You're talking. That's great. Mary said your dad was freaking out."

My dad.

We look out the window a second.

"Nice snow angel," he says.

I blush.

"And your bike's gone."

I have to change the subject.

"So what happened . . . with Dr. Williams?"

He clenches his fists and undoes them a few times.

"My hands and feet feel weird, kind of like they fell asleep. And my balance is worse. Dr. Williams checked me in, put me on some drug for a few days." He sighs. "It's getting better."

"It is? It will? Get better?"

The million-dollar question. The one polite people step around. Overlook.

He pulls away from me slightly.

"Not the way you mean. But it comes and goes, and it's worse when it comes."

I look back out the window. It's mostly a mirror now, reflecting the two of us, small on the couch, more terrible questions wedged between us, unasked and unanswered. But the moon's out there, spilling light all over the place, a searchlight, still visible through the glass.

Cal runs his hands through his hair, pushes it back. It falls forward again. He has the faraway look in his eyes you get when you're reliving something. The look I've been stuck in since last May. Then he squints a little, turns to me again, pulls me back into focus.

"Hey—just now—it doesn't mean anything. Doesn't have to, I mean, it doesn't have to be weird. I get it, Wren. You have a lot going on."

I want him to stop looking at me like that, to stop leaning away. I take his hand and put it back on my heart, hold it there. He feels familiar to me. Right.

"So you'd be done with school this year."

He looks at his hand. Pulls it away. Shakes his head.

"No. The program's five years. I was third year, design studio, pulling all-nighters. My feet started catching curbs, undershooting steps. Susanna's the one who called it. Freaked herself out on the Internet. She knew about my mom. One morning I woke up sick, and she panicked. Called my dad."

"Susanna's your girlfriend?"

A small smile. "Was."

I run my fingertips over his eyebrows. He closes his eyes. I want to kiss away the dark look shadowing his face.

He pulls away from me again. Looks out the window.

"We were doing this rooftop build-out of a community center in the projects. A green space right in the middle of these faceless towers crammed with people who would probably all rather live anywhere else. We got a lot of notice for the work, an offer to do an exchange, work on a project in Barcelona."

"But you didn't go."

He shakes his head. Bounces one knee. Stops.

"I left Cornell. Once it was confirmed, I couldn't deal. Susanna went to Barcelona alone. Michael came up"—he gestures toward the photo of him and his brother—"and we stayed in the city for the summer, went out, picked up girls, slept it off, did it again. I was an ass, angry and sick."

It's weird to think about Cal running wild around the city, my city, all summer while I was in bed with my face to the wall. I don't mention the letter on the table. He'll find it when I'm not here.

"Do you want something to drink?" he asks abruptly, leaning over to grab the crutches.

"I'll get it." I jump up. "What do you want?"

He doesn't answer. I find seltzer in the fridge and bring two glasses. Sit and watch the little bubbles shiver to the surface and pop when they hit the air.

"So," he says, after a while, "in August, my dad came down, told me to stop freaking out and get my shit together. Said I wasn't my mother. My brother had been talking to him on the phone and was, it turned out, afraid to go back to school and leave me alone." He pulls his face into an embarrassed grimace. Takes a breath and goes on, "My dad called some friends, lined things up, the internship, and here I am. A year off, he says, someplace less stressful." He looks at me with a sorry smile. "And you can see how well that's working out."

I'm not sure if he means me. We're quiet for a while.

"Anyway, I have to figure it out, handle it myself. I was starting to feel a little better when I nearly ran you over." Bitterness in his voice again.

"It's okay," I say quietly. "Nothing happened."

"Everything happened." He closes his eyes. "Dr. Williams had just told me not to drive on days when—if I'm not sure about my reflexes. I was so pissed, driving like a maniac."

Another long silence.

"What if I'd hurt you?" He lets out a long breath. Looks at me.

"You didn't."

He pulls me on top of him and we sit, forehead-to-forehead, nose-to-nose, breathing each other in.

a regular person

EVEN THOUGH IT'S LATE, when I get home, I open my laptop. First time since I moved here.

My sole remaining e-mail account's maxed out. 800 messages. Apparently mostly from Emma. Patrick's little sister's name a daisy chain looping through my inbox. September, October, November—it looks like she sent the same message over and over until my account filled. My stomach flips.

I close my laptop. I'll read it. But not yet. Then I open it again, do exactly what Susanna did. Research. It isn't pretty. I don't understand everything I read, but it seems like there are different types of MS, and from what he told me, Cal's is the best, if there is such a thing. His mom's was definitely the worst.

I go to bed late, try to forget what I read, and sleep badly. Finally around three, after watching the Patrick reel in my head and insomnia-dream mixing his face with Cal's, I get up and take a pill. Dark comes like an anvil.

Mary wakes me up the next day at noon.

"You skipping the library today?" she asks, poking her head in the door.

"Shit!" I sit up fast, head pounding. I'm sticky with fatigue. The pill had me down somewhere deep.

"You're talking!" she bounces on her toes a little.

"With the sun behind your head like that," I say, struggling to come to, "you look like one of those Mexican religious candles. Our Lady of Achingly Bright Light."

Mary laughs. Strikes a holy pose, the wide sleeves of the scarlet kimono-like shirt she's wearing falling in a graceful, light-shot triangle.

I flop back on the pillow and throw my arm over my eyes. Now I'll have to call Lucy Shepherd and apologize.

"Your phone's chirping."

She tosses it to me. Her eyes dart to the pill bottle next to my bed.

It's like I'm coming up from the center of the earth. I sit up again. My phone. Missed calls. From Cal. From the library. One from my mom.

"Will you call Lucy?" I plead. It's totally inappropriate, but my mouth carries on, begging her, "At the library? Will you call and tell her I overslept, and I'm sorry?" I'm so lame, but I can't stand the idea of calling her myself.

"Sure," she says slowly, eyeing me.

We're quiet a minute. Some requests cross the line.

"Forget it," I say, ashamed. "I'll call."

She gives me a conspiratorial smile, like nothing weird has just passed between us. "You were out so late, I thought maybe you wouldn't come home from Cal's . . ." She raises an eyebrow.

I throw a pillow at her.

"Your dad called. Some supplies came in for him near the airport. He wants me to get them so they're here when he comes back." She picks up the Larkin next to the bed, fans the pages with her thumb. "He says to tell you his show opened well, and he might not stay the entire week. He's inspired." Her face brightens even more—it's like watching the aperture blades on a lens twirl back to let in more light. "And he wants to get to work again!" She clasps her hands together and rocks happily on the balls of her feet. "It's great for me, of course. Anyhow, I'm driving in to pick up his stuff. Will you come? It's a long drive. We could hit some shops out there? Please?"

It's a normal request. But panic rises inside me anyway. My carefully constructed solitude is coming undone faster than I think I can handle. I swallow.

"Let me check my phone," I say. Hope she'll leave. Not press me for a decision.

She looks at the pills again. Back at me.

"Rough night?"

"Couldn't sleep."

"You know"—she waves a somewhat uncertain hand toward the little bottle—"when you first got here your dad made me go to the pharmacy and ask for sugar pills. He wanted me to switch them out."

I'm stunned. How could he ask her to do something like that? It's coming to me that I've underestimated how closely my dad's watching me. Like I'm a basket case. Which I am, I guess.

She hesitates a second. "He thought you might take them all. Or something. But the sugar pills looked nothing like your prescription, so I didn't do it."

My phone chirps again.

"But I told him I had. He was so worried about you, he couldn't get any work done."

She laughs a nervous laugh and her chandelier earrings flitter. She sits on the end of my bed.

"And then I was afraid you might, you know . . . I mean, I didn't know you . . . didn't know what you were thinking . . ."

I close my eyes and cover my face with my hands. I'm so embarrassed I could die. Too many people are mixed up in my stupid life.

She goes on, "And then I'd never forgive myself for not doing it. He'd never forgive me for lying to him. But I decided to trust you. Someone has to. You'll pull through this. You *are* pulling through. You wouldn't do that—hurt yourself, hurt so many people."

She sounds certain. Wonder if I could borrow that.

"I already did," I say under my breath.

Patrick's mother, for example. The first face I saw when I came to. Her relief. Holding my mother's hand. Worrying for me, us, when she'd just lost her son. I haven't said a single word to her since that night.

It comes to me like that. Flashes out of nowhere and so vivid I live them again. They pull me under. Make me lose my focus on the here and now.

"What did you say?" Mary tilts her head sideways. Reminds me of a bird.

Errands with Mary. An afternoon of it. It's what a normal person would do. Make an effort. Nothing else is working.

"Nothing." I rub my eyes, like I can make it clear away. "I might go with you. Can I run first?"

"I'll be in the studio. Bang on the door when you're back. It'll take us an hour and a half to get in there, an hour if there aren't any cops. Don't take a long run."

I get up and face the day. Call Lucy. Apologize. Promise I won't mess up again. She laughs and says with a high-pressure job like mine, a day off is just the thing. She doesn't sound mad.

My mom can wait. I try Cal. Voice mail. I leave a message. Tell him I'm going out with Mary and to call in the next hour if he wants me to come over or needs anything. I don't know if I'm supposed to be working for him now, or what. Last night seems like something from another life. Not mine. I pull on my running gear.

I leave my iPhone behind. Despite the crappy night's sleep, there's a new quiet in my head. The run works faster. I find my zone in the first mile. Scenes, thoughts, faces rise up here and there, behind this tree, or around that bend, but today I just watch them roll on by. The memories are like a Ferris wheel. I can ride it, go up to the top, feel the rush when everything seems like it'll fall away, but then, if I keep my eyes open, I see the ground again. Patrick fades, and I don't feel the crushing tightness in my chest or the ghost feeling of my seat belt locking me in, upside down, next to him.

When I get home and out of the shower, there's a missed call from Cal.

I call him back. Because that's what a normal girl would do.

"Hi." My heart's skipping around in my chest.

"Hi, yourself." He's cheerful.

"I wanted to hear your voice," I say.

Subtle.

"I know you went right home and freaked yourself out reading on the Internet," he teases. Clears his throat a little.

Caught.

"Yeah." There's no point trying to hide it. "I'm sorry. I had to."

"You had to." He's sarcastic.

I wince. Want to hang up. Say nothing.

"Sorry," he says, after a second. Sounds more pissed than sorry.

"I didn't know anything about it—I had to look. For instance, yours isn't like your mom's . . . ?" My voice trails off.

Silence.

"Right?" I want him to say something. Anything.

"So far." He's brusque. Changes the topic. "Aren't you supposed to be at the library?"

"Overslept. Not exactly a model employee. And now Mary wants me to run some errands with her. Go shopping." A perfectly normal day.

"That's great," he says. "You're going, right?"

"On my way out the door now," I say, woodenly. I can't loosen up. I wish this were going better, but I don't know what else to say. I remember what it felt like to have his hand on the back of my head, in my hair. Shiver a little.

"I'm glad you're going out. It's good for you. Between working and all your running you'll be like Lola from *Run Lola Run*. Did you ever see that movie? German thriller. This girl, lean, rosy-cheeked, kind of distraught, runs everywhere. No, wait, you're already like her."

"Shut up." I laugh, looking around the room for my wallet. I'll have to take more cash from my dad. Lucy hasn't paid me yet.

"Did you run yet today?" he teases. The smile's back in his voice.

"Of course. You should try it. It might do you some good."

It rolls out of my mouth before I can stop it.

He doesn't miss a beat. "That'd be more like *Fall Cal Fall*."

I die a thousand deaths. "Oh God, I wasn't thinking . . ."

He lets me off the hook. Laughs.

"I go to the gym," he says.

Mary sticks her head in. "Last chance, Wren, we've gotta get out of here."

Cal hears her through the phone. "Go, have a good

day. And do me a favor, Lola—don't stop talking all of a sudden?"

I hang up. Try to get my head together. My face is burning. I just had a conversation with a guy who likes me. A guy I like. I'm going shopping with Mary. Look at me. I'm a regular person.

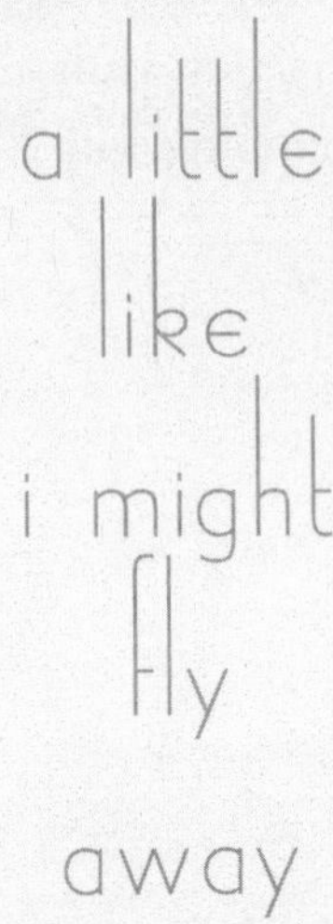

MARY SWINGS US by Mercy House so she can run in and grab a different bag and an extra pair of socks. It's an old wooden house on a lane just outside town. Over the door a weathered plaque reads MERCY CONVENT and just beneath it a more modern sign says MERCY HOUSE. I follow Mary up slightly sagging wooden steps to the porch. She pulls a brass skeleton key on a string out of her coat pocket and unlocks the glass-paned front door. We step into the silence of an oak foyer, surfaces polished to a shine, portraits lining the wall to the left, nuns in rows of black, smiling at an unseen photographer.

"What is this place?" I ask, staring at all the women's faces.

Mary walks past me to a desk near the back, leans across it, and pulls a letter from an old hotel-style mail cubby.

She turns and smiles. "You're kidding, right? You've never been here?"

Her eyes go to the envelope in her hand. Looks official. RISD logo on it.

"Zara and Jeb started it years ago," she says, kind of absentmindedly. "When the last of the nuns were moving into nursing homes. It's a retreat space for artists. C'mon, I'll show you my room. I just have to grab a few things."

I follow her through a wide, wood-paneled living room. The windows overlook a wraparound porch. In the side yard, I spy a gazebo that looks like it's seen better days. And a huge, fenced-in garden plot, covered with hay and snow.

Mary takes the steps two at a time. We come up to a long hall with six doors on either side.

"Bathroom's at the end if you need it," she says in a quiet voice. "My room's here." She opens a door with an eight on it.

"I'm okay," I say, following her in.

Despite the gray day outside, Mary's room is bright, a narrow space, plain, with one tall window overlooking the yard. A delicate lace curtain hangs before it, translating the light into something more intricate, lovely.

"Isn't it marvelous?" she says, clearly proud. "Honestly, it's the most peaceful place."

She throws her bag down on the bed and pulls open a few drawers in the bureau. Other than the narrow bed and dresser, there's little room for much else. A small lace-topped nightstand holds a reading lamp, a water glass, and her sketchbook. A rickety little desk leans before the window, its chair tucked neatly into it.

"I grew up in a house full of sisters," Mary says, smiling. "I had to share everything. I think Zara's brilliant for saving this old place, offering it to artists as a place to think."

While Mary rummages through her things, I look at the photographs she has taped up on the wall near her bed. More than a few shots of herself with a set of three other girls who look like sisters, and her mother, five variations on the same face, smiling through time from birthday cake-laden dinner tables, wobbly-ankled in skates on ice-covered lakes, honeycombed together on inner tubes floating down a small, weedy river.

"No dad," I say, before I realize I'm speaking out loud.

Mary's head whips in my direction and her smile falters for a fraction of a second. But just a fraction. "Nope," she says, looking at the pictures. "He missed out."

I don't know what she means by this, but it's the first time I've ever heard anything remotely resembling an edge in Mary's voice, so I don't ask.

Freshly packed bag in hand and brilliant blue socks peeping from the tops of her boots, she guides me through the house, down a set of back stairs, through a large kitchen where a woman and a man are working together quietly. Three fruit pies, two loaves of bread, and one tray of cookies are laid out before them in various states of perfection. Mary greets the bakers and grabs us apples from a basket in the pantry, and we slip out the back. The snow under our feet squeaks like Styrofoam as we make our way back around the house.

"It's pretty empty right now," Mary says, waving one gloved hand toward the upstairs. "The regular residencies are cyclical and this is a downtime. It was packed when I got here. The dinners were great. All the same, I'm kind of glad for the emptiness."

Her car's still warm and I sink deep into my seat. We're both quiet while it lifts and loops us inland through wooded hills. I'm still startled to find myself here with her, heading out. In one day, I've taken in more of the area than all the weeks I've been here so far. Finally she breaks the silence. "I'm so lucky to get to work with your dad," she says, casting a twinkly smile in my direction.

"Oh yeah?" I say. I really don't want to have this conversation. Not with Mary. Everyone sucks up to my dad.

She gives a bright laugh, like she's read something into what I didn't say.

"You don't understand," she says. "Working with your dad is a big deal. I'm just glad to be up here."

I look out the window. The landscape looks like it's the one rushing, pulling back and away. As we get further inland, the timber thins and yields to evidence of people. Drab gold and brown grasses lean, wet and bent. Mary puts on some music and sings along quietly. Snow sprinkles from the low sky in drizzly starts and stops. Beads away from us on the windshield as we cut through.

Mary does Dad's errands first, then we pull in by some shops.

"Ah, the city," she says with a wry smile, as if we've reentered civilization. I look around. The "city," as everyone here calls it, could fit in New York's back pocket, but Mary's on a mission and pulls us right up to a row of vintage shops and a great bookstore.

The store is packed, warm, and has that smell only vintage stores have.

"This," she says, holding a plum chiffon blouse up to me, "screams *look at my gorgeous eyes*!"

I wish I could laugh. I work up a smile instead.

She makes me buy the blouse, and another one, slate-gray cotton, kind of eighties style, with little rose-colored owls printed all over it. Already well-loved by someone, washed into a ridiculous thready softness.

"One blouse for beauty, another for wisdom." The cashier winks at me, twisting her pink hair into a bun she sticks in place with a pencil.

"Clothes don't fix everything," Mary agrees, "but they can fix a lot."

The bookstore's next. It's a densely packed warren of old books offering themselves back to dust. Mary drops to the floor near the back to sift through a collection of German art books.

I start to wander through the sagging shelves, look for poetry, but can't get past a vintage periodic table hanging on the back wall. It's identical to one Patrick had over his desk, and there I am again, listening to him plan it all out, his favorite game, the future. For him, more science. For me—he stumbled a little when he got to me, like my mother does. Wanted to box me in. Only what I wanted wasn't hidden, it was just messy. Uncertain. In my heart it could have been anything less prescribed, something open, different. Something that got me out into the larger world, watching people, the secrets playing on their faces. Something true. I wanted to see something true. Collect as many stories as my heart could hold.

My stupid heart.

As if she senses something, Mary appears and laces her arm through mine. Pretends not to see how my eyes have filled. She pulls me out of the store. We swing into the coffee shop next door for mocha lattes and scones, then back to her Subaru to head to the mall.

At the mall, I feel surreal, out of place. Mary leads me in and out of stores. I'm overwhelmed by the swath of faces we weave through, the biggest group of people I've seen since I left the city. Everyone out looking. A group of girls passes, laughing, but they don't sound happy. Men lean against the glass railings, stacks of packages near their feet, their eyes like slow clocks, inspecting the floor below. I used to pray to open up, used to worry that I was like my mother, too closed off or something. I hauled my camera everywhere trying to *see* more. Now it's like my lids are pinned back, nothing between me and—everything. How did I not see it? Pain is everywhere. I'm just another sorry story. All these people wearing smiles, dragging themselves around—do they all know already? Do they realize how fast the world can change?

I'm losing it. My phone buzzes in my bag. I fish it out. My mother. I drop down on a fake marble bench a minute, ignoring the call, and close my eyes. I tell Mary I'm done, I'll wait in the car while she tries on a few more things. She gives me a quick worried look but tosses me the keys.

One last errand for Dad on the way back. At least it's dark now, an enclosing relief. The lights in the dashboard are gentle, dim. We pull in to a shipyard. Mary runs up a few steps to a decrepit gray trailer-slash-office to get whatever it is we're supposed to pick up. She comes back out. It's still not ready. We'll have to wait.

"So," she turns to me, radiant. "It sounds like your dad is going to have his Swap Night party this year after all."

Like I have any idea what she's talking about. Or why it wouldn't happen.

"Swap Night?"

"You don't know what that is?" She's astonished. "He has them every year. I'm almost done up here."

I'm lost.

"Done?"

"My fellowship . . ." she says, cocking an eyebrow.

I shake my head.

"Your MFA?"

She looks at me like she feels a little sorry for me.

"No, the fellowship. You know I'm up here on fellowship, right?"

I didn't. It hadn't even occurred to me to wonder why she was up here. I thought she just was—one of my dad's regular people.

"I'm only here first semester. End of August through December. From RISD?" Her voice lifts at the end and she speaks a little more slowly, like she's talking to an impaired person.

That's me. Fresh out of The Home. I shrink in my seat.

"I knew that much, the RISD part," I say. "He's always talking about RISD."

But really I don't know anything. My dad's world has always been a given. People coming and going. Crowding around him. A full place, one that's never had much space in it for me.

"Well, it's a fellowship; I'm on a fellowship. To work with your dad. He chose me. He takes two fellows every other year. And it's almost done."

My heart sinks.

"My replacement comes on Swap Night. Get it? We swap. The party's legendary. New Year's Eve. I hate to say it, but it's part of why everyone wants to win the fall fellowship. The party. The contacts. There's another gathering at the end of spring semester, but apparently it's hard to get people to come up here then. This one's the best."

She eyes me like she's a little embarrassed of her ambition.

My mouth's open. I close it. Close my eyes. I'm blown away. I have no idea about anything. I haven't paid attention to anyone since I got here. A cold creeping shame climbs inside me.

"Swap Night. On New Year's? You know, good-bye old, hello new?" She looks at me, sad. Tucks a wisp of white-blond hair back into its arrangement on the top of her head. "You really didn't know?"

She starts the car again and flips on the windshield wipers.

The snow's coming down faster, closing us in.

"You're leaving?" I ask. I feel like an idiot. Of course she is. I'm the one not moving. I'm the one who got off the ride and is sitting here, sulking. It's what people do, right? Scatter? It's what I'd wanted to do.

She nods, squints up at the white coming down.

"But I'm just getting to know you." It's a whining, childish thing to say, but it's out of my mouth before I can stop it.

"Yeah, I have to get back down to school. It's not that far. You know, you could come stay with me anytime, Wren . . ."

She sounds like she feels guilty. Like it's her fault I'm so clueless.

Why are people even nice to me? I'm ill with shame. I've done absolutely nothing to get to know her, and here she is, feeling bad about leaving. Inviting me to visit, even. She should run fast and far out of here, no looking back.

I sigh and lean my head against the cold car window. How could my dad go to Berlin right now, at the end of her fellowship? Berlin. His opening. It hits me.

"Oh God! Mary, were you supposed to go to Berlin with my dad?" I feel sick.

She gives a little shrug. Won't commit. Looks over at the trailer like maybe she's noticed someone coming out or something. No one. She glances at the gas gauge and turns off the engine.

"You were—" I put my face in my hands. "You stayed back because of me."

I sink and sink.

"Your dad says I can come back this summer if I want, since he's been kind of distracted." She gives me a quick smile. "That's not usually how it's done, he said, but since this year—" She takes in a quick breath. "When I heard about your accident—I was so surprised he didn't cancel on me."

She says the last part quietly, like she'd rather not say it at all.

Of course. And I would be the reason he's even hesitating about having his famous party. I have to swallow back the crappy scone I ate with my mocha. He's been distracted.

She won't stop looking at me. Reading me. And I can't control my face. I'm too busy bearing up against the shame pounding at my center.

"It's my fault, really," she says, sounding a little nervous or something. "When I first got here, he was so distracted—I offered to help however I could."

And so she ended up keeping an eye on me, doing dishes and probably not getting anything useful from my dad. I pull my collar up high around my face. There's nothing I can say to her that will change anything. Mary was helping out in the hopes of actually getting some of what she came for. She drew the short straw. Had her fellowship when the artist's crazy daughter was in town. I tighten my scarf. Wish, wish I were back at the house. Or running. Anywhere but here, feeling like this. And that's just it. This is how it is. Always. To pay attention to things. People. It's too easy to fail other people. And the good-byes. You never have the time you think. It brings tears to my eyes. I blink them away.

I blew it with Mary; now she's out of here.

"So, my replacement is a guy. Nick Bishop," she says in a bright voice. "You'll like him. He's nice. Outgoing. Ambitious."

"Great." I couldn't care less about the new guy.

The snow slows. Melts when it hits the windshield. I watch it spin down lazy through the triangle of the floodlight between us and the shipyard trailer.

"I met him a few times. He's funny. My friend Sarah knows his roommate. Says he's got a good heart. Your dad liked him in the interviews."

I'm going to have to meet another person. I didn't even know my dad had done interviews. When did my dad do interviews? I would kill to be in bed right now. Last night's bad sleep is draped like a lead apron over everything. I've been so self-absorbed, it's embarrassing. I look at the shipyard office. No sign of anyone coming out to us anytime soon. I sigh. Make an effort. I tell myself that. *Make a damn effort.*

"Who are the other people, then? That work with you guys?" I ask. "The other assistants?"

She looks at me like she can't believe my question, then laughs. "You mean Zara, Anna, Jeb, and Mark? Anna's an independent artist who sometimes collaborates with your dad, not exactly an assistant, and Jeb and Mark—they're all artists in their own right, but your dad hires those guys to help out. You'd like them. They're cool. That's why I wanted you to come to Secret Cinema, most of them come. And Zara, well, you know—she and

Jeb run Mercy House together. I think it's been the same crew for a few years now. God, Wren, does your dad tell you anything?"

She's nice to put it like that. We both know he probably has.

"I haven't been paying that much attention." I shrug, like it's normal. "I mean, before now, I hardly ever came up here."

I stare at the place on the dashboard where the airbag pops out. Airbag. What a name. Like it's a balloon. Felt more like a brick wall. The airbags in Patrick's car—they didn't do him any good. I shiver involuntarily. It's cold in here. Heat seeps away so quickly when the engine's off.

"Well, Swap Night is legendary," she says, still smiling, like a strident grin will pull me out of the pit I'm in. "There are wild stories about the old days. But even now, everyone wants to come. He invites locals, friends from the city, people from galleries, art writers—we all hope. The new fellow comes up, with trustees from RISD. Your dad goes all out. Champagne, the works."

I wrap my arms around myself. Shrink into my coat. I wish I could disappear into it. Dad's errand is taking forever.

"I'm going to go ask them what the deal is," Mary says, with a frustrated look back at the little office. "Did you see what I found at the bookstore? Check this out."

She reaches in a bag behind my seat and pulls out a thick book. A monograph. My dad's work. It's heavy on my lap, which is good because I'm starting to feel a little like I might fly away. Like everyone else has solid lives, and I'm just a particle, passing through.

"Wren? Are you okay?" Mary asks, before she shuts the door.

I shake my head. Find words and force them out. "No, I'm fine. Just sad you're leaving. And I'm sorry I wrecked your fellowship."

"You didn't!"

A lie. She gives one more quick look at the shed, shakes her head, and pops back into the car. Turns over the engine.

"Wren, I didn't mean—"

"Distracted? God, Mary, have you gotten anything out of your time with him? You've been waiting on me since I got here." There's a painful strain in my neck when I swallow. "And I don't want to meet the new guy. I want you to stay."

It comes as a surprise. To both of us, I think. I want something. I want Mary to stay. And something else. I want Cal.

She covers my mittened hand with hers. Cranes her head into my space. "I've been happy here. Your dad—you know—that's life. I got to work with him, watch him work through a personal difficulty. It's not only sculpture I came for. That's the point of these fellowships. You live the daily life of your mentor, however they define it."

She taps the horn lightly a few times. No response from the office.

"They're so slow! Sorry," she says, leaning back in her seat.

I keep my eyes on the dash. Sweet, cheery Mary. I ruined her time up here. And now she's trying to make me feel better about it. The hot prickle of shame climbs the back of my neck. I keep my eyes on the snow falling through the light.

"I was serious when I said you could drive down and visit. We're in a big old house, my roommates and I, lots of room. It's a good group of people. My friend Charlie's a photographer—he can give you a rundown on the department. Come see me. I'll show you what life's like at RISD."

"Yeah." I nod, slowly.

But that'll never happen. I'm floating away. It's too hard to feel. I'm drained. Want to go home.

On cue, the guy comes out of the trailer office carrying a small piece of welded steel. Mary thanks him, chats a minute, effortlessly, then signs for the piece.

The drive home is quiet through the snow.

open your eyes

THE DARKEST NIGHT OF THE YEAR.

Darker for some than others. Patrick's family's approaching their first Christmas without him. I should call. I look at my phone, try to imagine actually doing that. At least once. And all those unread messages in my inbox from Emma—guilt, guilt, guilt. I'm weak. I roll over. Sleep a little more.

Finally, I drag myself out of bed like a ninety-year-old. Get in to work. Cal hasn't called in days. Not since Mary and I went shopping. My phone's as silent as a stone. He probably changed his mind. Had a chance to think it over and figured out what a mess I am. Came to his senses. Good for him. Maybe Mary weighed in after our chat in the car. Told him to save himself. I can't stop thinking about her, how much I failed to see. I don't trust anything I think I know now. I guess that's the price of sailing so far away. I probably misread what happened between Cal and me at his house, too.

I check my phone anyway. Watch the door at the library. Like it's ever going to be anyone other than Lucy. I can't call him. Mamie might have, she wasn't afraid of putting people into awkward positions.

No. I don't need to call. If I didn't misread it, it's obvious he's realized I'm a disaster. Not worth the trouble. I swallow that thought down like a brick. But it's for the best. This was exactly what I didn't want, anyway. All this feeling.

Lucy has me stacking books for her shut-ins, extra deliveries she wants to get out before we close for the winter holiday. Things are changing. Life is like that. While I sort books into patrons' piles, I run down how it's going to go. A silent script, stage directions: Mary exits, I work, Cal—I don't have one for Cal, but I find a way to close up again, get back to feeling like I'm not going to break apart at any second. Like I don't have my ruined, ruining heart exposed all the time.

On the drive home, I hear Patrick's voice in my head, the actual sound of it, so clear I almost swerve. Laughing at me. Then shouting when he realized I was serious, telling him I was done. I thought he'd understand. See it from my point of view. I'd been that girl for too long, Mamie and Patrick—my quirk to his cool.

I can hardly see when I pull Cal's Jeep in alongside my house. I sit with my face pressed into the damp wool of my mittens until I can breathe normally. I shouldn't be driving his car. Keeping it here. I should find a way to get it back to his place. Clear boundaries. Drop it off and jog home. Not now, though, not when I might risk seeing him. Maybe really early tomorrow morning.

I go in to the empty house, change, and head back out for a run. A long one. Up high over town, to the overlook. Nowhere near his house. Up near the top, the view pierces me so totally I have one of those flash thoughts about tossing myself into the ocean. Surrender to the enormous wildness, the water's churning gray force, the solid rocks. It doesn't seem so scary. The idea. It seems like it could bring a lot of quiet. Endless quiet.

When my phone rings it's so unexpected and out of sync with where I am that for a second I'm not even sure what it is.

"Darling."

"Hi Mom."

"I just had the strongest desire to hear your voice."

"I'm running."

She sighs, but lightly, like she doesn't mean to let it slip out.

"So you are, I hope it's a good run?"

"It's a good run, but I have to get back to it, Mom. I'm getting cold standing still."

"Of course, darling, don't catch cold. Call me later?"

I promise to call and head for home.

When I get back, Dad's in the studio, home from Berlin, and Mary's at Mercy House. I'm alone with the dimming daylight. No music. Everything I have makes me think of

Cal. I will myself not to be heartsick. It doesn't work.

Industry. I am my mother's daughter. I drag myself from the couch over to the sink to tackle some seriously neglected dishes. This morning's oatmeal is barnacled to the side of the bowl and, until the water heats up, seems like it's going to win the fight. Conquered by breakfast foods. A new kind of pathetic.

My phone rings. I almost ignore it. It's going to be my mother again. Only it's not. It's Cal. Cal's number. The fading light out my windows looks more beautiful than it's ever looked.

"Can you come over now?" he asks before I say hello.

I dry the bowl I've managed to scrape clean, wipe my hands, toss the dishtowel on the counter, and go fall into the armchair. Relief rivers through me.

"Yes," I say, trying to hide how happy I am to hear his voice. Fail.

"Everything okay?" I ask.

"Fine. See you soon."

He hangs up before I can say anything else.

Very mysterious. And it's like it's the first time a boy ever called. I spend a minute or two frozen with my phone in my hand, trying to figure out how his voice sounded. Not cold, I guess. Then I rush around my room trying to find the right thing to wear. Try on the chiffon blouse Mary made me buy. I can't do it. I don't know what I'm heading into. Better to be comfortable. I check out my hair. Brush it a few times, then finger comb it. I still remember how to do a few things. I leave it loose, soft around my face. Put on a little lip gloss. I don't want to try too hard,

I'll feel ridiculous if he says this is the last time I'll see him. Because, let's be honest, he's probably given it a little thought, is going to tell me he isn't into miserable.

When I pull up to the house, there are tons of tire tracks coming and going along the driveway. Company. Maybe still here. I cut the engine and sit a second, try to take a few deep breaths. Then I push the button and the garage door swings open. Only the silver car. No one else's. I let out the breath I was holding.

Someone clears his throat. Cal, leaning on the doorjamb, smiling at me. I spent the whole drive there thinking I can't do this, but there he is, looking at me that way he does. I climb out of the Jeep, throw my arms around his neck, kiss him.

He steps back, laughing. "You could knock a guy over, you know."

He opens the collar of my coat and kisses my neck. I feel it somewhere down behind my knees. I step out of my boots and he slips my jacket off my shoulders. There are no lights on in the house.

"What are you doing in the dark?" I try to make my eyes adjust. I'm shaky, jittery in a nervous, happy way. Relieved. I'm relieved to see him. Relieved he's glad to see me.

"Well, Rabbit," he says leaning on a crutch and ruffling my hair like I'm a puppy, "my dad and stepmom dropped in for a surprise visit. When I told them I was staying here for the holidays, they got worried. That's not what they said, of course, they were supposedly just passing through on their way to New York and wanted to say hello." He laughs. "Like this place isn't totally out of the way. My dad was just here, but I think Annie, my stepmom, wanted to see me with her own eyes."

"Sounds like my mother," I say, suddenly hoping she doesn't get the same idea.

"So they showed up a few days ago for a thorough parental check-up-on-the-sick-kid holiday extravaganza." He slides a hand around my waist, against the small of my back. "I showed them how fine I am."

"Yes, you are," I say, grinning at him. I'm ridiculous with happiness. It's a strange sensation.

He laughs. "I told them I wanted to stick around here this year. With you?" He looks at me like he's not sure if that's an okay thing to say. I press my forehead into his chest. Close my eyes. This can't be real.

"So they left. But Annie left something for us."

He slips his arm into the other crutch and I follow him through the dark house to the span of windows that overlook the water. "Stay there," he says, "and close your eyes."

I close them. This is more than I hoped for. He's glad to see me. Seems like he's feeling a little better. I squeeze my eyes a little tighter and take in a huge, happy breath. The first one in a long time.

He puts on some music, and then he's behind me, hands on my waist. I lean back a little against his chest. He kisses the top of my head.

"Okay. Open your eyes."

Hundreds of tiny lights before us. Strands of golden sparkles crisscross the terrace between the house and the water. It's like the sky loaned down some stars and they're dusting the bare limbs of trees, twinkling from small snowy tufts of bushes, lining the terrace all the way to the edge. It's another world. A dream of light.

"Oh . . ." It's all I can say. I wish I had my camera.

He tips my chin up, leans down, meets my mouth with his.

"My stepmom wanted to give us something beautiful."

Us.

It's been so long. But I want something, this. I want to be an us. With him.

He frees his arms from the crutches. Drops them onto the couch. Lowers himself to the soft rug on the floor. Pulls me down with him. It's a little awkward.

"Sorry," he says, voice tight a second. "Down's not as easy as it looks."

We lean back against the couch, face the lights. The lengths of our legs run hot side by side. Touching in a million places. He moves closer, pulls me to him, runs his hands through my hair, along my neck, then into my shirt. He presses his mouth against my throat, along my collarbone. I shiver.

"Is this okay?" he whispers below my ear.

It might be the first thing that's been okay for me in a long time. We slip down so we're lying before the windows, Cal on his elbow, over me, tracing my face with the backs of his fingers. I know this path, where it goes. I want to press myself into him, against him, be here, not there, disappear into this heat between us.

"Are you crying?" He wipes a tear off my cheek.

I am. Not now, Patrick, not now, not now.

"I'm happy," my voice breaks.

More tears. I cover my face. Impossible not to think about it, where this leads.

He pulls my hands away. Kisses the tears off my cheeks. Holds me close, his heart steady, sure, under my ear.

"It's just," I say, when I find my voice again, "everything's kind of intense for me right now. I'm not really sure what I'm doing. And I thought maybe you were done with me. You know, when I didn't hear from you." I wipe my face with my hand.

"Done with you—" Cal's arms tighten around me. "I wanted to give you some space. I told you all that heavy stuff—I wanted you to have a chance to back away."

He kisses my eyelids. My wet eyelashes.

Heavy stuff. He has no idea.

I take a deep breath.

"You make me feel like I might not be an entirely ruined person."

He starts to object when I call myself ruined, but I put my hand over his mouth. I think I need to say it. I need someone other than my parents to know.

"The night—that night—we were out at Meredith's beach house. A bunch of us. Patrick—my boyfriend—I broke up with him."

But there was something else.

Another deep breath.

"We kept it small on purpose, only the people we wanted out for the weekend, you know—" I laugh bitterly, remember how stupid and calculating I was. "I brought my camera with me, my swimsuit, some music." I pinch my eyes shut tight. I can see myself then, that stupid girl, I think I was planning to make pictures out of the weekend, everyone's last hurrah or something. Like it could all go exactly how I wanted it to. I would break up with Patrick, and we'd still all be close, like we were, have fun, one last time. Like life actually did what you willed it to. "I was done with my projects for the end of the year—"

I swallow, and for a second I can't talk—a great swooping silence alighting on me like an owl on the hunt.

There it is, in my bag, as clear as if I had shot a picture of it, the little white test kit I had tucked away.

Cal opens his mouth, but I shake my head. I have to say this.

"It ended up being crowded anyway. Rowdy. End-of-the-school-year stuff. Some other kids we knew were at a house down the beach, and we made a giant bonfire. This guy Meredith kind of liked brought a guitar. We were all drinking."

I can't look at Cal. I know what I'll see. The same look my mother wore when I woke up in the hospital.

"I know I didn't . . ." I'm choking on it.

There I am, wearing new shorts, the cool ledge of Meredith's parents' huge bathtub pressing against the back of my thighs while I sit, gripping the little white stick.

I force myself back here, try to stop crying. I'm wrecking this whole night, but I think I have to say it out loud.

"I know I didn't—I mean, the rational part of me knows it—"

But there it is again, the thing I keep running from. The way the second pink line appeared, slowly at first, then swift, solid. Complex mathematics, an addition, a division. One, then two. Doubling me. Splitting me away from my life.

"I killed us—" I choke on the words.

He tries to interrupt, stop me, shush me, but I shake my head, shake him away. "Cal, I was pregnant."

Now I have to look at him. Watch his eyes widen with surprise. Take me in, see who I really am.

"It was so unreal, I didn't tell anyone, Meredith—it was such a stupid mistake," I say. "I knew better. I was late. I'm never late."

I am crying too hard to say more. Great way to spoil a beautiful night. At least I'm reliable. Cal holds me close. Until I can breathe normally again.

"I panicked. I blamed it on Patrick. Because I wanted us to be done, I'd gone off the pill, but then he—we—" I wipe my face on my sleeve. "When I saw that second line, it was like everything I wanted was falling apart. Amherst, starting somewhere new, I was so close, so nearly out of there." My teeth are chattering like I'm cold or something. "Away from my mother, from Patrick and the way everyone saw us, even Meredith, all our habits. Suddenly breaking up seemed like the most important thing I could do. I had to do it."

Cal props himself up on one elbow. I cover my face.

"Cal, I wished it all away—" My nose is running now, tears down my neck, in my ears. "And it happened! I lost everything."

He pulls my hands from my eyes and kisses my palms. Holds me, says nothing. Lets me cry. But the words sink me. I imagine I'm shrinking to nothing. It gets easier to talk.

"I didn't tell Patrick about the test," I say. "Just that I was done. It turned into a huge fight. I was messing up the plan, his plan. We were supposed to travel together over the summer, then leave for school. No good-byes, whatever happened, happened. We agreed. He kept saying that over and over, *but you agreed*. He couldn't believe it. I started saying the meanest things I could think of, tried to make myself into someone else, someone he'd want to let go."

I close my eyes, remember realizing how drunk Patrick was, worse than me, how long I'd been in the bathroom staring at that test, while he'd been on the beach, partying. Someone put wet wood on the bonfire, and the smoke swirled around us, the smell still in my hair the next morning in the hospital.

"We were loud. Totally out of control. It wasn't a private fight. I remember spotting his little sister, Emma, and a few of her friends, wondering how they got out there. Patrick shoved me, hard, and stormed off the beach. For some reason we didn't collect keys that night. A bunch of us ran after him. He was so messed up. I got in the car just before he ripped out of there. I thought I could get the keys, or get him to calm down, make him pull over. But there was no time. We were going so fast. The front right tire caught the edge of the road and we flipped. Rolled down a little hill. We didn't hit anything. Just rolled until we stopped. And then it was quiet."

Cal keeps holding me. His breath is so steady it reminds me of waves rolling in.

"Patrick died right away. He wasn't wearing his belt. I couldn't get out of the car. Then I was in the hospital. My mom told me I miscarried. So my parents know. No one else."

Deep, ragged breath.

"She kept saying how lucky I was. I couldn't stand it. I couldn't stand anything anyone said. But they wouldn't shut up, so I did. Kind of a long time. Three months."

I let out the breath I'm holding. Look at the empty white ceiling.

"I just walked away from it—God—I wanted out of my safe little life so badly, to feel like I was living in the real world." A bitter laugh rises like bile in my throat. "I got my wish. The real world feels like hell."

Cal's eyes are on me. Steady. Witnessing my shame. I shut mine again.

"Everyone thinks I didn't get hurt in that crash. But I did. I deserve it, I know—"

"No." He holds my face in his hands. Stops me there. Firm. Eyes dark. "Look at me."

I shake my head, try to look away. "You have no idea," I say. "You never—"

"Neither did you," he cuts me off. "Wren, you can't do that to yourself. You made a mistake and got pregnant. Patrick made a mistake and got in his car drunk and angry. What happened is bad enough. The worst. But it's not anyone's fault or any kind of punishment. You can't think that or you'll take yourself down for good."

Take myself down for good. Maybe that's what I've been doing. Trying to do.

"It's never going to get better," I say.

"The facts won't change," he says quietly, "but you will."

"You don't know that."

Out the window, the golden lights twinkle like they're hopeful for us.

"It's already happening," he says sounding sure.

I wish I believed him. He's looking at me like he can see where I begin.

I close my eyes.

Patrick. We're in his car, flying down the Old Montauk Highway, my words pecking at him like little black birds, begging him to slow down, pull over, stop the car. Then I'm screaming. He's scaring me. The tire catches; the steering wheel jerks and spins. I can't take my eyes off it, how loose it looks, like it's unwinding itself, then those never-ending seconds we're in the air, and everything stops.

"Wren, come back," Cal whispers from somewhere faraway. "Please come back." His soft lips on my ear, my neck, my eyelids, my chin. "Don't disappear again. I want you here. Stay here."

I try to remember the Ferris wheel I imagined on my run. How things fall away, and you fall too, but if you stay with it, the ground reappears. I open my eyes and look at Cal. His beautiful face. How did I find him? How did we end up here? Lost and found in the dark and terrible winter woods?

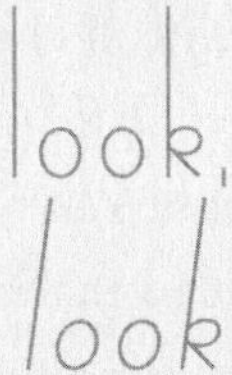

WE'RE EXPECTED at Mercy House. Christmas dinner. Everyone's invited. Even Mom. She declines, making me wonder if she is seeing someone, keeping busy while I'm gone.

Dad and I pick up Cal and head over early to help in the kitchen. Over thirty people are coming. Zara greets us at the door, bearing a tray filled with cups of mulled wine. Her hair is loose around her face, wild, golden, spilling down the back of her red velvet dress. She's voluptuous, seems conjured almost, nothing like the steady woman in the braid and work boots I see around the studio.

Cups in hand, we follow her to the kitchen where Lucy welcomes us, pink-faced over a saucepan of cooking cranberries and floury from what looks like the setup for three pies. Mary hoots a loud hello overhead and clatters down the back stairs in a pair of silver clogs, her hair twisted in little knots all over her head and tied with tinsel.

We're all given jobs. Dad's assigned to monitor the birds, a turkey and a goose Zara ordered for him because it's something my granddad made every Christmas, apparently, and it's not Christmas dinner without it. News to me. Cal's put to work on brussels sprouts with chestnuts. Lucy slides a stool over to him, which he takes without a word. Mary informs me that first I'll set the table, then I'm going to make dinner rolls from a huge bowl of dough she has rising on a long board by the ovens.

I slip out to set the table, grateful for this part of my assignment. The linens are bright, pressed, perfect. Mary guides me to the side pantry where all the dishes are kept. It's a mixed bunch of plates and bowls, a collection made from what appears to be countless other families' abandoned china. I count out all the pieces, lift them carefully to the table in stacks, even find the most delicate etched-crystal stemware for water at each place. Mary squeals when she slides open a particularly heavy drawer and discovers a trove of silver salt cellars. She disappears in search of polish.

I set the places carefully. Sip a little mulled wine. Wonder about all those nuns living here over the years. What were they dreaming of? I look up, in case there's a ghost of one of them, hovering, inspecting us as we fill their house, but the only apparition I see is my reflection in a mirror behind the table. My hair looks nice today—I dried it for a change—but my face is stern. I stick my tongue out at the grim girl's reflection.

I woke up this morning and realized I had nothing for anyone, no gifts, like one of those dreams where you sleep through a test or show up somewhere naked. It's like I thought I was going to pass through the holiday but not live it or something.

Dad rescued me when he heard my wail of awareness, blessedly did not say parental things like gifts don't matter and he was just glad I was here. Came into my room instead and after planting a firm kiss on the top of my head, dug in the closet until he found a box of photos I'd sent him over the years. Dropped it next to me on the bed. Walked out. I lifted the lid. Dangerous territory, the first image is Patrick, back just before we started going out, doing a handstand on the top of our stoop. Show-off. But then, like a gift, another photograph slipped out of the pile.

A little boy, flying down Twentieth Street after school one day, kicking along a box about his same size. I caught him, both legs in the air, face wide open in a lost-tooth grin, the box flying too, an urban kite, a few paces ahead of him. You have to look. I remember thinking that when the image emerged in the darkroom. Feeling my luck for having looked. This minute of something, of life, of the best part of it, revealed because I was ready, I was looking.

It's a good gift for Cal, something I love. I ran out to the studio where Dad and Mary were both working, early, and hard, and Dad broke away from what he was doing to help me frame it.

The table's set. Ready for a celebration, guests. I just wish I weren't one of them. Through the swinging door, I hear feet stomping off snow in the back, then the sounds of everyone welcoming whoever has come. It's quiet a minute, then they laugh hard about something. The newcomer's voice is especially high, sharp. Her laugh hits a certain pitch that startles me. I lean against the sideboard, try to relax, and fantasize about Mary's quiet room. The door to the kitchen swings open. Zara, humming *O Holy Night*, bearing a spoonful of pear-cranberry pie filling, strides toward me, lifts it to my mouth.

"You need this," she says, smiling. "I felt it. Nice job on the table."

I wander into the front parlor, savoring the sweet fruit. She follows, adjusting holly garlands draped along the mantels, straightening a candle in a silvery tree-branch menorah on the sideboard.

"Mary cast this," she says, running her finger along its delicate bends. "Gave it to us for the house. Have you seen her candlesticks?"

I shake my head. I haven't seen anything. Or if I have, I've missed it.

"They're another thing she does on the side. That girl. She's never done making." Zara laughs. "She worked so long on those popcorn strings." I look where she's pointing. An endless train of crisp white popcorn twirls around the green tinsel tree sagging in the corner of the front parlor. "I didn't have the heart to tell her they brought our mouse back."

She pulls me down on a settee. Sits next to me. "I had to take the bell off the Pope's collar to give him a fighting chance."

"The Pope?"

She laughs again. "Him." Points to the corner of the room near the tree, where a corpulent orange cat lies lazy before the fireplace. He focuses on us a second, then goes back to sleep.

"The Pope." I nod, handing her the empty spoon. "Of course. Hey, nice tree. Where'd you get it? 1950?"

Zara makes a small fist and socks me lightly on the arm. "Even up here," she says, laughing at her tree with a dismissive wave, "I can't bring myself to cut one down."

She stands.

"I have to get back to the pies. If you'd like, I can finish those rolls for you. I could do them in my sleep."

I nod, grateful. The rolls felt like some kind of test.

"I'll send Cal out." She waves her hand toward the two fireplaces, one in each room. "Do you suppose he knows how to build a perfect fire?"

I smile at Zara, banish the grim girl.

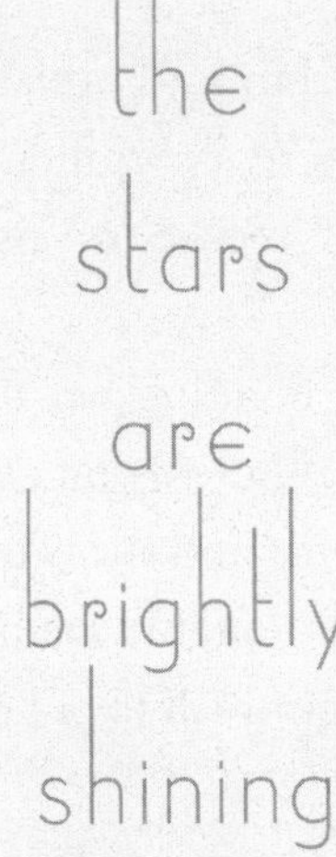
the
stars
are
brightly
shining

IT'S MIDNIGHT before we roll out of there, goose-stuffed. Cal, Dad, me. I drive. Cal's tired, and Dad's had way too much champagne, sancerre, vouvray, cognac. I've shifted into some other mode, new for me, quiet but present.

Silent night. It's been snowing while we were inside facing the fire, and the roads are softened by it. We make tracks between Mercy House and home like we're tracing a line on a map, one that points from one good place to another.

"Cal will come home with us," my dad announces. I glance at him in the rearview. He's stretched out like a sated bear in the back.

I blush twenty shades of red. Bless the dark truck.

"There are gifts to exchange," Dad qualifies his remark.

I sneak a peek at Cal. He's got his eyes on the road, face straight.

"Sorry!" I say, mortified. "I'll swing by your house," I whisper, "so you can get your car?"

He looks at me then, and I can see he's trying not to laugh. My shoulders drop with relief.

"Only if you want to get rid of me," he says, reaching across the vast front seat to slip his hand under my thigh.

Our house looks cozy when we pull up. Softened by great dollops of snow.

"Be with you in a minute!" my father says, crossing to the studio.

Cal and I lose our coats by the door and sink into the couch. I hop up again, move around, turning off most of the lamps and flipping the switch on the outside lights.

I rejoin him. Grab a natty quilt off the back of the couch and pull it over us.

"Lotta people," he says, reaching for my hand under the quilt.

"Mmhmm."

Before we can relax too much, Dad comes back into the house, pushing a green bicycle, its snow-covered tires marking a wet path to me.

"That's a serious frame," Cal says, pulling the quilt off and sitting up more attentively.

The bike is vintage, heavy, and sports a pair of rugged-looking new tires. A metal basket and a bell decorate the front handlebar.

"In case you need to make yourself known in traffic," my dad says, with a wink to Cal.

"Thanks Dad," I say, standing to hug him.

"Not so fast." He puts a hand up between us. "The real gift's in the basket."

He flips on a small reading lamp near the armchair. In the basket is a narrow gray box wrapped with an extravagant silk bow.

I slip off the ribbon and open the box. Inside, on a bed of moss-green velvet, is a necklace he made for me. A long filament of dark, bent-metal wire. He lifts it out, stands behind the couch, and lowers it over my head. Cal lifts my hair so he can clasp it in back. The wire runs around my neck and down my sternum like a rivulet of rain on a windshield, or a vein of something more precious. It ends in a rough-cut droplet ruby, wire-wrapped, suspended.

"I love it, Dad," I say, hopping up again to hug him.

Also in the bike basket is my gift for Cal. Dad's wrapped it in brown paper.

Cal lifts the wrap away from it carefully and looks at the image, silent.

"It's hers," my dad says, unable to help himself.

"Is this in Chelsea?" Cal asks, inspecting the image, looking up at me.

I nod.

His eyes go back to the photograph.

"Did you ask him to do that for you?" He looks up at me like I might actually have that kind of power over someone.

"It was total chance, dumb luck," I confess. "I was waiting for Meredith to pick out a cheap lipstick in Duane Reade."

"I love it," Cal says, glancing quickly at my dad and then

leaning toward me anyway for a kiss. He runs his hand along the frame a minute, considering the wood.

"And one from your mother," my father announces, handing me a small box. A discreet pair of diamond studs from Tiffany. Very her. Elegant, simple. I love them, too. It's strange to celebrate Christmas without her. I put them on, the first pair of earrings I've worn in months. They hurt a little going in.

Cal pulls himself up and goes over to his coat. Retrieves a slender package from the inside pocket. Joins me on the couch again, slipping it onto my lap.

I pull away the paper. It's a first British edition of Philip Larkin's *High Windows*. Somehow he knows I love Larkin.

My dad makes some noise about getting us all a little nightcap and moves away from the couch. I have a hard time looking at Cal. I'm so overwhelmed and glad to have him here, I think it might break me.

He knows this too and leans to slip a small kiss under my ear.

"Merry Christmas, Wren," he says.

My dad returns with three cordials of Chambord, raises his and says, "You kids are the holy night, raise your cups to all things that impart delight."

We clink the delicate rims like bells.

He sits in the armchair, clicks the light off again so we can see out. The real gift is time. Now. Each other, this night, and the wide, wide moon-silvered sea.

swap night

THERE'S NO DOWNTIME. In the few days between Christmas and New Year's, our place becomes a hive of caterers, art movers, people delivering cases of champagne. I slip out and away whenever I can. The library's technically closed for the week, but Lucy lets me hide out there anyway. She's in herself, doing what she calls spring cleaning, directing a floor polisher and hand washing the woodwork.

Mary is in the studio all hours, finishing things and getting my dad's help selecting which pieces to show the trustees. She begs me to come to her last Secret Cinema, a going-away party for her, I hear, but I decline. Even a silent movie would be too loud right now. Mary's leaving, and Cal's brother's coming up for the party. Both truths like birds in my chest flapping, trapped.

Only Cal seems to understand my heart's slamming away inside me, bruising itself against my rib cage, making it hard to find any rhythm at all. He doesn't pressure me to go to Secret Cinema with him or tease me when I run between our houses rather than take the Jeep.

Michael arrives on New Year's Eve, a few hours before the party. Cal asks me to come meet him at the house before everything begins, but I can't seem to bring myself back in from my run until it's too late to get over there and back and still keep my promise to Mary that we'll dress together. I text a lame apology.

Mary's face falls slightly when I stomp back into the house, flushed and drenched in sweat. She's been waiting for me, and behind her I spot a neat little row of vintage suitcases lined up against the wall of my room. Packed and ready to go.

"I'm heading right for the shower," I say, by way of apology for coming in later than I'd said I would.

"We have time," she says, brightly, even though we really don't have much. "Your dad kicked me out of the studio. He says I can't see it until the party." My room's lit, buzzing with her nervous energy. It makes me want to nap.

"Shower." She sets a flame-colored suitcase on my bed and pops open the brass latches. "I'll hang the dresses. You're going to love what I have planned for your hair!"

It's not a nap, but the shower's warm and quiet, and I use every minute of it to try to relax, tell myself everything's fine. It's Mary's night. Time to shine for her.

While Mary twists and pins my hair into loopy knots using vintage ivory combs and jeweled hairpins her grandmother gave her, the stars twirl themselves into the high sky. We zip into our dresses right as the first cars start to line the driveway. Finally my dad pokes a head in to let us know it's go time.

The studio's transformed. Looks more like a gallery than a workspace. Wire birdcages filled with candles dangle at various heights from the pitched ceiling, one of them made by my father, for Mary, with three little wire twist birds suspended inside it, a good-bye gift.

Candlelight flickers on every surface in the studio like light on water, alive. Everyone's more beautiful for it. And the place is packed. People I've never seen before. My dad and the trustees welcome people near the door, while servers make their way through the crowd, pouring champagne. Mary slips into a stream of guests who have come to celebrate with her. The studio is a bell, ringing with the sounds of a party. So many different voices, talking, laughing.

Cal and Michael are waiting for me and it's all I can do not to turn and run back to the house. I feel strange in my heels and it's difficult to walk up to that much attention. Cal takes me in, every inch of Mary's transformation. I pray not to fall before I reach them. It's a weird time to meet Michael, but here they are, grinning at me, brothers, handsome in dress clothes. Cal catches my eye and gives me a quick wink before he introduces us. They're so alike, yet just the slightest bit different, the way people sometimes look in drawings of themselves. Same dark hair, full mouth, nose—Cal's is longer, Michael's a little more round. But Michael . . . it's hard not to stare. Makes me feel guilty. It's like looking at Cal, stronger, healthier. Michael meets my gaze and I look away, worried he can see what I'm thinking.

Behind me a cork pops. I start, nearly drop my flute.

"Jumpy?" Michael says, smirking slightly.

I'm embarrassed. Before I can say anything, Cal slips a steady hand against the small of my back and eyes his brother. "It's a big night."

People gather near the other end of the studio. One of the trustees starts to talk about my dad, the fellowship. The din changes to a murmur, then shifts to whispers as people finish telling each other their stories, then at last to quiet. I try to focus on something other than all that breathing around me. Remember why we're here. Mary's last night with us. The new residents arriving and settling in at Mercy House, Mary's room already filled with someone else's stuff. Her bright row of vintage suitcases lined up against my bedroom wall like the tiles to a children's board game.

Standing by my dad's side in a shimmering metal-gray taffeta dress, her milky neck long as a swan's, Mary looks like a 1940s Hollywood siren. Some grandma working in the dinky hair salon in town set her white-blond hair in glamorous pin curls, and it ripples away from her face now in bright waves. Nick Bishop, the new guy, is at her elbow. Might be cute, it's hard to say. He has one of those faces that could go either way. He's Mary's twin in coloring, like my dad's put in a special order for cheery-looking fellows this year.

While Dad talks about Mary's work, Nick checks her out a little bit. Classy. He towers over Mary, leaning toward her, like she's his, his mouth pulled into the grin of someone having an adventure.

"Tonight," Dad finishes, lifting his glass to Mary, "and with special gratitude, we celebrate the fine work done by Mary Virginia Roebling."

The place breaks into noise. Cheers. Chiming flutes.

One of the trustees steps up. He speaks about the history of the fellowship and the value of building relationships between working and emerging artists. He thanks my dad for his continued mentorship of young sculptors, calls him an asset to the community. Finally, he turns toward Nick. "And in that spirit, please join me in welcoming Nick Bishop."

A group of people near us hoot for him. Definitely his friends.

"Mabry Fellows," the trustee continues, "are chosen from a competitive pool of applicants." He lifts his glass to Nick. "We congratulate Nick and wish him great success during his tenure here."

Applause.

My father raises his voice over the din, "Let the party begin!"

"Happy New Year!" Mary calls out, raising her glass to my Dad's, then Nick's.

Cheers. Some of Mary's friends chant her name from the crowd. She laughs. My father envelops her in a great hug, lifting her off her feet. As the three of them work their way into the crowd, she locks arms with Nick. Always looking out for people.

I clink my flute to Michael's and Cal's and we drink. Then Cal hands his glass to Michael so he can wrap an arm around my waist. We kiss. I'm self-conscious with Michael watching.

"Cheers, Wren," he says, lifting his glass when Cal and I pull apart. I can't tell what he's thinking. Feels like a test. I hope I pass.

My father strolls back toward us, Mary on his arm now, Nick following close behind.

"Wren"—he says, his face is rosy from drinking—"I want you to meet Nick. Our new Mary."

I raise my glass in a little wave. "Hello Nick," I say, flat, trying not to wince at Dad's words.

Cal shoots me a look that says *try harder*.

I give it a little more effort. "Big shoes to fill." Try to smile.

"Congratulations on your fellowship," Michael says, with a quick glance at Nick and a longer appreciation for Mary.

Cal, infinitely warmer, pulls his arm from my waist to shake Nick's hand. "I'm Cal, this is my brother, Michael." Without the weight of his arm I feel a little like I might float up to the ceiling and out a skylight.

Nick and Michael shake hands. Nick glances at Cal, his crutches, openly curious. My stomach twists a bit.

Then he catches my eye and shoots me a flirty smile.

"I'm really glad to be here," he says. "I've heard a lot about you."

I blush again. "I'm sure you've heard plenty." I sink 'em left and right.

Mary fills the weird air with a light laugh.

"You're going to have a great time working with John," she says.

"Yes," my dad cuts in. "Your drowned maidens were eye-catching."

"Drowned maidens?" Michael asks, looking at Mary.

She flushes with pleasure. "Nick did this series of figureheads—you know, carved for the prow of a ship? Only he worked from photographs of people lost at sea in famous shipwrecks. It caused a stir in Providence."

Nick looks pleased with himself.

"Indeed," my father says, lifting another flute from a passing tray. "I'm looking forward to a larger discussion about form and content while Nick's here."

Nick waves his arm around the studio, "I can't wait," he says. "Mary's series of hands back there is really strong, different from what she was doing when she left. Reminds me of Kiki Smith." He shoots a fast glance at my dad to see if the name-dropping has effect. "Not derivative, of course."

"Of course," Michael says, slightly mocking him.

"Mary's work," my dad says casually, lifting his flute and downing it, "will be unstoppable when she learns to attend it as selflessly as she attended us during her Mabry tenure."

It's surprising, almost cruel.

At my side, Cal flinches slightly.

My dad's words land on Mary's face, erase some of the high color there. Her hand flutters near her heart a second, like a bird just flushed from a bush. Michael stops another server, pulls two glasses from the tray, and slips one into Mary's hand.

"Art asks for everything," my father finishes, looking Mary straight in the eye. "That's harder sometimes for women."

He turns away, leaving us suspended in the wake of his remarks. For a second Nick looks unsure whether to follow or not. He does, but not before he gives me a quick backward smile and a wink. It's not lost on Cal.

There are so many things going on at once I think I might just slip out. Run away from all these people and their careless tongues. I'm afraid to face Mary.

Cal looks at me, then gets us two fresh glasses from a passing server's tray.

Michael raises a brow at his brother. "Watch it," he says.

"Thanks, Mother." Cal gives him a withering look.

I lift my eyes to Mary, who appears to be swaying slightly at his elbow, trying to slip happiness back over her shoulders like a fallen stole. Then she straightens a little, tosses her shoulders back, and smiles again.

"No sense letting that ruin the night," she says.

I'm speechless, watching her shrug it off.

"I like your work," Michael tells her, helping smooth it away, even though he hasn't left Cal and me for a second to look at any of her pieces. "Your hands are awesome." He grins charmingly. "I mean, I don't really know art, but those are fine hands."

Mary laughs. "I like you, Cal's little brother," she says,

slipping her arm through his. "Let's go have a closer look at my hands, then, shall we?"

They drift away.

Cal laughs. "Michael's happy now."

My dad's oldest friends from Berlin, Marta and Theo, join us. Marta wraps her arms around me from behind.

"Mausi," she says softly into my ear, "I'm sorry we got in too late last night to come say hello. Matthau sends his love."

"Marta!" I turn and hug her. Her arms around me are a relief. Motherly. I haven't seen Theo and Marta since they came to New York a few years ago for an opening.

"Marta, Theo, this is my friend Cal. And that was his brother, Michael." I gesture toward Mary and Michael.

Marta appraises Cal, kisses him on both cheeks, then turns to me, lightly touching one of the jeweled vintage combs Mary worked into my hair. "Theo, look how beautiful she is."

Theo embraces me, then claps Cal on the shoulder like he's thanking him for something.

"We've heard about you," he says in his wonderful accent. "You are the one who found John's little Wren here in the woods and brought her back."

I could die right then and there. I tip my glass again. Who cares if my face is the color of the dress Mary zipped me into. I forgot how great it feels to drink at a party—the bubbly's a lift, smoothing all the jangled edges.

"Wren"—Marta turns back to me after asking Cal a few questions about his work—"Have you given any thought to our offer?"

"Offer?" Cal's eyes on me.

I shake my head, "No," I say, "No . . ."

In truth, I'd forgotten about it. My dad mentioned it a while ago. The details are sketchy, like a half-remembered dream.

Marta explains it to Cal, "Theo and I suggested to John that Wren come and work with us, for a year, if she'd like. We'd teach her all about printmaking, she could take classes at *der Künste*, Berlin's University of the Arts."

I watch Cal's face for a reaction but he just looks polite, interested. Keeps a strong arm around me.

"I haven't had any time," I say, chest tight. Lift my glass and finish it.

"Never mind." She shakes her head and pats my arm. "In time. No hurry, no hurry. Your father says you're thinking of RISD. He thinks you'd be happy there. He never stops talking about your work, Wren. We have two of your photographs in our house. He's given us many over the years."

I must look surprised when she says that, because she squeezes my hand.

"Do what feels right, darling, when you're ready." She pulls me away from Cal, her hands on my shoulders. "It's marvelous to be young! You haven't lost that." She folds me into her arms and holds me a minute. Until I feel more like I can breathe again.

I love Marta. And she's asking me to come stay with her, them. Work in Berlin. It's a lot to consider. Another time. It's enough for me that I'm here, tonight, sort of dating Cal, getting up in the morning, working at the library, and thinking about more than my careful nothing each day.

Cal and I make our way through the crush of people and over toward a more quiet corner. I watch Mary move through the room, smiling, radiant. My dad hovers, introducing her, opening doors for her, looking almost like a proud father. She seems happy, unfazed, like all is forgiven and her night is going exactly as she hoped.

People begin dancing after midnight. One of Mary's friends hooks up a laptop and deejays. The studio's a pulsing disco, sound bouncing off all the metal, whirling everyone around. The tempo is deep in my bones, my sternum vibrating with the bass. My heart feels like it's skipping beats, being reset by everything around me, leaving me breathless. It's not a good feeling and isn't really helped by the fact that I've lost track of how many glasses I've had. In the far back, a lobsterman and his wife set up a table of fresh lobster rolls, whoopie pies, and a Down East bisque served in these crazy 1970s soup mugs, "my touch," Mary sings, whirling past us, gaining a grin from Michael.

After we eat, she spins by again, barefoot, her silver toes sparkling, and tries to pull me out to dance with her.

No way.

She pleads with her eyes.

My heart's doing that fractured syncopation. The hot, airless crush of people. More than one of my dad's colleagues has exclaimed over me in that syrupy way that says they know everything—about what happened.

I shake my head. Apologize. No dancing. I can't, not even for Mary. I'm already on the far side of the moon.

She grabs Michael instead. He starts to protest, but Cal gives him a little push, and he follows her into the crowd. We watch them grab hands before the mass of dancing people parts to pull them in.

Cal looks wiped out all of a sudden.

"Let's find a place to sit," I say. "I need to be somewhere quiet."

We slip around the back corner to the little office where my dad stashes everything. It's still really loud, but the absence of the crowd makes all the difference.

Cal sinks into a dusty armchair, setting the crutches on the floor. He pulls me by the waist onto his lap.

"Earth to Wren, Happy New Year."

"Cheers," I say, but I can feel myself leaving, lifting away to someplace more still. A year ago, it was Patrick and me together, his hand running over the silky slip of a dress I borrowed from Meredith. This is the first new year he won't see. It's a blow. I let go of the breath I'm holding.

"This is some dress you have on."

His eyes follow my new necklace down my sweetheart neckline. His hand brushes my breast. Stops my heart. He slips his fingers into my hair, freeing the combs and pins, pulling them out so it falls, warm against my back and shoulders.

"All I can think of is how much I want to pull it off you," Cal says, voice low.

I try force myself back here, back to him, feel this, but I notice how pale he is. The look Nick gave him when we met flashes through my mind. Uncomfortable. Makes me wonder if people look at him like that all the time, whether he notices.

"You doing okay?" I ask. "You look tired."

He groans, lets his head fall back against the chair.

I wrecked it.

"Don't do that," he says. "This is not how it's going to go, between us, okay? I'll take care of myself. Also, were you going to tell me about Berlin? Or was it some kind of secret? And who's Matthau?"

"Oh God." I bury my face in my hands, Cal's words registering more clearly now. "I'm sorry. Too much champagne."

I let my hair fall forward, a curtain between us.

"Matthau's their son. I was seven the last time I saw him. Cal, I honestly forgot about the offer," I say, feeling like a total loser. "My dad mentioned it to me when I was—" I'm at a loss. Sleepwalking through everything. "I didn't—"

"It's okay," he says, parting my hair and pulling my hands away. The annoyance fades from his face, and he traces the edge of my cheek with his finger. "Come on, this is a great party. Really, our first night out."

He lifts my chin, his mouth hovering over mine softly, lightly, teasing.

Then Nick Bishop pops his head around the corner. Kills the spell.

"Whoops," he says, spotting us, hands up like we've got him at gunpoint. "Sorry. Didn't mean to interrupt. Carry on."

He backs out of the room with a smirk. I decide he's not cute. I decide I hate him.

Cal's quiet. His face softens again.

I look at him for a minute. It might actually kill me, how much I like him. I have no idea what I'm doing, pretending like I'm ready for anything like this.

My fingers float over his face, along the bridge of his nose. I breathe him in.

Then we kiss and kiss and kiss.

The night is good and long.

clumsy

MARY AND MICHAEL burst back into the house just in time to see sunrise. They're trying to be quiet, but Mary wakes us up with her laughter. I'm tangled with Cal on my too-small bed and shaky from little sleep, but happy.

Happy.

We meet them in the kitchen to make Mary's going-away breakfast while light creeps like a promise over the edge of the Atlantic.

"Michael's riding down to RISD with me!" Mary beams at us when we join them.

Cal raises his eyebrows at me. Mary looks even happier than usual. If that's possible.

"Who wants a hangover omelet?" she calls out, moving toward the refrigerator.

Breakfast by Mary. I'm going to miss this.

"Step aside," Cal says, glancing at Michael. "We've got this one down."

"Yeah, Owen Brothers Special . . ." Michael says, following him to the kitchen.

They put Mary and me on fruit duty—washing and cutting strawberries, juicing oranges—while they pull out the rest.

"What's the secret ingredient?" Mary inquires sweetly.

"Motherless boys," Cal says, without missing a beat.

Michael hoots and high-fives Cal. "Black humor first thing in the morning. It's how I know I'm home."

"You get good in the kitchen." Cal laughs into Mary's surprised face. "That, and more egg whites than yolks."

"The protein," Michael says, like that explains it.

They bang through Dad's kitchen, making short work of peppers, mushrooms, cheese, onions, thawing some bacon Cal pulls out of the freezer. If it weren't for Michael's shorter, neater haircut, shoulder to shoulder like that, they could almost be twins.

"So," I say to Mary, "I never heard my dad come in. Do you think he's still over there in the studio, asleep on the floor or something?"

She looks at me funny, like it's a weird question. "He and Zara cut out before you and Cal left," she says, smiling.

The kettle whistles and she pours the jumping water into the press.

"Oh, coffee goddess, that smells great," Michael says. Like she's doing something amazing. He can't keep his hands to himself. Misses no chance to brush against her in our small kitchen space.

"Dad and Zara?"

I close my eyes for a second while I consider this disorienting information.

"You innocent." Mary grins and pours four mugs of coffee. Slides me one.

"He's never once, not since he left, told me about anyone he was seeing." I look up at her. "I thought he was a lone wolf. Solitary art man."

"I think it's been a few years now," Mary says, pouring cream into her own cup.

"I thought Zara and Lucy were together," I say, watching silky white whorls form on the surface of her coffee then sink.

This makes Mary laugh.

"You really didn't know?" She squints at me, the rising sun casting a rosy color on her face. "About your dad and Zara? It's not like they hide it."

"Why wouldn't he tell me?" I say. I'm starting to feel ridiculous, my words sounding, even to me, hideously naïve, blind, clueless.

"You've been pretty . . . occupied with your own stuff, I guess. Maybe he didn't think he had to announce it, that it would just be obvious." She shrugs.

She blows on her coffee before she sips it. Michael watches, under her spell, like the gesture might undo him. Her silvery fingernails catch the light.

"I think your dad likes to play it kind of loose, though," she says with a smile.

"Too much information." I pick up my coffee. Scald my tongue.

"Zara told me he comes to her place, but she doesn't stay here."

"Ugh," I groan, "Thanks for the mental picture."

Cal laughs. Reaches past me for a potholder.

"Nice double standard," he says. "You want him to be cool with us, but he can't have someone of his own?"

He slips a spatula under the perfect round of egg and folds it in half. Bits of cheese in the pan spit and hiss.

"Perfection," Michael says, eyeing the masterpiece. "Plates, ladies? We'll be eating soon."

"I don't know," I say, backing away from the heat a bit. "I guess I just haven't thought of my parents that way."

It occurs to me that I might be right about my mother not coming for Christmas. She's seeing someone. Has to be. Why wouldn't she? Maybe I've been blind to everyone else's lives longer than I thought. I close my eyes a second, try to imagine a man for her. No. She isn't seeing anyone. Can't be. She wouldn't have so much time to worry about my life if she were.

"Penny for your thoughts," Mary says.

"Not worth that much."

I pull the bacon off the back griddle and try to soak up some of the grease with paper towels. Sneak a sideways glance at Cal. Pale. He leans against the counter while he tends the eggs. Dark circles under his eyes. I keep my mouth shut. I learned my lesson last night. Still, he makes me want to pull him back to bed. I could handle a lazy day lying around together.

"Which one's Zara?" Michael asks, watching me watch Cal. He steals a piece of bacon. Mary slaps his hand.

"The one in that sculptural dress—all those little metal moons," I say. "I don't know, mid-forties, maybe? Walking around with Theo and Marta."

Now that I think of it, I saw them together a lot last night. My dad and Zara. After Dad was done making introductions for Mary, he and Zara made the rounds. And my dad looked happy in a way he hasn't really since I got here. I get that sick feeling again. I don't deserve any of this. All this attention from everyone else. Their worry. My stupid problems are taking my dad away from this—his life here.

"Oh yeah, what was with that dress?" Michael laughs. "All those metal edges. Looked sharp."

"I liked it," I say, a little surprised to find myself feeling defensive about Zara. "It made that little chiming sound when she walked around."

"I liked it too." Mary energetically backs me up. "She made that dress, and only the crescent moons were sharp, and she only put a few of those on. I adore Zara. And John, of course. They're alike," she says, with a romantic expression on her face. "They might be made for each other." She shoots a look at Michael, a coy smile, and then glances back at me. "You know?"

Michael shakes his head. "How can you adore him after that thing he said to you?"

Mary stares back at him a minute, her face falling slightly. "Yeah, that was hard. But he wasn't trying to be mean.

He talks like that. Says what he thinks. And he's probably right."

"How about you, Wren?" Michael asks, turning his eyes on me. "Do you buy your dad's line about what a mistake it is to look out for other people?" He hands Cal a pile of shredded cheese.

"Shut up, Michael," Cal warns, whisking it into a new bowl of eggs.

"That's not what he meant," Mary says, defending my dad, or me, maybe. "He was just reminding me to watch out—as a woman, I face different standards for how I'm supposed to live. Zara and I talk about that once in a while."

"I'm just trying to figure out if it's a family thing," Michael laughs, like he's only kidding.

"Who's hungry?" Cal asks, taking the bacon platter off the back of the stove and thrusting it at Michael.

I try to concentrate on gathering plates, silverware. Cal knocks his shoulder into mine, a comforting gesture. I look up at him. I can't believe he's here, with me. That I'm here. With anyone. I feel like I've lived years in a few weeks. Makes me happy and uneasy. I know how fast things change.

As if to emphasize that thought, Cal drops a stack of juice glasses onto the kitchen floor. They shatter against the tile. Glass everywhere. Loud. We're all startled.

"Shit." Anger flashes across his face. He looks at me. "Sorry, clumsy."

"We were up all night." I keep my voice light, give him a quick kiss, and reach for the basket.

Michael crouches near me on the floor, hands me some of the bigger pieces. Mary steps over us and sets the rest of the food out on the table.

"Do you have a dustpan somewhere?" Michael asks, gesturing to the remaining glinting shards.

I point him down the hall to the little closet.

"I don't see it," he calls.

I go back to get it for him, but he's standing right there, dustpan in hand. I'm confused a second. He grabs my arm kind of hard and looks at me intensely. His eyes aren't warm for me like they were for Mary a second ago.

"I'm watching you," he hisses, giving my arm a tight squeeze. "Don't hurt him, however crazy you feel. He really likes you. Whatever you do, don't mess him up. It took a lot for us to get here. Don't fuck with him. Please. Not now."

I'm stunned. Michael drops my arm, like it was something disgusting he touched, takes the broom from my hand, and walks back to the kitchen.

I lean against the wall, heart pounding. Try to breathe. I slip into the bathroom a second. To calm down. My stomach's in freefall. I splash a little cold water on my face. Look at my reflection. Everything's changing; I'm disoriented. Michael's probably right. I'm just going to mess it up, somehow. I don't know what I'm thinking, getting involved with Cal.

When I come out, they're at the table, laughing about something. Missed the joke. I avoid Michael's eyes.

"Bon appétit," Cal says, when I take my seat.

For a few minutes there's only the sound of silverware

against plates and the murmur of people passing dishes.

"Mmm," Mary says with a great sigh after a few bites. "What is it about breakfast after staying up all night? I feel like I died and went to heaven."

Died and went to heaven. Her words wedge themselves in my throat and for a second I'm afraid I'm going to cry. I look down at my napkin. Blink hard.

Things are okay. It's all okay. I repeat it in my head. It's okay, it's okay, it's okay. Time moves forward. I'll say good-bye to Mary, and it won't break me. I'll keep seeing Cal. Keep waking up. Going to work. I look at Michael. He shows no sign of having just torn into me in the hallway. I tell myself I'm lucky to be alive, to be eating with these people I'm starting to love.

it's so still

IT'S QUIET WITHOUT MARY. Too quiet. I don't mean to, but I catch myself expecting her in the kitchen, pressing some seriously powerful coffee, looking like a Technicolor sunrise. The house is dim without her. Even my father, normally so constant in his orbit, has a slightly deflated appearance. And as fast as everything around us lifted and swelled, suspended in Swap Night glamour, January pushes us ahead again, utilitarian in thick-soled boots. Nick and my dad disappear into the studio, establishing Nick's fellowship, my dad says.

I run farther every day. Try to forget Michael's warning. The look on his face. Winter is huge. The sky low and blank and endless. Pressing me down. Making it hard to breathe.

If I could find a way to shut it all off again, just for a little while, I'd be okay. Not caught like this, wide open between Cal and nothing.

After Michael leaves, Cal crashes. Not sick, he tells me over and over, just tired. I don't mind. I'm tired too. Used up. I just want to run and not think, shelve books and not think, sit and not think. On this morning's run, a dead bird in the snow brings me to my knees. It looked so abandoned—by life, by itself. I'm doing it wrong somehow, failing to take up the new year's offer of starting over. Because it's everywhere, working its way into everything—a looping conversation with Patrick where I explain myself. Try. Use words in the hope of making it end differently. I tell him I wished I'd waited until we were somewhere private, at home, in the city, away from cars and drinking and general insanity. I say I wish I'd been a better person, more honest about what I wanted, and sooner, and maybe then I wouldn't have slept with him again, after I knew we were done, after it was over, for me. I was pregnant—I'd tell him, he'd know—I was really scared that night. On it rolls, useless words while I'm brushing my teeth, while I'm tying my shoes, while I'm running past Mercy House, pretending Mary's in there, wishing she were, *I'm sorry, Patrick*, a refrain echoing into nothing. It's a meaningless exercise, my excuses pathetic, pointless. They fall like snow between us. It's never going to happen. I have to hold it. Alone. He'll never know. God, never is so long.

When I finish at the library, I head to Cal's. He called in sick to his internship. We lie, legs tangled, warm on his couch.

While he sleeps, I hold a book like I'm reading and watch him sleep or stare at the water. Or at his face. The winter light turns itself away from us.

My phone buzzes. I answer it fast so it doesn't wake him.

"Mamie, I hear there's a boy."

"Mother," I whisper, moving Cal's head carefully off my thigh and crossing the room to an armchair by the bookshelves.

"Darling, can you hear me?"

"Yes, Mom. I can. You've been talking to Dad?"

"Marta, of all people. She hasn't contacted me in years. I had to call you, it sounds like something hopeful? She said you look marvelous, well, that you were on the arm of some young man at your father's bacchanal?"

"His name's Cal," I say as quietly as possible.

"Oh I'm sorry, darling, did I call you while you're at the library? I thought you'd be done for the day."

"No," I whisper. "I'm at his place." I glance at him on the couch. He looks so relaxed, his arm up over his eyes. Then, before she can ask more questions, "He's sleeping."

"Sleeping?" I can hear her brow furrow.

"Not like that, Mom," I say, flinging a leg over the arm of the chair. "Cal has MS. Some days he has to rest."

Radio silence.

I reach up and twist one of the diamond studs in my ear.

"Well, I guess it's good you've found someone, some company," she says, finally, diplomatically. But I can hear it in her voice. Disappointment. This is not how she wants me to spend my time.

I slouch in the chair, press my eyeballs with my fingers.

"I ran into Ms. Gaffin yesterday," she says, her voice brisk, we're moving on.

Ms. Gaffin. Bly's dean of students and my former advisor. My heart hangs in my chest, frozen.

"She asked about you. I told her you were well, living up north with all those artists." She laughs lightly, but it comes out more like a little tight gasp. "She says Emma's doing better, playing basketball, blossoming in tenth grade. I thought you'd like to hear that. I know you were fond of her, too."

Now I need to hang up.

I walk back over to the couch. Curl onto the end of it, make all the murmuring sounds of accord I know my mother's expecting to hear, whisper something about going to make dinner, and let my phone fall to the floor.

I hold tight to the memory of the dead calm I made inside myself before Cal came along. Look at him again, stretched out long and lovely beside me. Shut my eyes. There's so little between me and the world.

When he wakes up, Cal stares at me a minute, then asks me where I am. Where I've gone. *I'm right here*, I lie. He pulls me closer.

Later, at home, I can't sleep. Can't stay asleep. My eyes fly open in the dead of night from the same dream, almost not a dream even, more like a thought I have that's so clear and real it wakes me. The car has stopped rolling. Even though I can't really turn my head, I know Patrick's dead. An alone feeling. He's not where he's supposed to be. I can kind of see his face, but he's not in it anymore. It's just his face. Less than that. Less than a picture of a face, even. Without life—it's the strangest thing I ever saw. I can't take my eyes off him. All his anger's gone. Everything. He looks empty. I can't believe how fast it happened. Then the spreading warmth between my legs, blood creeping up through my shorts, soaking the hem of my tank top. I think it's then I notice we're upside down. I'm very calm. It's so still. The airbags are everywhere between us.

It's the quiet that wakes me up, after all that noise—metal bending, glass popping, grinding, crunching—it's sudden, the silence, like a slammed door, the puff of air that knifes out between the wall and the jamb.

It happens every night now. I sit up, heart pounding. Sweating. Sick with it. We're always going to be together, Patrick and me. Only worse. Because it's really just me and me. Patrick's nothing. Words. Images. That's what it comes down to. I'm left with me. Our angry words hanging on the air like spider webs between branches, invisible until you feel them sticky across your face.

I think about the ocean, great erasing waves.

Then I take a sleeping pill.

1
mornin' sunshine

I'M GROGGY from another night of it when I stumble out of my room and find Nick at our table reading the Sunday *New York Times*, magazine and all. Where'd he get that? He's drinking what smells like a great, slap-in-the-face cup of coffee.

"Mornin' Sunshine," he says to me without looking up. Like this is our routine. Like he is supposed to be at my table, reading the paper, drinking my coffee.

He looks like he's just come from yoga or the gym. Healthy glow. For some reason this puts me in a foul mood. I've avoided him since Swap Night. Barely said two words. My dad seems happy to have him here, but today, this morning, I hate him. Just like that. He's not Mary. He's in my house, stealing my silence. Probably loves getting up early.

I resist reaching up to my hair and do a fast mental inventory instead. Flannel pajama pants. Check. Sweatshirt. Check. Not my usual T-shirt and underwear, thank God. I walk over to the coffee. Casual. Will not give him the satisfaction of thinking he's a surprise. Or interesting. The house is annoyingly bright, like it's on his side.

"Why are you here?" Manners. My mother would be so proud.

"Heat's out in the studio." Lays his cat green eyes on me with what I'm sure is a smirk, like he's caught me somehow. Every time I've passed him since the night he got here, he's turned them on me, questioning, as if he thinks after a few get-to-know-ya questions we might be friends.

"So where's my dad?" I ask. He's got to be around.

"He told me to hang in here till he got back."

"Back . . . ?" I ask, in my best annoyed tone. My head's a hammer from the sleeping pill.

"He had to run to town to get someone to help him whack the heating system or something."

This does not explain why he's sitting at my table. I stare at him.

He looks up, reads my face, and shrugs, waving his hand vaguely toward the door.

"He took my car. The truck wouldn't start." Goes back to looking at the paper.

The truck. Damn. I smack my hand across my forehead. This one's my fault. I saw the cab light on when I set out to run yesterday. Meant to turn it off when I got back. My lethargy equals one dead battery and breakfast with Nick. Perfect.

"News from the greater world?" he asks, sliding some sections in my direction. Like I'm going to sit there, next to him, with him, and read the morning paper.

"Where'd you get the *Times*?" I turn away, grab a mealy-looking peach from the fruit bowl, and pour a cup of coffee. It's a sad breakfast without Mary around.

"It's delivered? It was on the step by the door," he says, like it's obvious, and I'm some kind of bumpkin. It is. I am.

I'm losing my edge. If I don't get back to the city soon I'm going to turn into one of those rural people who don't say much.

I take my coffee and peach and head back to my room.

"Don't let me chase you off."

He rattles the back of the chair next to him at the table. Like a challenge. Big grin.

Now if I leave the room, he wins. Worse, I've played. I stop and take a bite of the mealy peach. Stare at him a minute. Witheringly. He doesn't flinch. Meets my gaze.

I shrug. "You're not," I say, and walk out.

Already a crap day. Nick, the minute I open my eyes. I'll have to say something to my dad about it. He can't just stick him here with me like this. I abandon the withered peach on the shelf, next to my coffee, and pull on yesterday's running clothes. They're a little ripe. Too bad for Nick when I pass him on the way out. I used to be on top of things like that. The simple science of clean clothes and smelling like a girl. Definitely need to get it together again in the laundry department.

I cue up my hard-ass-run playlist and lace my shoes. The woods await. I'll blow it all off. The jerk at my table, the bad night's sleep, an overbright day. I can make this feeling change. Will it to. Pound it out of myself on the trails.

"Hey," he calls, taking in my running outfit as I breeze past him. "Mind if I join you? It doesn't look like your dad's coming back soon. I've got nothing better to do. I'd love a winter run."

"I—" I stop to stare at him. Is he serious? Nothing better to do? I'm speechless.

"My shoes are in the studio," he says. "Let me grab them and my jacket, and I'm good to go."

Good to go. He would be. Like he's a sales rep from The Land of Good to Go. I let out an exasperated sigh.

"Fine," I say, as cold as I can. What else can I say? *No*, Meredith would tell me. *You could say no*. But he's working with my dad. So I can't. Or don't. What an ass, I think. A mantra. He's an ass. He's an ass. Gives me strength. Mary would probably grin at me and tell me to turn it into an opportunity. A challenge for a better workout. An ugly little smile crosses my mouth, does not make me feel better. I'll lose him on the trails. Run along the water's edge, make it as hard as I can.

He sprints to the studio and comes back seconds later, sneakers on and an annoying bounce in his stride.

"You lead," he says, with a flourishing bow, flirty.

He's an ass. He's an ass. He's an ass.

We set out.

"So—" he starts. We're on the highway shoulder. "Have

you figured out what there is to do up here in the off hours? Secret Cinema died, I guess. Sounds like Mary was the force behind that one."

Yeah. Mary the force. Poor Mary. I can't stop thinking about her spending her fellowship watching over me, probably wishing my dad would actually mentor her like he was supposed to. I don't answer. Let him run on the outside edge. Maybe a passing car or truck will pick him off.

He tries again, "Your dad thinks you might end up in art school? In the spring? Or next fall?"

God, my dad's talking to him about me? I shoot him another annoyed look. He's not winded in the least. That long-legged stride. Kicking his ass won't be easy, even with a home-turf advantage.

"I don't really like to talk when I run."

He shuts up and we fall into a decent pace. I cross to the trails after we get a bit farther south, where the coast opens up. We climb high into the wooded hills, picking our way up a path that comes out over everything. I can see Cal's house. Ours. The littler ones on the far side of town. Near the top, we run along a gravel road locals use. A few cars pass us.

I'm warmed up. Take him down closer to the water. A rocky trail along the coast. He keeps close behind me. It's icy, but I run a slower, flat-footed kind of stomp over the rocks to keep from slipping. It looks stupid, but I've perfected it, and I never fall. I don't look at him, won't give him the satisfaction, but I wonder if he's too vain to run like a duck. Maybe he'll fall into the surf. Icarus and his wax wings. I amuse myself imagining it. Then I curse him for still managing to fill my mind, even if we're not talking.

I really just wanted to get out here and get a grip. Alone.

Finally he slows his pace, drops behind a bit, so I can't feel his breath down my back anymore. Then, like a movie in my mind, a terrible scene unfurls, one where I stop, let him catch me, breathe hard against my neck, let him pull me down for a mad second, our legs twisting hot together, still vibrating from the run.

Only he's not the one making it up. It's me. I veer sharply left, drop down a hatefully angled rock, scrape my leg through my tights.

"Christ—" he calls out, following me, half laughing. Then a bit of a scramble when, I assume, he loses his footing.

I don't look back. That's what he gets for running with me.

"Hey, Wells, you're bleeding," he says.

"Shut up."

But I glance down near my ankle, and he's right. A bright, guilty trail.

I turn and go up the steepest incline I can find, back into the woods. My thighs burn. I don't care. I blaze a new trail through deep, hard snow. My feet punch loud holes through the untouched crust. Icy bits fill my shoes. I should've made him lead. He's probably running in my footsteps.

"You're hard core," he calls out finally, or taunts. Probably both. Does he think I'm doing this to flirt with him? He sounds a little closer to me.

"Head back if you want," I say.

Please. Turn back and leave me the hell alone. Get out of my head. I just want time. To run. Empty out.

He has no clue. Laughs.

"I'm good," he says. "Having a ball. Dish it out. I'll take whatever you're giving."

I'm not losing him, I'm encouraging him. I come to a dead stop. I can't run with this guy, the relentless cheer he clearly thinks is his charm.

"Whoa—"

He almost crashes into my back. Hand on my shoulder a second. Warm.

I whirl around.

"I'm sorry," I say. My voice comes out low, mean, "Did I give you some signal? Some sign that I wanted you with me today? Because I'm not sure how you got that idea."

My thighs feel like noodles. I'm shaking, from adrenaline, from trying to lose him, from using all my energy to tear around these hills like a madwoman instead of just being straight with him.

"I want to be alone," I say, blinking right into his surprised face. No time for manners now. I can't stop myself. "I wanted to be alone. This morning. I wanted to wake up in my house and not find you there, or here, following me, talking at me the whole way. If I led you on somehow, gave you a different impression, I'm sorry. If you're looking to win some kind of extra favor with my dad, you're looking in the wrong place." Curse my wavering voice. At least I didn't scream, let out the shriek boiling up inside me.

If I weren't so mad, I'd laugh at how shocked he looks.

And sincere. His eyes are freakishly green against his blond hair, against the bright sky. He must have been smiling before he heard what I had to say and now it's stuck there, that stupid grin, like a piece of food in his teeth. It's embarrassing. For me. Him. I want to punch it off his face. Mr. Easygoing. I hope his art sucks. Screw him and his happy life.

I turn away from him and run. I'm pretty sure he won't follow.

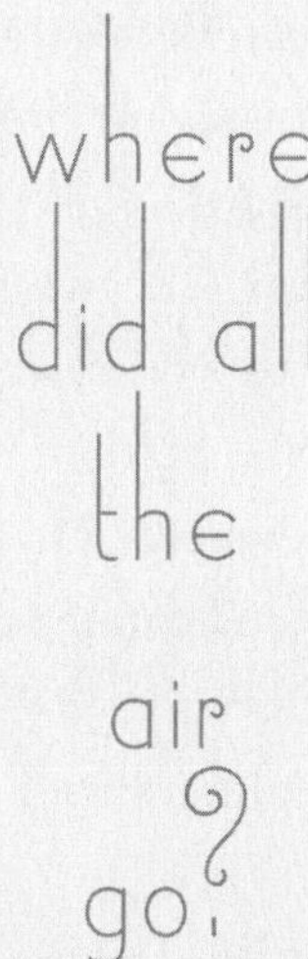

IT GOES FROM BAD TO WORSE.

When I get back to the house, a message from Cal. Cryptic. He wants me to come over as soon as I'm free. I really, really want to take a nap, but I take a fast shower instead and hop in the Jeep. Hope he's okay.

He's waiting in the garage. Leaning against the silver car. Looks very satisfied with himself, face broken into the kind of grin usually reserved for victory.

"It's a great day . . ." he says, when I pull in and get out.

Jingles his keys in his hand. No crutches. He looks terrific.

"You look happy," I say, smiling.

He walks over to me, curls and uncurls his fingers, then

catches my hand, lacing our fingers together. Pulls me close.

I laugh, back up, take him in. He looks so good. Flutter heart.

"Woke up feeling great. Better than I've felt all year."

He leans down and kisses me, long and slow. Lures my heart from its dark cupboard.

"Almost no numbness," he whispers happily into my neck, like it's bad luck to say it out loud. "My balance is good and I want to get the hell out of this house. Will you come with me? Go somewhere? Do something? Just drive? Let me take you out where I can see the sun on your beautiful face."

I nod. I'll go wherever he wants. I'm a little light-headed. Take a deep breath.

He jingles his keys again. Looks so happy.

"If it weren't freezing, I'd take you down by the water with a blanket and tear your clothes off."

I'm trying, I really am. It should make me feel great, what he's saying, but it doesn't. I'm flat inside. Can't shake it. I try to look happy, but I'm a terrible actor. His brow furrows.

"What's wrong?" he asks, deflating a little.

"Nothing." I shake my head. Force a smile. "So you're driving . . ." I try to joke, "Are you sure you don't want to take the Jeep for old-time's sake? Look for bikes on the road?"

It's a lame and even kind of terrible thing to say. He looks at me, puzzled, then shrugs it off. Takes me by the hand to my side of the car and opens the door for me.

I sink back into the comfortable seat and whisper a new

mantra until he gets in. It will be a good day. I will it to be a good day. My mood will lift. I want to believe it, despite all experience to the contrary. I check my phone for the time. The afternoon's half over, anyway. I can get it together a few hours for Cal.

We back away from the house. He drives like someone who's really happy behind the wheel. Steers us expertly backward down the snowy drive. I can't keep my eyes off him. That's a bonus. His hands are light on the wheel, like he's in an ad for a perfect life in a perfect world. It makes me shiver. Been there before. Didn't quite work out. But this is different. I'm good at lying to myself.

He points to the stereo. "Pick something," he says. "Something you want to hear loud."

We go fast. Out of the woods and onto the highway. The music drums through my body. I recline my seat a little and close my eyes while sunlight flashes across my face like a strobe through the trees. Try not to think about being in a car. With Cal. With anyone.

"Is this okay?" he asks, his hand on my leg, slowing the car a little. "Am I freaking you out? Driving too fast?"

"No," I lie. "I'm fine. It's fine."

"Are you sure? You're all right with just driving around awhile, being in the car together?"

I nod again. He needs to drive. I remember that feeling, flying out to Meredith's beach house, free of the city.

"It's okay," I say. "Really. Drive as long as you want." Not too convincing, but it's the best I've got from inside my dull fog.

He looks doubtful.

"Seriously." I make my voice more sure. "I'm just tired. Do your thing."

It comes out sounding a little sarcastic. I don't mean it that way. Besides, if he kills us going one hundred miles an hour on a winding road, it'd solve a lot of problems. For both of us. I slip my cold hand under his. My head's in a bad place.

"Something's wrong," he states, taking his eyes off the road to look at me for a second. "Did you run this morning?" Like he's asking if I took my meds. I close my eyes. Did I run.

"Yeah."

A little hammer of shame beats against me. Somehow it seems smart not to mention Nick.

"I'm sorry," I say. "Bad night's sleep." Another little shiver. "I'm glad we're out. That you're feeling better. Drive as fast as you want."

He looks at me again, unconvinced.

"I know you," he says. "Something happened."

"It's just a dumb mood," I say, entwining my fingers with his. "I promise."

We drive fast, slowing for sleepy villages, one-stoplight harbor towns full of people living their lives. What do they all do? Snowmobilers buzz by us, noisy on trails outside my window. Signs for blueberry barrens, ski hills, antique barns, and maple syrup dot the edges of the road. Below the sun, lazy and low, we swoop, dip, and curve our way south. Late-day light angles in on us. Cal flips down his visor. Puts on sunglasses. I didn't bring mine. I close my eyes against the light. For just a second.

Cal kisses me awake. It's dark. We're parked outside the only Italian restaurant in town.

"I'm sorry!" I straighten up, my heart racing.

"What for?" He kisses me again. "I got to drive fast. You got to sleep. We're both happy."

I stretch my back and neck. Hope I didn't sleep with my mouth open or bob my head up and down like some old guy on the subway. I reach up and feel my cheek. Dry. Good.

We're in a parking lot. Out my window, a red-and-green Italian placard outside the place reads LunaRossa Trattoria and Wine Bar. The lot's full. Everyone's out to eat, apparently.

"Hungry?" he says, gesturing toward the place. "It's campy but decent. Basic American Italian. Or we could go back to Stone's Harbor?"

Where we had such a great dinner that first night. No thanks.

"Here's good," I say, trying to put some cheer in my voice. "Small-town 'Eye-talian.' Nothing better."

Everything I say sounds bitchy. I push open my car door and the cold air hits me hard. I'm a terrible girlfriend. I have the slightly insane thought that I could jog around the little downtown for ten minutes or so, try to shake myself out of the heaviness I've been dragging all day.

"Wait." He comes around to my side of the car. "Let me get your door for you. You know, because I can."

He offers me his hand, and when I get out, he leans

me back against the car, an arm on either side of me, and breathes a line of kisses along my collarbone. I shiver. I want to press into him and disappear. Stop having to be myself.

"I know something's wrong," he says in a quiet voice right near my ear. "And I'm getting to know you well enough to know you don't want to talk about it. I'm fine with that."

"I don't even know why you like me," I say, the words out before I can stop them. It's the truth. I can't see what I have to offer that he could possibly want or need.

He looks surprised and a little pained. Quiet a minute. Then, "You looked as miserable as I felt the day we met. You had this look on your face—and then you tried to be so fierce. I felt like I knew you already, knew what you were going through. Scared. Angry. Everything all at once. I've been there."

He pulls my chin up so our eyes meet, kisses me.

"Stop looking so sorry. Everything's good. I had a great time driving a beautiful girl all around this damned gorgeous coast, listening to loud music in my fine car, and feeling like a regular person. So stop it, okay? If you're worrying about disappointing me or anything, don't."

I'm shivering. It's freezing in the damp wind. He pulls up my hood and kisses me on the forehead. "It's life. Our moods won't always sync up."

Won't always sync up. Every time he does that, acts like we have a future together, like there's an *us*, I feel a little quiver in my stomach. Bad and good. Usually good. Depending on how far out I can imagine my future.

I wrap my arms around his neck, open my mouth, and almost say *I love you*. Catches me off guard. I close it again. Stand on tiptoe and kiss him back. "You're the best." I breathe him in. I mean it. He is. And I might love him.

I pull it together and we head in for dinner—he's happy to talk. Tells me stories about windsurfing with Michael off Carro in the south of France. I laugh in the right places.

Then it all goes to hell. Just as the cannolis come, a square of a woman passes by our table on her way out of the restaurant. She has a weathered face, like she works on a boat or something.

"Wren Wells." Her voice is huge. The sound of my name fills the room. Startles me. "Did your dad get that part into his heater this afternoon?"

I still have a New Yorker's sense of anonymity. Can't quite get used to having all the townies know who the hell I am.

"Pardon me?" I face her, confused a second. "Oh, the heater. I'm not sure . . ." I look at Cal and raise my brows. No privacy in this place. "I wasn't home this afternoon."

I pick up a chocolate cannoli, hope she'll walk on.

She doesn't. She eyes me a minute, the cannoli, then Cal.

"Well, you and that new art kid sure were going at a good pace earlier today," she says. Hefty chuckle.

I set the cannoli down.

"I passed you in my car up on the old Dover trail. You were givin' that young buck a good chase." She laughs again. *Heh, heh, heh*.

I push my plate away. I can't even look at Cal. My face

is on fire. I can feel his eyes on me. I fold and unfold my napkin in my lap.

"Yeah," I say, lamely.

There's nothing else to say. Anything that comes out of my mouth at this point is just going to make it worse. I want the old crone to get the heck away from me and stop talking.

"He looked just like a jackrabbit," she says, laughing again. "Oh, you young people and your springy knees."

She nods to Cal and turns away from us to follow her partner out of the suddenly tiny and overcrowded restaurant.

Where did all the air go?

My lungs are pancakes in my chest. I try not to gasp for breath when I finally look up at Cal's face. It's like watching a time-lapse video on fast playback—passes from surprised, to incredulous, to hurt, to grim.

Breathe. My hands tug on my napkin, like I might pull it apart. Or, preferably, tear a hole in the fabric of time and step through it, out of here, away.

"Nick?" he says quietly, his question so much bigger than that.

Waves of something come off him. Disbelief maybe, but something else. Worse.

I can't even open my mouth. My heart is in it. I keep my eyes on my napkin.

"The new Mary? That's the art kid Miriam's talking about?"

Miriam. Fucking Miriam. I nod. Look at him, then my lap. Back at him.

He picks up his water, takes a drink, and looks right

through me. Like I'm not there. Invisible or something. I wish I were.

"I knew there was something. I don't—" He shakes his head like he can't quite figure it out. "You two went running? You and Nick? This morning, together?"

He keeps his voice flat. Even. Like he's trying to be casual, maybe, though it's obvious this is killing him. I try to find his eyes, but he won't look at me. It's like he's focusing on a spot just behind me.

Blood rushes in my ears.

"Nick Bishop." He nods slightly, his voice sounding distant. Hard. Filled with something I haven't heard in it before. Anger, jealousy, maybe both. Probably both. I'm queasy. Try to breathe through my nose.

"Yes. But Cal—"

He cuts me off. Looks at me like he's the one who just woke up.

"Nick Bishop," he repeats with the slightest sneer. "You didn't tell me."

"It was nothing," I manage. It has to be the lamest sentence in the history of all defenses.

He looks at me for a second. Then back through me again.

"This is why you're so tired today?"

"No—"

"Because you and Nick were out having fun on the trails?"

"Cal—"

"Did you take him south along the coast a bit, show him

the view? The spot where it's really steep? It's amazing down there."

I did. But not how he thinks. I shudder a little.

He's cold. Angry. Gone off somewhere far away from me. It scares me. He waves to the server for the check. Avoids my eyes.

I reach for my bag. He ignores me and hands cash to the nervous-looking kid who brings the check. Apparently it's not lost on the other people in the room that we're having a fight. The kid makes a speedy U-turn back to the servers' stand.

Cal rubs the bridge of his nose and looks around the room. Still won't look at me. Some of the townies are listening in. Trying to seem like they aren't. Miriam's remarks were not quiet. We'll be the talk of the town as soon as we leave.

It's too much to be trusted with someone else's heart. I don't think it ever ends well. I try again, my voice nearly a whisper, "It wasn't like I asked him to join me."

I want to explain to him how it went down. But that little fantasy I had sits there in my mind, mocking me.

He dismisses me with a shake of his head. He's pale. Whatever he's thinking has him pulled so far away from me right now he might as well be gone. Nothing I say is going to make a difference at this point. If I could disappear, I would.

"Save it," he says, looking around, away from me. His voice is more calm than his face. "I don't want to hear about it. Not tonight. You would have told me earlier if you'd wanted. I don't need to know."

I knew it would be like this.

Feel awful like this.

He pushes back from the table and heads out. I grab my bag and trip after him. He holds the door for me with a dark look on his face. He clicks the car unlocked and gets in his side with a slam. Starts the engine.

I can't make myself get in his car.

He leans across the front, pushes open my door.

"Wren, get in." His voice is tight, cold.

I can't. Try not to cry.

"What's the problem?"

"I'm—I'm just having a hard time getting in the car"—I can't quite catch my breath—"while you're so angry."

His face shifts from fury to something that looks like regret and hangs there a second, fallen, then recomposes itself. A more masked fury. Resigned.

"Wren, please get in," he says in a more controlled voice. "I'm not angry. It's fine."

He's lying, though, and as soon as I'm buckled in, we peel out of the lot and drive back to my place fast. I keep my face turned away from his and silently recite all eight lines of Larkin's "To put one brick upon another," the rhythm and repetition forming something sturdy around me.

"I'll bring the Jeep to you another time," he says when we pull in.

Dismissed.

Hot splotches bloom on my cheeks. Shame. Or something. It's dark. He won't see them. I could throw up the dinner I just ate.

"Cal—" I try again, reach for his hand. He moves it away from me, grips the wheel.

"No, it's fine," he says, voice clipped. "You want to run with someone from time to time. I get that."

So cold.

"Cal, you're making this into—"

"I'm not making anything into anything." Strain on his face in the moonlight. "I had a good day, thanks for coming out with me."

He speaks like I'm an acquaintance. Doesn't look at me. His eyes are fixed firmly on something out the windshield. He doesn't lean over to kiss me.

I sit there a second longer, in the space where our kiss would have been. Stunned. Then I throw open the car door, get out. I close it with what I hope is a bit of a slam.

Fucking shitty day.

bad to worse to worst

SO IT'S NO SURPRISE, then, when I turn and notice my mother's car parked behind my dad's truck. Of course she'd pop up for a visit now. Today. Tonight. Unannounced.

My parents' two cars tell the whole story. Divergent paths. Their philosophies of well and good. The behemoth, his 1970s rattletrap Wagoneer with broken seat belts hemmed in by her compact luxury coupe, known for its superior safety features. The kind of car that saved me.

I sit a minute by the front door on the freezing step with my face in my hands. Why is she here unannounced? Is she going to tell me I have to move back to the city with her?

I need a minute to absorb what happened in the car with Cal. He thinks something's going on with Nick and me.

This stupid, stupid town, stupid me. Why didn't I just tell him? I didn't tell him because I thought it would make him feel bad—that Nick could run with me when he can't. I felt guilty and I was trying to protect his feelings.

Exactly what he asked me not to do.

Michael called it. I wreck everything. God.

I run through the day in my head, beginning with Nick. Our run. Just thinking about it makes me feel sick. I should have called it quits right then, turned off my phone, climbed back in bed. But no. Instead I was Wren Wells, world's worst date, starting with a lie, checking out in the car, deathly dull at dinner, and now this.

Behind me, the front door opens.

"Wren?"

Dad. Using his soft voice. He's on to me, has some kind of freaky mind power or something. There's no hiding allowed. Roll a car and lose your privacy forever. I keep my hands over my face.

He puts his hand on my back, crouches near me. "We heard the car pull up. What are you doing sitting out here? Come in." Pulls my hands away from my face. "Are you okay?"

I look at him. He feels sorry for me, I can tell. But he's not going to make me explain. It's a good thing about him.

"Your mother's paying us a surprise visit."

I take his hand and stand up, brush snow and birdseed off the back of my jeans. Remember Meredith dropping me off drunk one night, after we snuck into an art opening in Chelsea and over-helped ourselves to plastic glasses of cheap white wine when I was supposed to be home with my mother, having dinner with a few of her colleagues. Meredith hung out of the cab, shouting after me as I stumbled up our stoop, "Put a smile on it, Wells! This is gonna be fun!"

Fun. What else could go wrong?

"Okay," I say, following him in.

"Wren. Were you just sitting out there in the cold?" Worry voice. My mother hugs me. Presses my face into her perfectly bobbed hair. I feel painfully young all of a sudden, and her hug is good. I could stay in it forever. She smells the same no matter where we are. Mom-ish. Soft. Comforting.

"Mom," I say, choked up, "you're here." It's the best I've got.

I kick off my boots and go into the living room. Away from her eyes, which are X-raying me, trying to figure out what's going on. I flop on the couch. Dad slips a mug of tea into my hand and settles down in the armchair. Awkward silence. Our little family reunion. Now all we need is a parental quarrel—a perfect end to a perfect day.

"It's just a casual visit," my mother says somewhat formally. "I decided I was going to get old waiting for another invitation after that nor'easter, and I had a few clear days on my schedule, so I took it upon myself to drive up and see how you're doing." She scrutinizes me. "You're thin," she says.

"She's healthy," Dad interjects, trying to help me out. "She runs a lot."

"Yes," my mother says, making a face that's the polite

version of an eye roll, "I know, John. I know all about the running."

Here we go.

"But you can't run away from things forever." She talks like this. Random comments wind around to demonstrate her point. Her important point.

I eye her. She's trying to see into me, stare me down. She'll win.

I stand up. "Mom, I've had a bad night. I'm going to bed. I'll see you in the morning."

I hate how hurt she looks, but I can't take another word out of her. Anyone. Not tonight. I have no idea where she'll sleep and I don't care. Just as long as it's not in my room. I walk out of there as fast as I can. No looking back. Sorry, Dad.

The sleeping pill can't work soon enough, and then it does.

A HAND ON MY SHOULDER. Shaking me.

"Wren," Dad says, "wake up."

"What's going on?" I ask, worried for a second.

"Nothing." He pushes my hair out of my eyes. "I just thought you might like a little time to resurface before your mother comes back to spend the day with you."

My lids are heavy. Swollen. It's weird he's in here. Sunlight fills the room. Mary and I were going to make curtains. Dark ones.

I swim back up. My mother's here. To spend the day. And she didn't stay the night. Oh blessed be my brilliant and kind father. He reaches down and hands me a sweatshirt.

"Where'd she go? She's not here?" I ask, pulling it over my head.

"She had a room already, at the B&B. Said she'd be more comfortable there, privacy, clean bathroom . . ." He smiles at me, winks. "You know your mother. She spared me the awkwardness of inviting her to stay here before I even had a chance to feel it."

I flop back against my pillow. "Why's she here?" I ask. "Did you . . . ?"

"Call her?" He shakes his head. "Nope. We've only been checking in by e-mail since things with you seemed to—seemed like they were looking up."

He rubs a scratchy hand on the leg of his work pants.

"I'm going to be in the studio today, Zara and Jeb are coming to help with fold-forming, but I can leave Nick with them and stick around if you need me to."

I've been mad at my dad off and on over the years for choosing art over us, but moments like this make me forgive him everything. He's not the most constant of parents, but he gets it. Gets me.

I shake my head. "It's okay, Dad," I say. "We'll be okay. Thanks for getting me up, though, I'll run before she gets here."

"Better hurry. Knowing her, she's on her way."

I throw my arms around him, hug him tight.

"Wren—last night—everything okay?" he asks.

"I don't want to talk about it," I say, kicking back the covers and slipping out of bed.

My mother pulls in just as I'm heading out. I wave

and take off before she can say anything.

Despite the early sun, the day's frigid. It's like that up here. Permafrost. Brightness definitely does not equal warmth. I have a hard time finding my stride. Focusing. Cal. It comes back. His face at the table, like he could read me, see what I'd imagined. My stomach drops. I have to stop a minute. Catch my breath. And my mother, waiting for me back at the house. I try to run again, but trip a few times, throwing my arms and back wildly to catch myself, and finally, wrenched and sore, I give up and turn around. Winter running requires focus. My head's not there.

Mom's in my room when I come in, folding my clothes and stacking them on the shelf.

"Honestly, Wren," she says, looking around the room wearily, "doesn't your father ever have someone in to clean?"

So her. It almost makes me laugh. Almost.

"I could find someone up here for you," she says, "if you'd like?"

She's trying to be gentle, not to overwhelm me.

"Is that something you'd want? A person. To clean? I'll line it up before I go back to the city."

I don't really care either way. That's part of the problem, I guess.

"If it makes you happy, Mom," I say. "But I can also just get my shit together and clean up once in awhile."

"Language." She winces. I'm not supposed to swear. I'll have to watch it or she's going to think she needs to stay longer.

She pulls the sheets off my bed and tosses them into the

laundry basket that's been neglected in the corner.

"No clean ones," I say. I never got around to buying a second set of sheets.

A big sigh from her. "Well, then. It's a good thing I came. We'll go out and get a few things today. I don't suppose there's anywhere in this town to buy that sort of thing? And do you need towels, too?"

She looks in my bathroom and shakes her head.

"How have you been living like this?"

"I make do." I keep my towels clean. Clean-ish.

"Shower," she says. "Then we'll set out to find a few things."

And that's how it goes. I leave my cell phone behind so I can't check it every few minutes to see if Cal's called, and then I spend a full day shopping with my mother. She makes me get some new clothes, sheets, towels, and even offers to buy books. She's trying. Manages to keep most of her opinions to herself, aside from one remark about young women who live only in jeans and sneakers and forget how to ever make themselves look presentable. She even holds back on the when-are-you-going-to-wake-up-and-start-college conversation. At least for most of the day.

"So, what have you been doing with yourself up here?" she asks. We're eating out. At Stone's Harbor, in town. Where Cal took me the first night. Great memories.

I don't answer.

She repeats it. The million-dollar question. Her face is a picture of concern. I wish we were troubled about the same things. It'd be so much easier.

I look around the dining room. People seem to be ignoring us. Of course, she had to take me out. Said it that way. Had to.

I can't say anything she'll want to hear. I used to be good at it. I toed the line. But I can't pull it off anymore. There's no good answer. Nothing that will make her stop worrying. I've been living. That's the best I've got. Feels like a lot.

Tap, tap, tap. Her finger on the table. I look at it. She stops. It's her tell. When she's scared.

"I don't know, Mom."

I push my food around my plate. I'm disappointing her. I used to do what she asked. I was responsible, and she left me alone. It's not that I didn't want to be close to her, it's just that I wanted to keep some things for myself. She has her ideas about how things should be. My life. How I should live it. So I started to tell her only the things she would want to know. We took a vacation together, every year, three weeks in August, then came back to our routine. She felt like an awesome parent, and I was almost out of there.

"I read," I say, finally. It sounds lame. Like I'm apologizing. Which I kind of am, I guess.

She makes no effort to hide her dismay. Stiffens her back against it, gets even more erect if that's possible, and resumes the tap, tap, tapping. Like she's pushing some kind of button that will take care of things. Patch me back up again.

"I work at the library. And I run."

"You read and you run. I see. That and this boy fills a day?"

I nod. That's why she's here. I should save her the trouble, tell her not to worry. Cal. Us. It has to be over. I totally wrecked it. My stomach dives. I let out a breath. Maybe he's called. Doubtful. Silence from his end of the world. Since he dropped me off.

"Your father told me a little about your new friend," she says, putting a perfectly forked leaf of lettuce into her mouth. "The architect's son."

I stare at my asparagus, the fillet, the little winter salad. It looks like a mountain of food that will be a lot of work to choke down. Everything seems too hard. I want to call Cal but I can't. I couldn't take more rejection.

"They used to live near us, you know, in the city. Harry Owen and his wife, before you were born. When we were all just starting out."

My heart races hearing her say his name. Like she could make him appear.

"Their lives sure took a turn for the worse."

Big sigh. Lifts her wine glass.

"Lives do that," I say.

I poke the fish with my fork. Poor fish. Too low on the food chain. I push it through its sauce. Lift a bite to my mouth. Chew.

She looks at me long and hard. Here it comes. Something. I don't know what, but I'm pretty sure I won't like it.

"Work with me just a bit, okay, darling? You've always been such a strong spirit, you get that from me." She raises her glass and takes the smallest sip of wine, does a quick pat of her mouth with her napkin. "Wren, it's not a good idea, right now, for you to—I want you to go see someone."

She's looking at me with such tenderness I almost don't hear what she's saying.

Then I do.

Sink inside.

"What are you talking about? What's not a good idea? Someone?"

She eyes me again, and I spot something like fear there a minute.

"Fall in love in a place like this—before college, before—I think you're in a precarious situation right now—I want you to talk to someone. Go see someone. If you're going to stay up here awhile longer."

She won't say it. Looks at her wine. Smoothes her already perfect hair.

If she won't say it, I will.

"You think Cal is a step in the wrong direction and you want me to see a shrink."

I stab my asparagus.

"You can't just walk away from Amherst after you worked so hard to get in there." It hisses out of her like a tired snake, the old argument. Brought back from the dead, my tremendous future, and now she thinks Cal's the bad guy.

"Mom. You have nothing to worry about on the Cal front," I say, closing my eyes. "Came and went." I try to breathe evenly. Keep my heart from doing its painful little trot.

She takes in this bit of information without comment. Forges ahead on her mission.

"Art schools, even, if you're planning to go—I've been

talking to people at RISD, your dad and I have—they could have taken you the end of this month. They'll welcome you next September if you'd like. We just need to let them know our plans." Sighs. "I won't insist on Amherst if you're sure, you're positive it's not right for you, even though I think it would be better to begin with a solid liberal arts foundation before you pursue other—"

I cut her off.

"Mom."

She ignores me.

"Wren, it's too early for you to set down roots—"

This is so absurd, I snort, choke a little on the haddock.

"You need to be a little bit more forward-looking."

Forward-looking. Laughable.

"You can't pass all your days staring into space. It's not healthy. There is a time for grief, but now you need to move past it."

It's terrible when you can tell you're scaring your mother. If we weren't out in public I would put my head down on the table. I can barely imagine getting through this evening, much less planning anything long-term. Looking forward. I just want to be alone. Remake the quiet mental space I had going until I met Cal.

". . . or we could find you a job," she's saying. "A real one. Another apprenticeship somewhere. Up here, if you insist. Something interesting. Something to give you some purpose, a challenge."

This room is stuffy. I'm sucking in all the wet breathy air everyone else is letting out. The steam droplets on the windows make me want to gag. I used to be a regular person. I miss her.

". . . sitting around idle like this."

She's still talking.

"It may be preventing you from moving on, in fact."

She holds her hand out for mine. I'll cry if she touches me. I keep my hands on my lap. She looks resigned.

"This is supposed to be the time of your life, Wren."

God, is she getting choked up? I will die now.

"Your friends have moved on, are growing up. You can't just sit it out."

Moved on.

"Patrick's not moving on, Mom," I say, suddenly angry.

I reach across the table and finish her wine in one swallow. Startles her.

"Yes, well." Sigh. "I'm so sorry about that. That can't be helped."

She avoids my eyes. Like we're discussing something better left unsaid. It has to stop. This conversation. I have to let her win. That's how it goes. I fold just to end the conversation.

She reaches across the table and pats my hand. Lingering near her empty wineglass. Caught.

"But you can, move on."

And there it is. Her finale.

I close my eyes. She thinks I need a challenge. If she only knew.

She reaches into her purse and pulls out an envelope. Her heavy stationery. Slides it across the table.

"I've done some research. Asked for recommendations. In there you'll find the name of a psychiatrist at the university. Dr. Lang. He's well-regarded. You have an appointment with him next week. He's expecting you."

She folds her napkin, sets it near her plate. Her move's played. We may still be sitting here at the table, but dinner's over. I wonder if this is how she brokers deals at the hospital. I don't touch the envelope.

"Mom—"

"There's a check in there for you. You'll need to start a bank account if you're going to stay here awhile yet."

And there's the concession. She's letting me stay. She could be a strike breaker.

"Put the money into an account and use it to pay Dr. Lang and for your expenses."

No fight. Just terrible conditions. I should have known.

"Mom—" I try again, but I have no idea what to say.

"Your dad knows people," she says, "and I have a few contacts. Friends of friends. We can find you something, get you a real job somewhere. Something good to do during this gap year."

Gap year. That's how we're spinning it. Like it never happened.

"We'll get you a car so you can get yourself out of that house during the day and start living like a normal eighteen-year-old."

"I have a real job," I say. "Dad was right about the library. It's been good. Fine." I'm a few paces behind her.

Big sigh.

"Why is it when you think it comes from your father, it's a great idea, but when I suggest something, you shut me out? Your job"—her voice is a bit withering here—"at the library was my idea, not his. And when I first brought it up to you on the telephone, you didn't take calls from me for three days. Mamie, your father hasn't lifted a finger on your behalf in years. He pours all his energy into those students of his. You'll forgive me if I find it a little difficult to see him as your hero now."

I drink some water. Can't look at her.

She takes a deep breath.

"There must be some people around this town other than the unfortunate boy you may or may not be seeing." She casts a quick, doubtful glance around the restaurant. "Kids your age who do things. Whatever it is you and your friends did when you were home."

"We did what you wanted us to do, then we had parties, Mom. We drank and had sex."

I say it to shock her. It's mean of me. I feel mean all of a sudden. Enough to break what I thought was our agreement. I did largely what she wanted me to and she looked the other way. As long as I was careful. Careful. That turned out to be the big catch.

Her face falls. Like she might cry. Then recomposes itself. It's a little like watching a computer delete a file.

Now she'll back off the real-job business. I know a thing or two about negotiation—learned from the best.

"So," she says, trying for a brighter tone, "you'll show up for the appointment with Dr. Lang and let me get someone in there to clean that house once in a while." Like she's not asking that much. Another negotiating trick.

I look at the small candle on our table and try to breathe.

"Wren," she says, a little desperate, "I love you."

I blink back tears.

"Let him help," she says. "Dr. Lang. Let him help you find your way through."

Find my way through. What choice do I have? Any of us?

According to Larkin that's the kind of question that brings the priest and the doctor running.

I had to give in. She loves me. And she can't leave until she feels like she's helped somehow.

In her car on the way back to Dad's, fallow fields and barrens flashing past my window, I imagine her running with Larkin's doctor and a priest, her coat whipping behind her like wings. My mother, coming to map a route out of this dark place I'm in.

way too fast

I HOLD ON TO NOTHING. Patrick had this Zen Buddhist thing for awhile, walked around saying stuff like *The only constant is change*. Acting really mellow in the face of everything. I thought it was ridiculous. Disconnected. Lacked passion. Anyhow, it's my new plan. Let everything slip through my open fingers like sand. Mom's visit. Sand. The fight with Cal, sand. Cal in general—sand. The past, the present, the future, all shifting, I hold on to nothing.

Dad's back in the studio, keeping Nick busy and away from me. He thinks it's funny, the whole Nick-following-me-on-my-run thing, but that's because I don't tell him how it ended. About Cal. I don't want to talk about it. It's over anyway. Sand.

Nick tries to smile at me when we cross paths. I ignore him. He is, my dad says, when I tell him not to let Nick into the house, an exuberant student. Of course he is. God. Nick's just the kind of person my mother's hoping I'll find and hang out with. Mr. Positive. If there's a scene here, he's found it.

Other than my mother, my phone doesn't ring. It's okay. It didn't seem real anyway. Me and Cal. Us. It wasn't real. I repeat this to myself when I run. *It wasn't real*. I practice all my old tricks. Run. Stare at the water. Clock in and out at the library. I'm too messed up to hold anything together with another person. I put aside my books and say these kinds of things to myself like poems. Out loud. And I can do that because I'm in the middle of nowhere, alone in the woods, alone in the empty library, alone, alone, alone.

The day of my appointment with Dr. Lang comes way too fast. Mom calls me about fifty times to make sure I'm really truly going to keep it. Calls Dad, too, as added insurance that I'll actually go. And now he wants Nick to drive me to it in his car. He thinks it's safer than me taking the Wagoneer. There's no way in hell I'm going to ride to any shrink appointment with Nick Bishop, though, so I stare at him cold, like one of his poker pals, and say if he wants me to go, he's going to have to let me take the truck. It's only an hour away, anyway. What could happen? Only I don't say that last part because that's just the kind of humor neither of my parents find funny.

But I go there, in my head. Imagine it. A wreck in that truck would be grisly, that's for sure. The heavy green-and-brown hood popped open, steam rising cinematically from the engine—me, who knows where, tossed through the windshield or something. I know it would be nothing like this. I know it would be unbelievably loud and smell like hot grinding metal and melting plastic, and I know how fast a person can slip out of himself. But that's the part that might not be so bad. The truck would probably look beautiful to people passing by, in that desolate way a crashed car can. I shake it away. No way is he going to give me the keys if he so much as sniffs a thought like that on me before I leave.

Another bright day. Too many of them up here. Bright and cold as hell. Spring's a fever dream. We're frozen in place under a high-up thin, blue winter sky. Cloud free. Sun flash off the water. Blinding snow. It's all so present, demanding. People say New York's intense. I don't think they've really paid attention to nature. The crowded streets are a buffer in New York. They give you a different sense of scale. Up here I'm a speck on the lens of the vast, glaring natural world.

"I have triple A," my dad's saying. Hands me his keys. "And your phone's charged?" He's overworried. I wonder if my mother's back to filling his inbox with nervous speculation.

Nick comes out of the studio. Perfect. I roll my eyes. He takes note.

"Sorry to interrupt." He's lost some swagger. "But I know you're driving in to an appointment," he says. "You probably know where you're going, but I thought . . . if you wanted to take my GPS, just as an added, you know, something?"

He doesn't even look at me when he says this. This is the first time we've spoken since I tore his head off in the woods. I scared him off good.

I open my mouth to refuse, but my dad answers before I can.

"Great idea, Nick," he beams, reaching out for the device. "Then she'll know exactly where she is if the truck stalls or something. Good thinking."

Like Nick's a genius. I decide not to point out that almost everyone has maps on their phone. My dad doesn't even bother charging his.

Mr. Sunshine leans into the truck and plugs in his GPS.

"It's easy to use," he says, stretching in through the door to start the engine. "After it finds a satellite, you just put in where you're going, and it'll talk to you the whole way."

"Great." I lean against the side of the car. There goes my quiet ride.

"Only if you want." He pulls himself back out of the car and points to the little screen. "You can just read the directions if you'd rather."

He glances at me and leans in again to switch it to mute. Exuberant student.

"Thanks," I force myself to say. He's trying to help. I wonder what my dad told him about my "appointment." Nick turns back to the studio.

"Dad." I look at my worried father. "I'll be fine."

"I know, I know." He squeezes my arm like he hasn't just been standing here sweating it out.

"I've driven this thing before. I don't know what you're

so stressed about." I look at my sneakered feet.

"I know you don't want to go to this." He takes a deep breath and flings an arm around my shoulders. "I know your mom's making you. Just be careful and take good care of yourself when you're there, okay?"

He's worried about the actual appointment. Now his worry makes more sense. I find it comforting. An ally. Dad thinks the idea's bogus too. Doesn't really seem like his style to have another person tinkering around inside his head. I feel a surge of relief. Someone, at least, trusts me. Gets it. I don't need fixing, I just need time.

I give him a long hug and climb into the truck.

"The tank's full," he calls out as I pull away from the house.

Of course it is. And the tires are probably new and just filled. I open the window and wave until I curve away.

The drive's too short. It's just me and the rhythm of the heavy tires on the road. Nothing like my luxury, curve-hugging ride with Cal. The Wagoneer shudders over sixty mph, so I go slowly, and still the miles fly by, carry me closer to having to talk about it. Closer to letting someone help me "find my way through." A lock I don't want to pick. A map I can't follow. Not now. I think about skipping my appointment, chucking my phone out the window, slipping away. Drive to Canada, maybe, or at least until I run out of gas, but that would kill my parents with worry, and I don't want to give them any more grief. It shouldn't be so hard to live without messing up other people.

Dr. Lang's office is two rooms on the third floor of an

old building on campus. Near the university's department of architecture. Of course. Everywhere little reminders. I shake Cal from my head and take the stairs up. The office is near the end of a large hall. A door with his name on it pushes into a tiny airless waiting room, no receptionist, no window, no art, nothing. Like a holding cell. I swallow a huge urge to laugh, break out in an hysterical laughing fit. It's just me, two chairs, and one of those enormous droop-leafed office plants that somehow manages to grow under windowless fluorescence. I sit and bounce my knee. No magazines. Who doesn't put magazines in a waiting room?

I check my watch. I'm on time. Low voices sound as if they're approaching the dark wood door in front of me. And then it swings open. A young woman strides out, slips past me quickly, and leaves. Too fast for me to see her face. If she looked happy or not.

"Mamie Wells?" a voice booms from the inner room. "Please come in."

Dr. Lang is a fat man with a kind face, a bit older than my dad. He looks like a well-dressed academic. He sits behind an enormous antique-looking oak desk adjacent to a long leather couch. Bookshelves line the room, some books, a boxed Freud action figure, one of those weird mossy-looking air plants. And unlike his terrible little waiting cell, thank God, this room has windows. Huge old ones overlooking the quad.

"Good to meet you," he says, lifting his girth from his chair a moment to lean across the desk and shake my hand.

I don't know what I expected, but formality of the

handshake makes my eyes fill. This guy's serious. And unlike the sessions I had right after the accident, I'm going to really remember this one. I sit on the couch. Look out those windows. Skyward. Imagine Cal at Cornell, on a quad like this one. Walking to one of his classes. The treetops are bare.

"So." He pats a fat orange file on his desk. "Coming here wasn't your idea, was it?" He clears his throat. A deep sound.

"No."

"Are you here under duress?" He doesn't look at me when he asks this, he looks at some notes instead. That orange file is mine. He has a file on me already.

"No. I mean, I'm here. It wasn't my idea, but I came."

He writes in the file. Lifts a page, reads something. I wonder if my mom sent my records up to him. He reaches to his left and picks up another file, a blue one, pulls out more papers. Slips them into the orange sleeve.

Then he lets the file fall shut and looks at me. Sets his pen down. Folds his hands on top of his stomach.

Silence.

I stare him down. This seems like a trick. Like under his unwavering gaze, I'm just supposed to spill. No thanks. Whatever I say will be reshaped, lobbed back. I remember that much. Mom cycled me through more than a few of these kinds of appointments.

"How are you?" he asks, finally.

What a stupid question.

"I'm fine. And please call me Wren."

I clear my throat. It feels tight and unreliable.

"Okay, Wren. You had a calamity last year, I see." Gestures to the file.

Calamity.

"Your mother seems concerned about how you're dealing with that."

I nod.

"How do you feel you're dealing with that?"

What kind of questions are these? This is what we're paying for? A shrink from central casting to ask me the psychological equivalent of *what's up*? I look away from him.

"I'm fine," I say again. "I mean, I'm—how do you want me to answer a question like that?" Anger creeps into my voice. Tips my hand. He knew it would. I see his game. Dr. Lang, one; me, zero.

He leans back, executes another silent doctor move.

"I'm fine." I say it with more certainty. Maybe this is how it works. This is the trick. He'll get me to repeat *I'm fine* so many times that when I leave I'll be convinced, happy, well-adjusted. I'm fine, I'm fine, I'm fine.

"Your friend died."

A calamity. Tears start pouring down my cheeks, even though I'm not crying. My eyes are doing their own thing.

"And there was more, too, wasn't there?"

I nod.

He waits.

"We were in the middle of a fight. I wasn't hurt, really. It made me sad. It makes me sad. I just want to be quiet awhile. It made me sad."

I have a second of panic that I'm going to start repeating that and not be able to stop.

Deep breath.

Another.

I run the sleeve of my sweatshirt over my eyes.

"How are you sleeping?" he asks after a minute. Picks up his pen.

"Like a baby," I lie.

"Really?" he says, "Because I have it in my notes that you have a pretty regularly filled prescription of a benzodiazepine. Do you experience panic attacks?"

I shake my head. Doesn't sound like something I'd want in my file.

"When are you taking the pills, then?"

"I take them if I wake up in the night. Which happens sometimes. Or if I can't fall asleep. That's all."

My heart does a weird little beat. I pull my sleeves down over my hands.

"You sound defensive," he says, appraising me. "No need. I'm not accusing you of anything. You're taking them when you need to. That's exactly what you should do."

He makes a quick note on a notepad while he says this to me, without taking his eyes off my face. It's weird, a little amphibian or something.

"Have you noticed a recent change in your sleep patterns or your appetite? Your day-to-day general energy level?" Eyes on me.

"I feel the same way I've felt since I came up here."

"And how's that?"

I'm silent.

"How do you feel? Since you came up here?"

"I want to be alone. Quiet. I want it to stop being everyone else's business how I deal with things."

He nods. "I understand that."

Writes some more notes.

I exhale. I've been holding my breath. Can't seem to get it right. Breathing.

He leans back in his chair and then forward again. It makes a tired squeaking sound.

"I'm going to ask you a few questions to assess whether or not you might benefit from taking an antidepressant."

I shake my head. No way.

"No?" he says.

"They made me take one after the accident. I hated it. I felt dull and weird."

He checks my file again, more notes.

I start to bounce my knee. Look back out at the bald treetops. Fight an overwhelming urge to ditch this appointment now. Stand up, say thanks but no thanks, and walk right out his door. Free.

"Would this have been during the period of time in which you were electively mute?"

Electively mute. God. There's a name for everything. I look at him like I don't know what the hell he's talking about.

"The antidepressant," he says. "Were you taking it during the period of time in which you did not speak?"

I nod. Then shake my head.

"The time line's a little sketchy for me," I say, finally. "I stopped taking it as soon as people stopped watching me swallow everything."

I close my eyes. Remember how calm I felt then. Quiet.

"And when did you begin speaking again?"

"August, I think? So my mother would let me leave. I wanted to leave the city. Come up here. She wouldn't let me go if she thought I was totally off the deep end."

He raises both eyebrows. Here we go.

"And that's how you felt? Feel?" He looks right into my eyes like he's going to mesmerize me. "Totally off the deep end?"

I could laugh. Out loud. At him. Instead another tear slips out. I summon my inner hard-ass. Fail. More tears. Without taking his eyes off me, he slides a box of tissues across the desk. It makes him look like an alien or something when he multitasks like that. It's spooky. I take one of his tissues and ball it up. Wipe my cheeks with the back of my hand.

"I'm fine."

He sighs. I don't think they're supposed to do that. He makes another note in my file. I want to tear the thing off his desk and stuff it in my bag. It's mine. More knee bouncing.

"Your mother mentioned that you'd had another period of mutism more recently. I'm curious, what do you feel those do for you? The times when you stop speaking?"

I'd do it now in a heartbeat if I could find my way back into it. I don't tell him that. How it shows up. Waits for me. That it shrinks other people. Buys me some space to breathe. I tunnel backward into myself and feel better. Far away from everything.

Long silence. He waits like we have all day.

"I guess it makes me feel insulated or something. Like I don't have to answer to people if I don't feel like it."

"Wren, have you thought about suicide?"

My body jerks at the words. Like he's shocked me.

"Like I would tell you," I say, before I can stop myself.

Doesn't faze him. He keeps his eyes on me.

"Do you have a plan?"

I look away. I don't have to do this. Sit here. Answer these questions. I don't even have to come here again. In fact, I can probably leave right now. Tell my mother it went great. He can't report back to her, I'm eighteen. I have a right to privacy. Doctor-patient confidentiality.

"Wren, I asked you if you had a plan to end your own life?" His voice pulls me back from the angry storm in my head, eyes calm on me. He's prepared to wait it out.

I'm silent. Can't open my mouth. I don't. Haven't. Of course I don't. No more so than the next guy. But I can't say it hasn't occurred to me.

Then it occurs to me that maybe the next guy never thinks about things like this. That I am way more messed up than I think I am. I sink a bit into his couch.

"I have an ethical obligation," he says gently, "if I feel you're at risk, to intervene. I know we've just met, and you're not here entirely of your own volition, but if you'll bear with me while I establish a few things, then we can get down to finding a way to help you feel better."

Feel better. Not likely. It seems so totall
point. Only I don't know what the point is, either.

"No," I say, finally, "I don't have a plan." I cross a
uncross my legs. "I mean, who hasn't thought about it once or twice?"

I suddenly want to convince him that I'm fine. Don't want this conversation on my record.

"I'm not scheming about how I'm going to end it all," I say. "Besides, it would kill my father, my parents. I couldn't do that to them."

He nods at the mention of my father. "You're close to him? Your father?" he asks.

"I guess." I shrug. "Now." Now I'm in his orbit. Only I'm not sure what that means anymore, really, to be close to someone. It occurs to me that I'm really not close to anyone, not right now. Makes me feel a little strange.

"Okay . . ." He drags out the word while he makes more notes. Doesn't look at me this time, at least, while he's writing.

"I mean, my mom and I are close, too, I guess, but Dad's different. He's more laid-back. Doesn't pressure me to do stuff."

More notes. He nods while he writes. Whether he's recording something I've said or making notes for himself is unclear. I shift on the couch.

"Did I pass the test?"

I'm going for snide but fail. I sound sincere. And there are no take-backs.

He looks over his glasses and gives me what I'm sure he

thinks of as his reassuring smile. Like we're in cahoots and have just had a moment. Dr. Lang sets the pen down and leans back in his chair. Crosses his hands over the top of his stomach again.

"So, why don't you tell me what's been going on? Why your mother suddenly feels you need to see a psychiatrist."

"It's not sudden. And it's because she's that way."

I feel a wave of hate toward her for making me do this. Sit here. With this guy.

Silence from Dr. Lang.

"I made a mistake. An unbelievably stupid misstep, and then we crashed, and she can't just let me off the hook awhile—to deal. She's probably mad at me. She's the one who needs to be in here talking about everything."

My hands are fists in my sleeves.

He nods at me slowly, like he's processing something.

"By 'misstep,' you're referring to your pregnancy?"

He must have read the whole damn file before I got here.

I nod.

Silence.

"I was so close to being done, high school, childhood—"

Tears.

"I'm never irresponsible. It was so stupid. I have no excuse for it, either. I did this one totally dumb thing, and it wrecked everything." I want to dissolve into this couch, shrink up and blow away. I wipe my face with my sleeve.

His pen rises like a judge's gavel, hangs there a minute.

"Is it possible," he says, setting the tip to the page, "that on some level"—he drags the words out while he writes something—"On some level you allowed yourself to get pregnant in order to conflict with your mother's plans for you? She tells me you two had some struggle over your choice of schools?"

It takes the wind right out of me. He thinks I did it on purpose? It's all my fault, everything that happened. And he can see it as plainly as I can.

"It's just something to think about, for you to chew on until we see each other again."

There's no air in here, in me, because the doctor is breathing it all up. Great sucking breaths that tear away all my defenses, all the ways I'm hiding. I close my eyes. Open them again, fast. I don't want to give him anything else for his notes.

He sets the pen down and looks up at me, smiles. How can he smile at me, knowing who I am?

"This is a good start for us, Wren. We have options. Sometimes grief leads to depression. In some people. We'll keep talking, once a week at first, then every other week until we feel like we have a handle on things. I'd like to explore with you some of your thoughts about the accident you were in and how you feel about your role in it."

I shiver. Pull on my coat. We're near the end. He said so himself.

"You're a strong girl," he says, glancing at my coat. "I can see that. We'll work together until you feel you have a better perspective on what happened. Okay?"

He eyes my face for a response. I couldn't move it out of its stony shock if I wanted to.

"Before you go, let's see if we can't get you up out of the bottom, reconsider your options. Something mild, better suited to you than what you took before?"

I nod, dumb. Start to get up. He raises his hand to stop me. I sit down again.

"Your reaction to what's happened isn't uncommon."

I nod, sure, whatever, because I'll never get out of here if I don't.

Encouraged, he goes on, "I'm talking about another antidepressant. You're working very hard right now; it doesn't have to be so hard."

I nod again. I want to get out of here so badly it tastes like metal in the back of my throat.

He flips open the orange file. Consults a fat handbook. More questions. About my weight. Energy. Sleep. Appetite. He draws a little diagram on a blank sheet of paper. About the brain. How different drugs affect it. There are lots of arrows up and down.

Finally I leave his office, shaky, clutching a handful of new prescriptions and an appointment reminder card.

I cross the quad to the parking ramp. Look at the papers in my hand. Sleeping pill refill. Pocket it. Two kinds of antidepressants. Appointment reminder card. Chuck them in the first trash can I pass.

The steering wheel vibrates under my hands when I hit seventy. I need some fast miles between me and that appointment.

Do you have a plan?

Do I have a plan. I keep my hands firmly at ten and two

like they taught us in driver's ed. Try not to look into the headlights of every oncoming car. I could never take another person out with me. But his words are like an itch.

I have to get a grip. I'm losing it. I pull onto the shoulder. Open the window. Let the icy air hit me.

I can't shut it off. The feeling that everything's ruined. My life. Patrick's. His family's. Cal, Mary's fellowship—I ruin things. I'm done for. I can't go back to who I was before. Back to being clueless. Like there isn't an ax over all our heads all the time.

I can't see any way out—I'm stuck between my old life and what? No matter what you do, what you want, how much you want it, it ends badly. For all of us.

I pull back onto the road. It's dusk already and Dad will start watching for the truck soon.

it was dark

When I get back, the studio's lit up bright, and it's quiet in the house. I'm glad. I take a long shower, then sit with my legs under me in the dark by the window and watch the moon on the careless water.

The appointment clings to me. Makes me feel icky, ashamed. Sitting across from Dr. Lang. The way he kept looking at me—like I'm the kind of person who has to be looked at like that. By a shrink. All those questions. I want to pack up and disappear. But there's nowhere else to go.

My phone rings. Breaks the quiet. So loud I jump. Dig it out of the bottom of my bag. It's Mary. Hail Mary, Holy Mary.

"Wren!" she says. Her sunny voice.

"Hey." I try to make my voice sound normal. I pull off one notch above totally flat.

A pause. She misses nothing.

"Everything all right?" she asks.

"Of course. I miss you! What's going on?" I deflect her question, a little more energetic this time.

"Oh, nothing and everything. You know. I'm back. Settling in again. It's good to be here. But I miss you guys, of course—all of you. Your dad, the studio crew, Cal."

I'm silent at the mention of Cal. Nothing to say.

"I haven't heard from you, what's new?"

I swear she brightens in inverse relation to how dark I feel. We either balance each other or cancel each other out.

"Not much."

I try to laugh. It's the gospel truth. I stretch my legs. Yawn. It's just me and my reflection, hanging out. Good times.

"My mom came up for a couple of days. So there was that. It went okay, I guess." I try again. "Mostly we just miss you. Dad keeps calling the new dude Mary. Drives him nuts."

I'm sort of making this up, but I have to say something.

"That's funny," she says in a kind of weird voice.

Silence.

She's calling for a reason. I should have known.

"So . . ." she drags the word out a bit.

"Yeah?"

I wish she'd just drop it on me already. Cal asked her to call. Wants her to tell me he's moving on.

"I was on the phone with Michael the other day, and

he said he thought maybe you're seeing a fair bit of Nick Bishop?"

Of course. I lie back on the floor. Wish I could laugh. Ask which bits he thinks I've seen.

"So, he's fitting in well?"

Mary's voice goes up at the end of every one of her sentences like she can hardly believe what she's saying.

I say nothing.

"Are you there? Wren?"

I'm so frustrated I could scream. Despite my efforts to shut them all off, apparently I still have feelings.

"I'm not seeing Nick," I say, tightly.

"I didn't think so!" She lets out a long breath. Sounds so relieved.

Even though I know the answer I say, "Is that what Cal told Michael?"

She lets out a nervous little laugh.

"Come on," I say. "Did you really think I was seeing Nick? I don't have that much energy. The sun doesn't have that much energy."

She laughs again.

"Is that what Cal said to Michael?" I have to know.

"I don't know. Michael just told me he talked to Cal, and he sounded bummed."

I fling my arm over my eyes. I'm so tired.

"Michael pushed him on it, and Cal said something about you and Nick hanging out? You guys running together?"

I want to hang up. Sleep. I can't keep my eyes open.

"I told him I was sure it was nothing," she goes on. She wants to make it all okay. "But Michael's worried about Cal. Not that it's your job to—"

I cut her off. "This is exactly why I didn't want to get involved with anyone."

I thud the back of my head against the floor. Thud, thud, thud. Feels good. Calming, somehow.

"What did happen? Between you and Nick?" she asks.

"Nothing!" I'm exasperated. "The guy's an ass. I'm sorry; I mean, I know you think he's nice and know him or his friends, but he's annoying, to me."

"So you're not into him."

"No! The heat was out in the studio, and he showed up at our house to wait while my dad ran out for a part. I was going for a run and he followed me. Uninvited."

Thud, thud, thud.

"I knew it was something stupid like that," she says happily, sounding relieved. Everything's right in her world.

"Some woman from town saw us and mentioned it in front of Cal. He freaked out. I haven't heard from him since. End of story."

"I told Michael he had it wrong—things were so good with you and Cal. You were coming back to life around him." She sucks in her breath. "I didn't mean it that way, just that you seemed happier when you were with him."

She's right. I was. And I wrecked it.

"Well, it doesn't matter because it's over now. Cal practically pushed me out of the car when he brought me home that night. Couldn't get out of here fast enough."

"He was probably just confused. I'm sure it's not that bad," she says.

"No, I blew it." I press the bottom of my foot against the huge window. It's icy cold. Hurts, almost. I like it. "I don't know why I didn't just tell him. I wasn't thinking. I thought it would make him feel bad."

"Just call him," she says. "Straighten it out." Like it's so easy.

"No." Thud, thud. "I can't. He's probably relieved to be done with me anyway. I can't deal with it. Hear him say it."

"God, you're so dense. Don't you see how he looks at you?" She gives a little sigh.

The spot on the back of my head is starting to hurt. I roll onto my side. Press my cheek against the cool floor.

"So . . . you and Michael?" I'm a master of distraction.

"He stayed two days when we drove back. I'm going down to see him at Johns Hopkins next weekend!"

Her voice is like a song. At least someone's happy. I press the balls of my feet against the window again. It feels good to push against something solid.

"Your younger man," I tease.

"Oh, he's plenty mature enough for me," she says.

No doubt. He's mature enough to think he knows what's best for his older brother, that's for sure. Hell of a watchdog, that Michael. I sigh. He had me pegged.

"He thinks I'm bad for Cal," I say.

"No . . ." but she's uncomfortable. We both know I'm right. "He's just worried about him. I guess it was bad last year when Susanna left. He thinks Cal's not used to . . . everything yet."

"Two ruined people."

"You're not ruined," she says, bright again. "You just think you are."

"I wish you were still up here. I'd let you do my hair."

She laughs. "I wish I were too. School's good, and it's great to be back, but you live in an amazing otherworld up there. Sometimes I feel like I dreamed it."

"It's dreaming me."

I'm not sure what I mean by that. But it feels right. Like something is shifting. Waiting for me. Pulling me back.

"Call him, Wren," she says.

I sink into the feeling. Mary's voice sounds like it's coming over the wires from far away, an old-fashioned long-distance telephone call. Scratchy. Faint. Static on the line.

"Call him," she says again. "Okay?"

She's little, tinny, breaking up. Or it's me.

"You want to, right?" She won't let me go without a promise.

I don't want anything.

I can't say that, but it's true. I really don't. Don't want to feel anything. Hurt. Or hurt anyone else. I don't want to see Cal's face looking at me, disappointed.

"Wren?"

"I'm here." I try to pull my eyes back into focus. "I'll call. In the morning. Okay?"

I'm a ghost. It's a ghost's promise.

whose woods

WE HANG UP. Mary's happy, thinks she's restored order in the magical world she imagines I live in. Pushed me toward the break in the trees.

My phone rings again. Dad.

He saw the truck. Glad I'm back. Am I okay? Yes. He's done in the studio but wants to go home with Zara. Is that okay by me? Quiet pause. Sure. Whatever. I don't really care. I don't say that part. Yes, I tell him. Go. Do I need anything before he heads out? No. Do I want to talk about it? No. A package came today, it's on the table.

I roll my head up from the floor, peer over there. A big white envelope. What has my mother done now? Probably enrolled me somewhere for second semester.

I want to hang up. I'm so tired.

Instead I say I'm fine Dad, it went well. Everything's great. Go, go. I promise I'll go to bed early. Soon. Now, even. I'll get a good night's sleep. See you in the morning.

Everyone knows what I should do.

Wish I did.

I grab the envelope off the table. It's been forwarded here from my dad's gallery in the city. No return address. Not my mother. I slip a finger under the flap. Pull out a stack of papers. Only it's not papers. It's photos. Big ones. A grainy black-and-white of Patrick and me on the beach at Meredith's. Near the bonfire. His face open in a wide smile. Patrick with Emma on his shoulders on the Staten Island Ferry. I took that one. Emma and me on the stoop of my house. I drop them on the table. Sink into a chair.

A little note in Emma's puffy handwriting sticks to the top of the last one.

I wish we'd never met.

She doesn't sign it.

This is what she's been trying to e-mail me.

I push away from the table. From the photos. Put my head in my hands.

I stand. Go to bed. My limbs are strangely weighted; I feel like I could black out, almost. But the minute I close my eyes, it starts. A buzzing inside me. Emma's right to hate me. I have been a stupid, thoughtless person. I can't stop seeing her note. Repeating it. The photographs. Then Patrick's face, empty, next to me in the car.

I sit up. Flip the light back on. Try to read. It's a waste

of electricity. The words on the page aren't nearly forceful enough to be heard over what's screaming inside my head. I click the light off and look at the stars. Wish I were closer to them. I get up and shove my bed up against the window. For a better view.

Finally, I take a pill. Then I wait. Fidget. Hot. Cold. Hot. Cold. For the first time ever, it doesn't work. I get out of bed. It's hard. Or too soft. I'm all over the place. My stomach growls, I can't remember the last time I ate. I go get an apple. A piece of bread and jam. Very Little Red Riding Hood. I'm a character in a grim forest. All I'm missing is the red cloak and a basket with a checkered cloth. And the wolf.

I pace the house.

Something is rising in me. Like excitement, kind of, only scary. I'm scared. Whatever this is might take me over. I'll never find my way back again. It's loud in my head. A chorus of disappointment. Emma. Patrick. My mother. Dad. Meredith. Mary. Michael. Cal.

Cal.

His eyes the other night. The line of his mouth when he dropped me off. I can't get it right with anyone.

I try to sleep again. After an endless hour, I can't stand it anymore. Being awake. I roll out of bed, go into the bathroom. Shake another pill into my hand. Then a few more. Then the whole bottle. I look at my reflection in the mirror. I look wavy, wild. What am I doing?

I pick one out, swallow it dry, and push the rest back into the bottle. Return to my room. Lie down. I can't stay still. Sit up again. I wish my dad were home—someone else in the house. I have so much energy. Like I could light the room if I could find a way to let it out. I look at the clock. It's past midnight, what my mom calls the witching hour.

My running clothes are in a pile in the corner. I pull them on before I can change my mind. My heart's going a million miles a minute. It hurts. I have to get out of the house. It's like I could lift right out of my body. The pill isn't even touching me. I can hardly tie my shoes.

I sprint out the door, barely taking time to pull it shut. There's a light on in the studio. Nick. Working late. Or maybe Dad asked him to stay, check up on me. The idea makes me want to scream. I don't. I don't want to make him come out. Have to explain myself.

The woods are dark and deep. It's a line from something. Famous. A poem. We had to memorize it in school—something, something dark and deep? Obviously too long ago for my memory. I can feel the rhythm of it but not the words. Which is how I've been living lately. Impressions. Gestures without meaning.

The woods are dark and deep, and I run through them until I can't feel anything anymore. Boughs dump wet snow on me when I crash through. The scarlet branches of bare dogwoods whip my arms and face. I lose sight of the trails. I'm a fucking pioneer. I'm going to kick nature's ass. I tear through deeper and deeper parts of the woods. Like if I'm fast enough, the forest might open up and let me in for real. I run until I'm burning. My lungs screaming in my chest, my muscles on fire. My heart's a machine.

Finally, finally, I come back down into myself again.

Calmer. I laugh. It worked. Screw Mom's shrink and his measured words. I can still get out. I can outrun the terrible tide of feeling that comes over me and pulls me under. It's all I needed to know. To calm down. I can still get out and away.

Something big flies overhead. My eyes start to focus, take in where I am. Branches snap as something else cruises through. I'm lost. It's really dark and everything looks the same. I try to be quiet, listen for the ocean. Then I could find the highway, follow it home, but the only sound is my blood roaring in my ears and my ragged, thundering heart.

I close my eyes. Wait for my breath to slow. Now I'm tired. Cold. Maybe it's the sleeping pills. I keep my eyes closed and try to walk, will myself homeward like some kind of animal. I fall. Tear my pants on something hard on the ground. Open my eyes again. A rock. My leg's so cold I hardly feel it.

I think I hear a truck. Ahead of me. Maybe the highway. Across it, water. Home. It's very quiet. The trees whispering hush.

I go toward where I thought I heard the truck. Close my eyes from time to time to listen. Hear another. I'm right. I come out of the woods at the edge of the highway a mile or two south of our driveway. Freezing. Shaking pretty badly. I'll have to run again if I'm going to make it back. My body protests. My muscles are wasted. I do it anyway.

Take that, Dr. Lang. Here I am, saving myself. So I guess I do have a plan, after all. Stick around, hope things get better. But this is the coldest I've ever been. I'm starting to trip over my feet. My legs are wooden, one hand burning, the other numb. Is this what it's like for Cal? I can't imagine it. I'm staggering, but still running, getting closer. I focus on that. Getting closer. Run to the rhythm of it. Get-ting clo-ser. Everything's familiar now. The moon is high and bright, and I pretend it's midafternoon. I'm running with the heat of the sun on my shoulders. The sun is always a surprise when I come out of the woods no matter how many times I do it. Bright, clear warmth after the muffled dark.

The road brightens ahead of me even more. It takes me a minute to realize it's headlights. A car pulling up behind me. Then a voice. Cal's.

"Wren?"

Disbelief. Both of ours.

I turn and look at the car. He's standing on the passenger side. Maybe I'm hallucinating. Who's driving? I try to ask, but I can't talk. I'm shaking too badly.

He leans back into the car, grabs a crutch, and rushes to me.

I can't form words. My tongue's frozen in my mouth.

"Wren?" He pulls off his jacket. Wraps it around me. "What are you doing out here? Do you know what time it is?"

Time. Somewhere deep inside me, this is funny.

"You're freezing. Have you lost your mind?"

Even funnier.

"Say something." He shakes me by the shoulders. Rubs my arms. I feel that. I'm pretty sure, now, that he's real.

Then the driver door opens and a dark-haired woman steps out. Très chic.

"Cal?" she says. "What's going on?"

Cal pulls me toward the car. "It's Wren, Susanna," he says.

Susanna.

"She's freezing. We have to get her warm."

Now everything's clear. Mary and Michael know nothing. Cal's not pining away for me at all. He's moved on. I wrench my arms away. Knock him off balance. He catches himself against the car. Reaches for me again.

A burst of adrenaline shoots through me, electric. I drop his coat, look at him for a second, and take off into the woods on our side of the highway.

It's a relief. I'm the one to walk away. No more loss for me. Not this time. I'll get myself home. Without his help. I'm almost there anyway. This is what people do. They look out for themselves. Don't cling to ridiculous ideas about love and being saved by it. I'm such a fool. How many times do I have to reach for the happy ending before I realize it's not there?

And then I'm not cold anymore. The opposite. I'm lit from within. More right and true than I've ever felt before. On fire. I pull off my jacket and drop it on a scrubby bush.

It's like an amazing dream. The moon's a spotlight over the water. Beckons. I have to see it. Get to the ocean. Listen to waves hit the rocks. Be close to something real.

I turn away from the direction of our driveway and head toward the shore. I can hear Cal calling my name, her, too, and then their voices get smaller, farther away. I keep running.

The tiered rocks are an amphitheatre in the tangible world. They're all I need. I climb down a little, slip once. An old, wrecked fishing dory is pulled up on a flat spot. Looks like it's been there forever. A place for me to rest a little. I'm so tired.

Then more voices.

My dad's. A woman's. My dad's again. Crashing through branches behind me.

I get out of the boat. Not sure where I'm going. Away. I slip on the icy rock. My foot's in water. Someone grabs me, hard. I have a second of the most complete clarity. Like I'm waking up from something. Then I pass out.

beacon

I OPEN MY EYES.

Nick.

Close them again.

Open them another time.

My father, his face a strange mask.

Cal.

Zara.

Nick again.

Some guy I don't know. Another one. Their mouths all moving. Soundless.

Cal's face. Terrified about something.

Close them again.

For a long time.

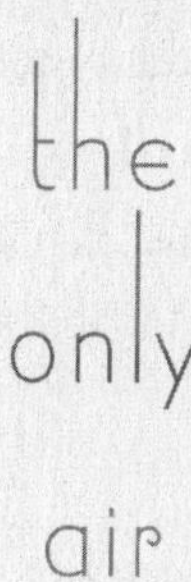

THEN: "Well, if this is what seeing a psychiatrist does for her, I'm sure as hell not asking her to go again."

My dad.

And: "I am not close-minded, and no, I don't know what they talked about. She didn't say."

I can't hear the other person. He's on the phone.

"Well, Lila," he says, "I don't push her like that. She'll tell me what she wants to, when she's ready."

Long pause.

"I did not abandon her. We divorced. Don't blame me for this," his voice rises, then changes to an angry whisper. "It was a mistake, I admit, staying out last night, but this thing didn't start up here. On my watch."

Sun on my face. I don't want to open my eyes. Then a warm hand on my arm. Squeezing. A blood-pressure cuff. Shit. Now I know where I am. I'm never going to get out of this one. Not again. Not like before.

I try to sink back into sleep, whatever's out there can wait, but it won't have me. I'm awake. Have to open my eyes at some point. I wonder if you can have elective blindness. Doubtful.

It's bright.

My dad's next to the bed, his back to me, looking out a little window. Teal blinds topped with a fat floral swag. Sun levering through. A small-town hospital room.

The nurse catches my eye and winks. She looks at me like she knows I need time to come to. Keeps her mouth shut but stays close, near the head of the bed. I'm under what feels like a hundred blankets. And still cold. An ache. Deep. But it's morning. And I'm here in it.

I pull one hand out and cover my eyes.

"John." The nurse's voice is kind. "She's awake."

My dad whirls to face me, says, "She's up. I'll call you later." He squints at his phone a second, ends the call, and shoves it in his pocket.

"Sweetheart, you were pretty cold."

He starts to cry. That's the worst. Seeing your dad cry.

I notice an IV taped to the back of my hand. Panic a little. Look at the nurse. I want to yank it out. What are they giving me? My other hand hovers near it, nervously. She steps forward, places a calm palm on my forehead. Looks into my eyes.

"Don't worry about that, honey. It's just warm saline. You needed a little extra help last night. We'll take it out soon."

She pats my arm and looks at me with such kindness, I start to cry.

"I'll let you two talk."

Dad sits heavily on the chair near my bed.

"Wren, what happened?"

Grabs us both tissues from a box above my head, blows his nose into one, sounding like an enormous trumpet. Used to startle me when I was small.

"What were you doing out there like that?"

I stop crying. I'll never be able to explain myself. He's looking at me like I'm not who he thought I was. It's the worst.

"Cal said he found you running on the highway. It was the middle of the night."

Last night seems like a lifetime ago. Blurry. I felt really bad. I remember that much. Wanted to crawl out of my own skin.

He sags, "You're quiet again."

"No," I find my voice. "Dad, I'm not. I'm sorry. I'll talk. I don't know what to say, though." I take a breath. "I couldn't sleep. Couldn't stop thinking about stuff. The package from Patrick's sister. There were photos . . ." I start to cry again. "I thought a run would make me feel better."

"I should have been there." He pats my hand, a little shaky, squeezes it. Looks so sad.

"And it did. Make me feel better." My nose is running.

"It made me feel great, clear about everything, like I'm going to be okay, but then I'd gone so far from the house. I don't know, I was kind of lost. I found the highway and was heading home when Cal and his girlfriend came along."

My stomach twists. Susanna. The way she looked at me like I was a wild thing from the woods. A child. A messed-up, sloppy kid.

"I'm sorry, Wren," he says, wiping the new tears from my face with his thumb. "This is my fault. I didn't know you were feeling so bad. I wasn't thinking, spending the night at Zara's. I should have known you might come back in rough shape from your visit with that shrink."

I pull apart the pulpy tissue in my hand.

"Cal called us when you ran away from him on the road. He called Nick at the studio and went chasing into the woods after you."

He shakes his head like he's living it again.

"Nick stayed at the house, in case you came back. Zara and I met up with Cal and searched for you. It was his idea to check by the water. He said you liked to look at it when you were feeling bad."

Cal knew that about me. It gives me a little shiver thinking about it. About being important to someone. Him.

"We went down the rocks from the house and headed south until we saw you. You looked ready to take off again." His eyes fill and his face is pink. "I got my hands on you and pulled you up. Zara and I carried you back to the house." He looks at me. "Nick had an ambulance waiting. And it was a good thing he did—you were pretty cold, kiddo."

He exhales, ragged.

"I'm so sorry, Dad." It's all I can say. I am. I am the sorriest person there could be. I don't know why I can't get it together and be normal. Stop hurting everyone else. "I didn't mean to cause so much trouble."

"It's okay." He kisses my forehead. "I know. We'll figure it out."

He reaches for the tissues and blows his nose again. Loud. I raise an eyebrow at him. He laughs, pulls me to him for a rib-crushing hug.

"Now, it's only fair," he says, letting me breathe again, "if it's okay with you—Cal's been waiting out there all night." He cocks his head toward the door. "Can I let him in?"

He's here. My stomach rises and falls like a diving bird.

I nod.

Better get it over with. Cut him loose. He's had enough. Doesn't need to go down on my sinking ship.

My dad leaves and lets Cal in. Tall and beautiful. Purple shadows around his eyes. Like he's been up all night. I sit up a little more and scoot over on the bed. He sits next to me. Pulls me into his arms.

Heaven.

Makes it harder. I have to get this over with. Open my mouth and tell him I'm sorry I'm a disaster. My throat closes. Keep it short and sweet. I swallow. Hard.

He presses his face against my neck and takes a huge breath, like he's going to breathe me in.

"I thought you were going to die," he says, finally. "There are animals in the woods, Wren. Wildcats. Wolves.

It's winter. What were you thinking? This isn't the city, you know, there's *nature*."

His arm is so tight around my shoulders it hurts—his heart pounding against me.

"I'm sorry."

"Your lips were blue. Your whole face. When your dad and Zara brought you out of the woods—by the time we got back to the house—"

I have to know where we stand. Now. So I can let go.

"Where's Susanna?"

He looks at me like it's a bizarre question. Left field. Shakes his head. "At the house, maybe, I think, I don't know, I haven't talked to her."

At the house. His house. She's staying with him.

"She's here—back from Spain?"

He relaxes a little against my pillow. Looks at me. We're side by side. He's holding me like he's going to warm my whole body with his.

"You and Nick . . ." he says, slowly, like he's weighing the words.

Here we go.

He runs a hand through his hair. "I want you to be happy; I don't want to hold you back." Looks at the ceiling.

Susanna's here. He's going to move back into his life. I close my eyes.

"There's no me and Nick," I say. "I tried to tell you that, but if you want a way out—"

"A way out."

Bitter laugh.

"How can you not get it?" He makes me look at him. "You're the one of the most intense, real people I've ever met. I feel good when I'm with you."

I start to cry. Relief or something. I can almost let myself hear what he just said to me. Feel it. Almost.

"Nick was nothing, he followed me that morning," I say. "I didn't ask him to."

"Your face—you looked so guilty when Miriam was talking to you," he says.

"I'm not interested in Nick. He's annoying. Too cheerful."

Cal laughs.

"I sent him every signal I could that I didn't want him along, but he didn't get the message. I had to stop and yell at him before he let me run in peace."

I twist the edge of the blanket in my hand. Remember Nick's face last night, didn't look cheerful then. He looked scared. I freaked out a lot of people. I close my eyes.

"I should have told you."

"You can't protect me," he says. "You have to let me deal with my crap my way. Yeah, it makes me jealous thinking about you and some other guy running. But if you hide stuff—" He shakes his head. "Trust me, my imagination's worse than the truth."

"I'm a failure of a person."

"Shut up." He laughs, knocking his shoulder against me gently. "Everyone is."

"Don't laugh."

"Why not?"

"Because I'm a mess. Because you don't need more trouble. Michael warned me not to screw it up. And I did anyway."

His body tenses. "Michael did what?" he asks, his voice sharp.

"Forget it," I say. I don't want to make him mad at his brother.

"No, tell me."

I shake my head.

"Wren. Tell me." He looks down at me, eyes dark.

"At breakfast. After Swap Night. He took me aside. Told me not to mess you up."

"He had no right to say that. To say anything to you."

"He's right, though."

"What are you talking about? I don't know who the hell he thinks he is."

"I hurt everyone around me. I'll hurt you."

"Maybe you will. We'll probably hurt each other. That's how it goes. For everyone. But people need to stop treating me like I'm going to break."

I look at the ceiling. So this is it. Life. Love. We spend all this time reaching for each other and mostly we end up hurting each other until it's over.

"Stop that," he says, reading my mind. "Get that look off your face." He kisses me.

"Susanna?"

"What about her? She wrote few weeks ago. Asked to see me when she was back in the States." He looks at me. Kisses the tip of my nose. "We were together almost two years."

"What does that mean?" I knot and unknot my fingers on top of the blankets. They feel like sandpaper, all pale and splotchy from the cold air.

"It means it's over." He turns my face to his. "But we ended on such a bad note. Before. I thought we should say good-bye."

"Is that what she wants?"

"I don't know what she wants, exactly. I'll talk to her about it after I get some sleep."

He rubs his face. We lie there a minute. He's so warm.

"I wish you'd called me."

"Back at you, Rabbit," he says. "Two stubborn people."

"Maybe you should try to fix it with Susanna. She looks very normal."

Cal laughs. "Old life," he says. "New normal. And I didn't call because I didn't want to pressure you. I thought maybe if you were happy with someone else—you have enough going on without another complication."

"You're not a complication." I lean into him. "You're the only air I can stand to breathe."

Cal reaches up and pulls the little blue curtain hanging between us and the door, then he scoots down farther on the bed, pulling me to him, close, tight, solid.

no agenda

CAL WANTS TO STAY until they release me, but Dad insists on driving him home. They both look dead on their feet.

Once they leave, Dr. Williams comes in. Introduces himself. Pulls up a chair and crosses one long leg over the other. Wide-wale cords, worn chukkas, total New Englander.

"Wren, were you trying to hurt yourself last night?"

Straight shooter, too.

I shake my head. No. I don't know.

"I was freaking out. I thought if I got out for a run, my head would clear. And then I got cold and things kind of fell apart."

"Do you panic a lot?" He looks at me the same kind way the nurse did. Disarming. I could weep.

"No? I don't know," I say, my voice a little unreliable, "I guess. Maybe. Sometimes I freak out. I have to do something to make it stop. Running usually helps."

He nods, asks me if I take anything, nods again. I tell him about the other prescriptions from Dr. Lang. The ones I threw away. It's easy to talk to Dr. Williams. Doesn't seem like he's thinking anything more than he's telling me. Like he has no agenda.

He pats me on the arm. "My dear, people go through things. Feel anxious, afraid. Some more than others. Antidepressants help sometimes. I'll give you one if you change your mind."

Just like that. No big deal. No ponderous scrutiny. He reaches my chart from a hook on the wall and makes a little note in it. The shortest entry in my East Coast paper trail.

"I want to check in again in a week. Your fingers and toes were pretty white when you first got here, but they pinked up nicely. Keep them warm, rub them, stimulate the circulation. You might notice a slight burning feeling, sensitivity to hot and cold water, but that should pass."

He stands, smiles at me. "You were one lucky kid last night," he says. Lays his hand on my forearm again. Gentle pat. Cue waterworks. He looks at me kind of ruefully. "You'd started removing your clothing. People can do that with hypothermia. Think they're hot. It's a fatal mistake. I'm glad we got you in here when we did."

I can't talk. I nod. Wipe my eyes on the blanket again. He leans and reaches a fresh tissue for me. Walks to the door of the room.

"Where's your dad?"

"He took Cal home. He'll be back."

"I'll try to catch him when he gets here, but if I don't see him, you can tell him we'll let you leave if you promise to go home, eat an enormous bowl of hot soup, take a long bath, then get into bed. Rest will do you wonders. Wren, you're going to be fine."

"Okay." I'm not sure if he means from nearly freezing to death or fine in general. Either way I hope he's right.

"And no more midnight runs, all right?" Laughs a little, crinkly around the eyes. Like it wasn't so awful, what I did, like it might even be a little easy to laugh at.

"No more night runs," I promise.

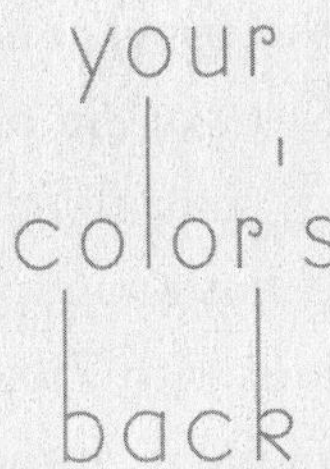

DAD AND ZARA come back with fresh clothes and take me home. They squeeze me between them in the front of the truck, wrapped in a quilt Zara brought, like I'm going to freeze on the way back or something. I feel really stupid, but I guess I owe it to them.

When we open the door, the house is flooded with sun flashing off the water. I stop a second, look around. I was so close to not seeing this again.

Emma's package is gone. Someone's cleaned. My bed's back in its normal spot. Clothes off my floor, washed and folded. And Zara's put quilts everywhere. Like the heat's gone out and we might all have to huddle together to survive. I take the longest, hottest bath on record and change into fresh sweats, a tank top, and a sweater. Then my robe. Truth is, I'm still cold. And tired.

The two of them sit on the couch like they're not watching my every move. Zara reads. Dad puts on some music, pretends he's reading the paper, but really just stares out the windows. Finally Zara goes into the kitchen and starts knocking around. Brings me a mug of chamomile tea. It's weird. Dad and I don't hang around the house together, and certainly never before with Zara, but it's clear they're not going into the studio today. It's intense, all this togetherness. Finally, I tell them I'm going to lie down. Assure them I'm fine. Don't need anything.

I have the nicest dream that I'm sleeping in Cal's arms. It wakes me up with a smile. I can't remember the last time I woke up that way. He smelled so great, felt real. And then it is real. I open my eyes, and he's there, pressed against me, asleep, holding me tight. In the dusk-lit room I feel something that might be the most piercing happiness I've ever felt. I relax into his arms and shut my eyes again.

The next time I wake up, it's early evening. Cal's awake, still pressed against me in the narrow bed, propped on his elbow, watching me. Smiles when I open my eyes. Plants a soft kiss on my forehead.

"You're still here." I flush with pleasure. The aching chill's gone.

"Couldn't keep me away," he says.

"My dad?"

He moves his head in the direction of the living room. "Out there. Having dinner, I think."

"When did you get here?"

"I didn't want to bother them by calling, but I couldn't stand waiting, so around three I got in the car and came over. Figured he'd tell me to leave if he didn't want me around. They were asleep on the couch together. I woke them up. I had to see you. At home. Pink."

"I'm not pink," I say, laughing a little.

"Well you're sure as hell not the white-gray you were last night," he says, with a pained look.

"Your color's back, too."

I'm a smart-ass. I can't stand the look on his face, so I try to make light of things, pat his cheek.

Makes him mad. He catches my wrist.

"Wren, you don't get it. It's not funny. When you took off like that"—he shakes his head—"I didn't know what to do. What you were going to do. And then I found your jacket on the bush—"

He looks so grim, I wish I could disappear.

"I had you there. With me, and then you were gone. I wasn't sure where—how we were going to find you—"

He drops back on the pillow and looks up at the ceiling. Takes a deep breath. Lets it out again.

"Don't ever do that again," he says.

"I won't." I make a tent of the blankets and climb on top of him.

"I'm." I kiss him on the top lip. "Sorry. I'm." Kiss him on the bottom lip. "Sorry. I'm." I kiss him on both lips. "A freak. And I didn't mean to scare everyone."

He pulls me down tight to him, and we lie like that

awhile, our hearts pounding against each other.

We're hungry when we finally come out of my room. Dad and Zara are ready to call it a night. Dinner's on the table, a chowder Zara made, and a dome of Dad's sourdough. Rock-hard crust, soft inside, bread like it's the only food you need. The house smells terrific. Like people live in it and are happy.

We kiss them both good night. Dad holds on to me a minute, then passes me over to Zara, who brushes a little hair from my eyes, then hugs me herself. No one says anything, thank God, about how this almost wasn't.

Cal fills the bowls and I bring them to the table.

"So, did Susanna go back?" I ask once we're seated, eating. I mean to sound casual. But don't pull it off. Can't look at him. I tear off a piece of bread to dredge in the chowder.

"Not yet," he says, tasting his.

My stomach drops, cold.

"So she's still here, now? In town?"

He nods. Takes the chunk of bread out of my hand, spreads some butter on it, hands it back to me.

"At your house?"

I set the bread down. He picks it up and sticks it back into my hand.

"Eat," he says, looking at me sideways. "She's still here because I was out all night and asleep most of today. By the time we had a chance to talk, it was too late for her to get on a charter, so she's leaving in the morning."

I drop the bread.

"She's alone at your house, and you're here with me?"

He nods. "Where else would I be?" Puts the bread back into my hand. "Will you please eat? I'm not going to talk to you about this unless you eat something."

"Fine." I take a bite and chew, purposefully. Like I'm in a commercial for bread. He rolls his eyes at me.

"She came to tell me I should come back to the program. That they'd take me. Let me go overseas, finish Barcelona with her."

Even though he's sitting here, with me, not her, two hot spots appear on my cheeks. I knew it.

My stomach drops. He shouldn't stay here, she's right, he should go back to school.

"And?"

"And what?" he says.

He points to my food. I dip the bread again.

"I said no." Sighs.

"Just like that?"

He drinks some water.

"She didn't take it too well. It wasn't exactly the civil good-bye I had planned. She was pissed I was out all night, that I was planning to come back over here again."

My face is still hot. I can't put more food in my mouth. I look at my hands in my lap. Think about what he's saying, what he's still walking away from. I look up at him.

"Cal, she's right. You should go back to the program. You don't need to be up here hiding out. My dad told me about last night—how you came after me. If you can tear into the woods after someone like me, you're not too sick to stick with architecture."

His eyes. Tonight they're dark gray. While I talk they move from annoyed to thoughtful. He fixes them on me in a way that makes everything else fall away.

"I know. You might be right. I'm thinking about it, going back to school, but not because of Susanna. Or Barcelona, for that matter. It's something I have to figure out, for me, what I am going to do. It was a mistake to let her come up here. Brought up old feelings, expectations, plans. That's her life now, not mine. It was dumb, but I thought we could end it better. Or something."

"So you just left her there?"

"Believe me, she wasn't going to come over here," he says.

I shake my head.

"That's not what I meant, and you know it. She's alone? At your place?"

"Wren, I left her at the house for me, not you." He takes my hand, pries it open, sticks the spoon in it. "I wouldn't be anywhere else today, tonight."

I stare at him. This can't be my life.

"I needed to be with you—know you weren't about to fling yourself into the ocean or get eaten by a lynx."

He runs a hand through his hair, pushing it back from his eyes. It falls forward again.

I must still look incredulous, because he says, "She'll be fine once she calms down. There's food, clean sheets, a car is coming for her in the morning. I said good-bye."

He tears off a small chunk of bread and tosses it in my bowl. Chowder splatters on me.

It's a lot to take in. He left her. To be here, with me. Maybe this is what it's supposed to feel like, love, steady in the face of things.

We eat in silence. Beyond us, the ocean's moon-bright and loud.

After we clean up, we slide, holding hands, on sock feet back to my room, climb quietly into my little bed.

Just before we fall asleep, he whispers, "You have promises to keep, and miles to go before you sleep."

It comes to me.

"Robert Frost," I mumble, on the edge of a dream.

"You were trying to say it last night."

Pulls me toward him, tight. We fall asleep.

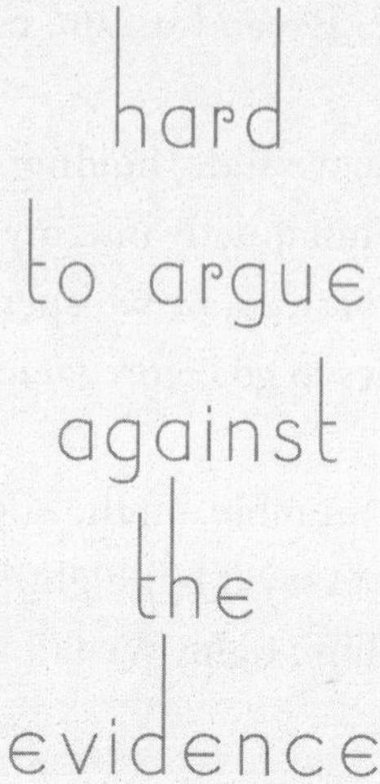

hard to argue against the evidence

THE LIBRARY DOOR swings open wide and a blast of frigid air races across the floor to my ankles. My bones are cold still, holding an ache like a grudge.

"John," Lucy says, looking up, smiling. She tucks a wisp of gray hair behind her ear and cocks her head over to the reference desk where I'm standing, trying to repair a collection of nursery rhymes that came back to us, four pages so exuberantly read they're nearly torn from the book entirely.

"What's going on?" I ask, my heart racing a little. It's bizarre to see Dad in here.

"Nothing." He smiles, striding toward me. "This place smells good, doesn't it?" He looks up at the vaulted ceiling, inhales deeply.

I nod, eyeing him. Out of the studio midday. Something's definitely up.

"Zara and I are making lunch at Mercy House. We'd like to spring you early, have you join us. If it's okay with Lucy, of course."

Lucy laughs, peering at us over the top of her reading glasses. "I think I can handle the rush," she says, waving her arm around the empty space.

I look at him a minute, let him know I'm on to him, I know this isn't a casual lunch. His eyes crinkle around the corners and he laughs.

"Come on," he says, "don't look at me like that. Get your coat."

I follow him to Mercy House in the Jeep.

He pulls around to the back of the house, and I follow suit. He takes an old key out of his pocket and lets us into the back pantry, right off the kitchen. We kick off our snowy boots on the mat and slip in past the warm ovens in our socks.

Zara's at the long worktable, waiting for us.

"There you are," she says, looking up. "I'm making thirty potpies."

She gestures to rows of small round oven crocks, topped with golden pastry, and floury circles of dough at her elbow.

"Wren," she says, "Would you mind washing your hands and using that brush to cover these with the egg wash?"

I look back at my dad. I have no idea what's going on. Something's coming, though, I know that much.

"Sure," I say, moving to the sink.

My dad strides to Zara and gives her a loud kiss.

"Full house?" he asks.

"And then some," she says, with a laugh. "It's good I'm—"

He cuts her off. "Let's finish these pies and then sit and eat, shall we?" It's like he's nervous.

I stand next to her elbow and paint egg wash on the edges of the filled dishes. My dad drops the dough rounds on the top and crimps them to the bowl with a joy he reserves for the kitchen. I follow him with the brush again and coat the tops so they'll brown and glisten when they're done.

Zara does a fast count, then, satisfied, moves to one of the ovens and pulls out a tray with three lovely pies on it.

"These," she says, "are ours. You guys hungry?"

I am. I am hungry. It's a good feeling.

We wash up and take seats at the end of the table.

"So," my dad starts, after we've all had a few bites, "we're making a few changes." He eyes me. "In our routine. All of us."

Something curls inside me. Tight. Hard. Consequences. Apparently you can't accidentally freeze yourself and expect to go back to normal.

"Wren," my dad says, "it's not that we don't trust you."

My stomach falls.

"John." Zara puts her hand on his arm.

He looks at her, starts again.

"I know what happened—it was a mistake, a misunderstanding about the weather, and so on."

He's beating around the bush, like my mother does.

Avoiding saying something. Speaking euphemistically. And it's about me. What I did.

I feel ill, the chicken on my fork is the color of a damp bandage, the peas pale.

Dad clears his throat. Here it comes.

"I've asked Zara to come live with me, us, move in, to try it for a while."

He takes a sip of water and then keeps the glass raised before his face. Prismatic. Looks at me over the top of it, squinting across the shine.

Even though I like Zara, all I can think is that he's trying to ditch me or something, pass me off onto her, like I'm too much to handle. It's sour inside me.

"Well, that's a big step," I say, sarcastic. "Congratulations. I'm so happy for you both."

Zara looks pained.

"Come on, Wren," he says, plunging his fork into the pie again. "Don't take it that way."

"How am I supposed to take it? You're only doing this because you don't trust me. Can't we just put it behind us? Have everything to go back to normal? Or whatever it was before the other night?"

"It's not about you, and it's not that we don't trust you—" he starts.

She puts her hand over his. They both fall silent. Their silence makes it worse.

"That's such bull, Dad. Why don't you just say it?" My voice is louder than I intend. "It's not that we don't trust you," I mimic, feeling ugly. "It's exactly that you don't trust me." I turn to Zara. "Have you considered his sudden commitment to you is because he needs a babysitter for his crazy daughter?"

It's a cheap shot. I would take it back if I could. I watch her face, expecting to see hurt. Instead she looks sad for me.

"Wren." My dad sets the fork down, wipes his mouth, fixes his eyes on me. "Zara and I have been talking about this for a long time. I should have included you, let you know more about my life. I guess I thought you had enough going on. You're angry. I see that. I've made mistakes, I know."

He pushes away from the table, goes to a cabinet near the refrigerator, and pulls out a bottle of wine. Pours himself a glass. Raises an empty glass at Zara. She shakes her head no.

"And now that you're up here—I'm trying. We'll be around more. All of us. The house is too quiet. You're alone too much."

I let out an exasperated breath. I want to push away from the table and walk out of the kitchen. But it would totally prove their point. Loose cannon. I sit tight.

Dad comes back to the table. Sits noisily in his chair.

"Eat."

I pick up my fork. Use it to scratch at a bit of baked-on crust.

"Sometimes," Zara says, her voice soft, "when people are depressed, I think it's because they're not able to say something, something true about themselves."

Her words fly through me. Shear a path that hurts. I

don't really know what she means, but it feels like she's telling me something big, important, hard.

"This is a good thing, Wren," my dad insists. "I don't think you need a babysitter. I think you need some family."

"It's a little late for that, Dad."

I shove away from the table. My chair scrapes across the floor. It's loud. They both startle like I've swung at them. Suddenly I get that they're afraid of me, or more precisely, for me. I lean against the cupboard doors. Cover my face with my hands.

Dad clears his throat.

"You came up here because you were in trouble. I've been too absent. I want to know more about where you are and what you're doing. I want us to spend more time together."

Tears slip down my cheeks. Now he wants to be a full-service dad. How'd I get so lucky.

"You don't trust me," I say, ashamed, wiping my face. Apparently I cry all the time now.

Neither of them says a word.

My dad lifts his fork, spears a bit of Zara's food. Talks while he chews. "Get your hands back on your camera and start a photo project. Organize a shooting schedule, work with someone. I'm not trying to be rigid here—"

"I'm already working at the library." My energy's gone. I'm the only one fighting.

"I just want you to be less isolated. Make something. Do something so you're not just drifting in your own thoughts."

"If we're done, I'm going home. For a run," I say quietly.

My dad keeps his face expressionless. Says nothing a minute.

"What, now I'm not supposed to run anymore? Not allowed?"

I stalk over to the counter where I left my keys. Snatch them up, furious. Then turn around and face them.

"I'm not planning to off myself," I say. "If I were, I wouldn't be standing here right now." I'm shaking, I'm so angry.

"You almost weren't standing here right now," my dad says quietly.

He wins.

"Enjoy your run."

CAL'S JUST WALKING AWAY from the front door when I pull up to our house.

"There you are," he says, smiling.

I put my head down on the steering wheel instead of getting out.

Cal comes over.

"Wren?"

"I just fought with my dad. I don't think that's ever happened. Not that I can remember, anyway."

"Come on," he says, pulling the car door open. Offering me his hand.

I slip past him, into the house, into my room.

"Do you want to talk about it?" he asks, leaning against my door frame.

I don't answer. I bend over the stacks of clothes on the shelf, pulling through them, looking for something to wear running. My clothes from the other night are still sitting stuffed in the bottom of the plastic bag the hospital sent home with us.

"What are you doing?"

I look at Cal for a second and then shake my head.

"You don't trust me either," I say, finding another pair of running pants. I stalk off to the bathroom to change.

"Wren, wait," he follows me.

I stop in the hall, yank my jeans off, one leg at a time, inside out. The gash on my shin from my wipeout has bloomed yellow. Looks like a sad banana.

"He asked Zara to move in."

I glance up at him. He doesn't look surprised. Relieved maybe, instead. Makes me angrier. "They're handling me." I say it as witheringly as possible, even though I'm not even really sure that's what's making me so mad. It's another change, another thing to get my head around. Why is this so hard? It makes me feel like the crappiest person in the world.

"Come on," he starts, watching me like he heard everything I just thought. "You know it's more than that, her moving in. They're not doing it only for you. And having been handled myself, when I was having a rough time"—he takes a deep breath—"It doesn't feel great, I know, but that doesn't mean it's not a good thing."

"You're on their side."

"I think you're having a hard time, and what happened the other night was scary."

Cal looks directly into my eyes, like he can catch me, hold me still, press his point into me, like I'll take it better with all his insistence.

I turn away from him, disgusted.

"Please don't be mad."

"Why not?" I yank my hair into a ponytail and head back into my room. He follows. "A woman I barely know is moving into my house to keep tabs on me. And you think it's a great idea. What's not to love?"

I turn to face him.

Cal sways a second and sags against the wall.

I drop my sweatshirt on the floor and reach out to him.

"Cal?"

He closes his eyes a minute, both hands pressed against the wall. Nods.

"Balance sucks today," he says like it's no big deal. An annoyance.

Great. I'm making him sick. Sicker. All my anger leaves me.

"I'll skip the run today. It's too soon anyway. It'd probably feel like shit. We'll go back to your place, lie around and read?"

I slip my arms around his waist. Want him to open his eyes and look at me again.

"I'm sorry," I say, starting to feel a little scared.

Nothing.

"It just feels bad, Zara moving in. Being watched all the time. Like you're all babysitting me. Like I'm not trusted." I let out a little laugh. "But it's hard to argue against the evidence." Try to keep it light.

Finally, finally he opens his eyes. Looks at me.

"Stop apologizing already. Go for your run. And no one's babysitting you." He kisses me. "We'll go back to my place when you're done. We can talk more then."

I pull away from him and go back to digging through my stuff for socks. I try hard not to entirely destroy the neat piles Zara's made for me. When I look up again, Cal's still leaning against the wall, eyes closed.

"Are you sure you're all right? I mean, I know I'm not supposed to say it, but you don't look so good."

"Yeah." He sounds annoyed. "Peachy. Just trying to get the room to stop spinning. I'll lie on your bed and read while you're gone."

I grab his arm and pull him to the bed. Stretched out, he's almost longer than my mattress. I select *The Blue Estuaries* by Louise Bogan from a stack of books my mom bought and hand it to him. I'm supposed to be casual about this. It's his deal. Takes all my willpower to pull on my socks and not climb onto the bed next to him.

"Nice legs," he says, sounding more like himself. Watches me while I do a few quick stretches. Lying across my bed like that, he reminds me of one of those marble-carved knights you see at the Victoria and Albert Museum in London. Life-size, stretched out on top of a sarcophagus. I shiver. Pull my sneakers out of the bag and sit on the floor to tie them. They're stiff with something—saltwater, maybe. A hazy memory. Lots of them pushing in. My heart sinks. I dig around for my phone and earbuds.

"Where are you going on this run?" Cal asks, rolling

onto his side and propping himself up with an elbow.

"Your house and back. I'll take the trails to your road, then back again. Nowhere near the water. I'll be fine. I promise."

"Susanna's gone," he says with a wry smile. "You don't have to check. Do you still have to run?" He's teasing me, but it's there on his face, a twist of worry. Like I'm setting out to finish the job.

I blush.

"I'll keep my ringer on loud if you want."

He laughs like we both know that's over the top, a ridiculous concession, but nods anyway.

I'm out the door.

Alone.

My first real minutes of solitude since I ran into Cal on the highway. I can still see the look on his face, on hers. Makes me sick. After I warm up, clear the house, and cross the road, I lean against a tree and try to breathe a minute. What was I thinking? I can't make it out in my mind. How did I come so close? I didn't mean to. I remember feeling hot. Like I was just going to sit and rest awhile, cool down. An involuntary shiver shakes me so hard I grip the tree. They're right not to trust me.

I could throw up.

I went for a midnight jog in the dead of winter in a desolate forest in the upper northeast. If I read that in the news, I'd say whoever did it was either really stupid or had a death wish. Makes me dizzy for a second. Like maybe I can't even trust myself. Like maybe I'm losing my grip. Lost it.

I start to cool down. Get a chill from sweat. Feels worse than normal.

I get back on my route. The forest is more beautiful this afternoon than I've ever seen it. All the boughs slipped into their white sleeves. In some spots the branches make lace against the sky.

Patrick will never see this. I imagine myself not seeing it. Not seeing anything. Cal's face. My father. The end of possibility. Stops me in my tracks.

It's huge, how close I came. Flips my hungry stomach. I retch what little I ate of Zara's lunch onto a bush.

What if it happens again? I panic and do something crazy? I only wanted to stop the feeling I was having. Made stupid decisions. Really stupid decisions.

I push a handful of snow in my mouth and start to run again. Get warm. Hit my stride. It comes to me that maybe I need them not to trust me. So I can stop trying so hard to keep it together. Let someone help me out.

Zara's words at lunch about saying something true keep bubbling up. I used to sometimes wish I could use pictures to speak instead of words. Carry around a stack of prints and hand them out to people in response to questions. *How are you* might be answered with a close-up of a girl's make-up-ringed eyes, watching a group of boys on the subway, trying to figure out if they're hot or hostile. Or responding to *What's up* with a photo of your best friend flirting with your boyfriend, just because she was bored. Today, right now, this moment would be a long shot, the photographer maybe leaning out of the open side of a helicopter, high, so there's a little fear in it too, and way, way, way down below, a girl, making tiny tracks in the woods, still imagining an escape.

The gagging feeling climbs my throat again. If I can't count on myself, what do I have? I feel weak. Stupid. Embarrassed. Ashamed.

My mother. My poor, worried mother. She sounded small on the phone. Wrecked. That voice she used with me in the hospital after the accident. Sweet and soft, like when I was little, scared in the night. Dr. Lang was a misstep. She said that. Like maybe a midnight run through the frigid woods was part of his therapy plan. Like somehow it might be someone else's fault, had to be, other than mine. Shame heats my face. This kind of thing would never happen to her. How am I such a mess? How did I come from her?

I pass the spot where I crashed my bike into the tree. Where I met Cal. Then I keep running on and on through the bright white woods until I'm at his house. It looks deserted. Susanna's gone. Like he said. And he stayed with me.

a routine

MY DAD AND ZARA don't mention the terrible lunch. Maybe I'm wearing the shame of it on my face or something, but they both act like everything's cool, forgotten. We start by having dinner together, the three of us, sometimes four with Cal. Then Zara moves in. A little at a time. When they're done for the day in the studio, she and Dad take his truck to her place and bring back some of her things. Clothes, a few paintings, a chair. She's super careful about it with me. Asks me if I mind if she straightens things up a little. Organizes the place here and there. Moves the furniture around in the living room. Knock yourself out, I tell her. We're polite with each other.

She's an early riser, and when I get up, she's at the table

with the paper, coffee for me, and breakfast. She likes to cook and she's good at it. Biggest breakfasts I've ever had. I skip eating the first few mornings, but then she starts knocking on my door asking if I want to join her for some beans and eggs or whatever's on her menu that morning. Quiche, crêpes, homemade fruit compote—it's something serious every day.

At first I can hardly look at her when we're one-on-one. I'm so embarrassed she's here. About why she's here. How I reacted to the news. But Dad doesn't do breakfast, so it's just the two of us. I keep my eyes glued to the *Times*, but I don't really want to see what's there, either. The terrible news of the world. It's quiet. Strained. For me at least.

About a week in, I say, "I'm sorry I've been such a huge pain—"

She's one of those people who looks at you totally calm, which always makes me nervous or like I'm going to cry.

"Nope," she says, very matter-of-fact, digging into a grapefruit. Grapefruit and homemade yogurt. Which I didn't even know you could make at home, if you didn't have a goat.

She shakes her head. "You're not a pain. On the contrary. I think you're good for him. Us. Shook things up. He was set in his ways."

This is a surprise.

"How long have you known my dad?"

"Do you mean how long have we been seeing each other?" She raises an eyebrow at me. "You can just ask me, you know. Whatever you want to know. He's your dad."

"Okay. How long have you been seeing my dad?"

"About five years."

Five years. Blows my mind.

"He didn't tell me," I say. Push the paper away. Look out at the sun on the water. Another bright day up here.

"I know. He's like that. We both are. Neither of us moves too fast. We should have talked to you, though, when you first got here. I wanted to. I wanted to welcome you up here. Especially since he was determined to keep his commitment to the fellows, but he didn't think it was a good idea. He thought you were in rough shape, had too much going on. I should have pressed him harder. It was a mistake."

So matter-of-fact.

I take a few bites of the yogurt. It's good. Not too sweet. She's stirred little bits of marmalade into it.

"Anything else you want to know?" she asks, eating.

"Are you from here?"

She shakes her head. "California. I moved east when I was in my early twenties. Following my heart."

"But not for my dad."

She smiles and shakes her head. "No, not for your dad. He was with you guys, and I was married then. Someone I met in college. I moved out here for him. He was a singer-songwriter."

"And you divorced?"

She sighs a little. Pushes her hair behind her ear. Looks faraway.

"Yeah. It got complicated. He traveled around, we were apart a lot."

"Do you have any kids?" I imagine a van load of stepsiblings.

A sad look flashes across her face. Shakes her head again.

"We lost a baby, our son. He was stillborn. I took it hard. Chris, my husband, went back on the road. We couldn't face each other. After a year or so, I suggested the split, and he was fast to say yes. I moved on."

I'm always stomping right into other people's soft spots. I curl and smooth the edge of my placemat. Look up at her. She doesn't look shattered or anything. She looks like she's waiting for another question.

"So, are you going to have a kid . . . with my dad?"

She looks amused and I feel a little stupid.

"No, it's too late for me, and your dad's too old to start another family. I—it's okay. I had other chances to try again, after my son, but I didn't. I figure that means I didn't want it enough."

She sets her spoon down. Looks at me. I squirm a little. It's like an emotional X-ray.

"Wren, I know something about grief," she says.

Time for the pep talk. She'd been cool up until now. I brace myself.

"It's something people don't understand until they've lived through it."

She sips her coffee.

"You're still in the first year," she says finally, quietly. "It's really hard the first year. I didn't care about anything after I lost my son. I let go of a lot—my marriage. But it gets better. Eventually. You come around. It doesn't go away. You learn how to live with it—all of it."

Not what I expected her to say.

I'm trying not to cry. Holding my breath. I let it out.

"Are you an artist too?" I ask in a weird voice. "I mean, on your own, when you're not working with my dad?"

She takes the topic change right in stride.

"I paint. But I don't have to do it all hours like he does. I'm more of a maker. And I have Mercy House, of course. I like to be busy. How about you?"

I shrug.

"Your dad's pretty proud of your photos. Did you know he's got a little book of them in the studio?"

I had no idea. I shake my head.

"The ones you send him by e-mail. Every few months he selects one or two and sends them to a friend of ours, a printmaker. Hitoshi prints them for your dad. Last year he stitched a bunch of them into a little book. Gave it to himself for his birthday." She winks at me. "You should tell him you want to see it."

My dad has never said a word about this to me. I'm speechless.

She gets a twinkle in her eye.

"Your dad's got a lot more going on than he shows," she says. "His heart's huge—you guys are alike that way."

I stare at my food a minute.

"I don't know what I am. If I'm an artist or not," I say. "If I should go to art school. I've always made stuff. My dad gave me a camera when I was nine, a little Instamatic—I've used one ever since."

"I hear you have a big collection."

I nod. "I have a few. Old Polaroids, a Minolta, a couple

of really cool ones from Germany and Russia. Some toy cameras. I buy them at flea markets."

"You know, there are a lot of flea markets up here. Maybe we'll head out one day and hit a few. Do you use them?"

"If I can. Sometimes I sort of shoot through them with my Nikon. Patrick messed with one so it could take a digital back."

Then I stop. Patrick's name slipped out as if he were alive. Then, the cold stab of remembering he's not. I swallow, hard. Force myself back on track, "Each camera makes you see the world in a different way. Like, what is it we see, really? What is what we're looking at if it changes with the thing we use to see it? I used to love that."

I look up at her. She's listening, like I'm saying something interesting.

"I thought it was so important. That I was—so important." I shrug, try to straighten up a little bit, sound sure. "It seems pretty stupid to me now. I mean, if I were really an artist, wouldn't it be killing me not to be working? Because I couldn't care less. About working. Seems like a waste. Pointless. Making stuff."

Patrick was so proud of himself after he hacked that little toy camera to work with my Nikon. I still have that first hybrid photograph somewhere. His broad smile.

I open my mouth to say more, then shut it.

"There," Zara says, "you don't have to do that—stay caught there like that."

She stands to clear the table. Then sets the dishes down. Touches my shoulder.

"You can't make anything if you're lost to yourself. You'll want to again, it's who you are. Wren, grieving is hard. Complex. Takes its own time."

She sits next to me and puts her hand on mine. It's awkward. I swallow hard. Sit up a little straighter. Tight throat.

"And you can cry when you need to, you know. I watched you choke it back just now, when you mentioned the lovely thing Patrick did for you. No one up here expects you to hide it. The thing about grief is that you have to let yourself feel it. Even the worst parts. Especially the worst parts. Pass through it. Let it pass through you. It's your strength—your humanity—your openness to your feelings. Even when you think you might not come through."

The worst parts. She knows everything. She must.

I put my hands over my face.

"But you will," she says softly. "When you're ready. This was big, kiddo. You just need time. I've been saying it to your dad since you got here. Telling him to relax, trust you, to call your mom off, to let you just *be* awhile."

Zara's been my secret defender.

"And Wren?"

I look up at her.

"Don't forget your follow-up appointment with Dr. Williams today. Lucy knows you're coming late."

I'm astonished. I don't know anything about anything. I had a fairy step-artist.

I thank her for breakfast and push away from the table. Time to take care of things.

breathe

DR. WILLIAMS' OFFICE is warm. The waiting room is already full—an old quavering woman, who keeps making an *ohhh* sound when she breathes out, like part of her is slipping away with each breath, an even older man next to her, shifting the contents of one plastic bag to the other, a younger woman in the corner, cracking the pages of a celebrity magazine who eyes me when I come in, and makes no attempt to stop staring at me while I wait, and a tired-looking mother with three coughing kids. I perch on the edge of my seat, willing the nurse to push through the door, call me in.

Finally I'm up, she lets me into a small room with an examination bed, a sink, a little wall-mounted desk, and a stool on wheels. I perch on the papered end of the table, hope he won't want to rehash the other night.

Dr. Williams comes in all smiles and washes his hands.

"Beautiful morning, isn't it?" he asks, sitting on the stool and rolling to the little desk.

"I guess," I say, trying to smile back at him.

"You guess," he repeats, flipping open the front of my file, glancing at it for a second, then flipping it shut again.

"Well, you're looking a lot better than you were the last time I saw you," he says, like he's proud of me. He rolls toward me on the stool and takes my hands in his. Turns them over, squeezes the ends of my fingers. "And how are your fingers and toes? Any sensitivity? Any issues?"

"Nope. Really, everything's fine."

He raises his stethoscope to his ears. "Lean forward for me and take three deep breaths. I'm going to have a quick listen to your chest."

I lean forward and he places the stethoscope on my back.

"Did you know," he says, after he listens to me breathe a minute, "deep breathing stimulates the parasympathetic nervous system and that's good because it helps counteract your response to stress?"

I shake my head.

"The trick is to face it, not flinch. You can close your eyes if you like, then breathe in through your nose, a big breath, deep, then count it out slowly."

"Okay," I say, my mind in so many places after talking to Zara it's hard to concentrate on the instructions.

"Your chest is clear and you're looking much better,

Wren," he says, leaning back, patting my knee. "I'm happy to revisit the idea of an antidepressant, but deep breathing is always good in a pinch." He winks. "Any questions or concerns?"

I shake my head. What am I going to say? Since I nearly killed myself running like a crazy person at midnight in the woods I've been experiencing a slightly disorienting bit of self-doubt? My dad no longer trusts me at the house alone and has adapted his entire life to make sure I don't do anything stupid?

I look up at Dr. Williams. His eyes are light, soft at the edges, wrinkles from smiling fanning out in the corners.

I shake my head again, force another smile. Then I close my eyes and take a deep breath, like he said, hold it, then let it out slowly. This earns a huge laugh from Dr. Williams, who stands, picks up my chart, and moves to the door.

"We're already busy this morning," he says, writing something on a slip of paper and handing it to me, "but it's great to start the day with someone bright and well like you. I'm here if you need me, okay?"

"Okay." I nod. A finger of sun stretches through the top of the window blind and lights his forehead in a way that makes him look sainted. I smile.

"Oh, and Wren," he says, half out the door, "will you ask Cal to give us a call?"

I look at the paper. In huge letters it says BREATHE, and below that a cell phone number. Another person looking out for me.

Bright and well. I turn his words over in my head.

meredith

I SMELL HER BEFORE I SEE HER. A little clutch of summer flowers. *Drôle de Rose*, a Parisian scent from her grandmother. The one thing Meredith hasn't changed since we were little.

A packet of letters tied with a ribbon slips along the length of the reading table to me. Then another one. I look up. Meredith. Sitting at the far end. Here. In my small library. Nearly swallowed by an enormous, dark-blue, arctic-tundra-caliber parka and a pair of fur-topped boots. I didn't even see her come in.

I close the book I was reading and look over at Lucy at the front desk. She raises an eyebrow, picks up her coffee, and walks to the armchairs in the back corner.

The bundled letters sit in front of me, relics from the lost land of friendship, or maybe missiles. Not sure which. Feels like I wrote my last one a thousand years ago. I did.

"Hi," she says, quietly, when I meet her eyes.

My mouth is open. I close it. She's a visitor from another life. I press my palms on the cool table top. Orient myself.

"Hi," I say back.

She starts to cry.

I look at the letters.

"I kept writing," she says. "One each Wednesday. There are a few extras because I wrote more when you were first in the hospital and everything was crazy—when you wouldn't speak." She wipes her face with her scarf.

Yeah. Crazy. When she yelled at me. Knocked me down hard when I was already down so low.

I touch the ribbon on one of the stacks. It looks like some of the vintage stuff she kept from when we cleaned out her grandmother's findings shop. A sapphire filament criss-crossed and bowed around each of the bundles, like she tied them up with a strand of sky.

I'm speechless.

"You're here," I say finally, my voice breaking. It's the best I've got.

She nods, teary.

I stand up. Walk over to her. We hug.

"I made your mom tell me how to get here," she says, her mouth pressed into my shoulder. "I know you still want to be alone, and all that—"

I nod.

"But it's getting too long. I had to come and see you. For myself."

"I'm sorry," I say.

I am. I'm sorry for everything. For disappearing.

"You're talking," she says when we finally let go of each other.

I nod again.

"Can you leave—here?" she asks, gesturing to the library.

I look over to where Lucy's sitting, in the corner, drinking coffee, pretending not to listen to a word we're saying.

"Go," she says, without looking up. Waves her hand toward the door. I give her ten seconds before she calls Zara to tell her Meredith's in town.

I put the letter bundles in my bag, grab my coat, and we're out the door.

Meredith has one of her parents' cars. It looks funny, out of place in this little town, parked rural style, angled into the spot. Clean. No winter's worth of salted snow crust in the wheel wells like everyone else's up here. She probably had it hand washed for the trip. She clicks it open and we get in.

"Where am I going?" she asks.

Good question. There are precious few private places in this tiny town.

I direct her to the Chat 'n' Chew. It's small town right out of a made-for-TV movie. Lots of birch and gingham. Lobster tchotchkes. Embroidered tea towels for sale. Someone's idea of cozy. A bakery case bears dense wedges of gingerbread, snickerdoodles, whoopie pies. And like most places in town at this time of year, it's largely empty. We get hot drinks and pick a table.

I can't stop shivering. I'm amped up and sad. It's surreal. I can't think of anything to say. My old life and the new one are pressed up against each other, tight. I squirm on my creaky chair. Can't get comfortable.

"I'm glad you're here," I hear myself say. But I'm not sure if I am.

"Me too," she says. Looks down at her cup. "I miss you."

Her voice is quiet. Small. We've never been awkward with each other. It makes her seem like a shrunken version of herself.

"I went over to your house. The first day of winter break. Surprised your mom. She let me stay for lunch."

My mother loves Meredith. Her poise. She says it like that, *Meredith's poise*. She has no idea. Meredith can be poised, especially around parents, but she was also the devious mastermind of everything we weren't supposed to do and did anyway.

I sip my latte. The milk's scalding. My tongue will be wrecked for a day or two.

"She told me you were doing okay—better," she said, "but that you still didn't want me to send you letters?" It's a question. She looks like she's going to cry again.

"I'm sorry," I say. I can hardly make my voice come out. I fight a moment of panic. What if I stop speaking all of a sudden? What if I can't control it? What if it just happens and I can't make it stop?

I look at her face, and there I am, on the edge of her

parents' bathtub, clutching my wrecked life on that little white stick in my hand. I can hear her voice, outside on the beach. Laughing. Flirting with the guy with the guitar.

We're quiet a minute. The air between us is heavy with everything, her letters sitting there like some kind of evidence. All the ones I never read, never wrote back. I look at my hands. Breathe carefully, in, out.

"Where are you?" she asks after a minute.

I look up at her. Burst into tears.

"I don't know," I choke. "Here, I guess."

If I could answer her question I wouldn't be sitting up in the north woods at the Chat 'n' Chew. I'd be a freshman at Amherst, making new friends, learning new stuff about myself, about the world, my place in it.

"Do I really have to call you Wren?" she asks.

I nod. I'm having a hard time stopping crying. Making more noise than I want. Drawing attention. I thought I was starting to feel a little better, but here I am again, sinking fast.

She sees. Does a quick change.

"God, *Wren*," she emphasizes it, stage-whispering, a glint in her eye. "*Stop it.* The weird ogre-looking guy over there from The Home is staring at us."

Saves the day.

I laugh.

"Ever kind to the less fortunate," I say, blowing my nose on my napkin. Deep breaths. Rein myself back in.

"Oh, come on," she says, feigning dismay. "You *know* I care."

"I can see." I nod, pointing to her jacket, feeling my way back into our way of talking. "Thinking of others and prepared for the worst—I'm pretty sure a family of three could withstand the cold in that jacket."

She flicks some of her milk foam at me.

"I think about you a lot," I say when I'm sure my voice will hold steady. "But I couldn't talk. I still kind of can't. I can't explain it, Mer. I felt like I was going to die if I didn't get out of there. Sometimes I still feel like that, up here, even."

She looks out the window a minute. It's snowing. Again.

"I really wish you'd trusted me more, I thought you did," she says.

I watch the snow drift down. We both thought a lot of things.

She clears her throat. Looks right at me.

"I'm up here because I need you back. It's time for you to wake up, be my friend again. I can't have it like this anymore. It's been months. If this is the way it's going to be—you don't get to just fade away."

She spins her cup on the saucer a little. Breathes. Lays it on me.

"You have to say it to me. Say you're done. We're done. If we aren't going to be us anymore—" She looks away from me, shreds her napkin into little strips. "I have a bunch of new friends at school."

I know what she wants me to tell her. And I do. I say it. Because that's how it works. Because she's here and right now I can't face what would happen if I said anything different.

"We're still us."

And when I say it, for a second I think it's true. It feels true. But maybe it's not; maybe it's an old habit. Either way she's right. I faded away. From everything. Her. Myself.

"Oh, Art School," she says, resurrecting an old nickname, "you have no idea how much I needed you. I was freaked out about everything—everything changed. Going away—I thought we'd go through that together. My parents weren't there for me—you know—and my brother's a total loser."

"I'm sorry," I say again. I am, I think. I am. I've been a bad friend. I take a huge breath. "I came up here because I couldn't stand being anywhere else."

Silence. I guess I sound defensive. She reaches up, undoes and reties her pony. Not that it needed it.

I pick at a sticky bit of something on the tabletop. "I just don't see how people can ignore all the terrible things that happen and shove on with life."

"Well, they just do," she says firmly, rewrapping her scarf around her neck. She's so used to having the final word. Thinks she still can, that it means something to be so sure. "Wow." She breathes out, looking at me like she's really seeing me, as I am now, for the first time. "Wren. How did you get so messed up?"

Patrick died ten inches from me.

I was pregnant.

I close my eyes. Press my lips tight.

"I didn't mean it like that—Wren—" she says.

I open my eyes and look at her again.

"I don't know when I'm going to feel better. I'm just trying to live up here. Trying to wake up and not feel like everything's pointless."

"Everything *is* pointless, you idiot," she says, sounding more like herself. "I don't know why that's bothering you now, all of a sudden."

We sit there a minute, then she leans toward me, drops her voice to a whisper, "Can we go back to your house? I need to stay the night at least, and Mr. Hunchback over there is giving me the creeps."

I laugh. She wants me to.

"I'm here," I say again, to make her feel better, more comfortable. "A little out of my mind, but here."

Her face softens when I say it. Looks less afraid. She looks like my friend again. The one I've known since we were little. The one I loved. Love.

But the thing is, I don't know if I can go back to being Meredith and Mamie. If I want to. My heart's pounding. Like it could come out of my chest, leave me. Like I might run out of here, chasing after it.

you're a freak

NIGHT SLIPS IN when we aren't looking.

"You drive." She tosses me the keys. "You always drive."

She looks at me, horrified for a second. "You do still drive, don't you?"

"Of course." I can leave the Jeep at the library overnight.

She gets the deluxe tour of beautiful Main Street. Quick and dirty. Then we fly down the highway, past the turn-off to Cal's road and on to ours. I pull in slowly along the muck-rutted drive.

"Christ," she says, looking out the window as we pass some of Dad's piles of scrap metal. "I think we were thirteen the last time I was up here. Remember that? Your mom had some big work deal she couldn't change, and we took the train up for that long weekend? She was so worried! Man, what did she think was going to happen? We were all excited, and then it was just a regular weekend. With trees." She looks around. "I forgot how pretty it is. Is your dad the same?"

"Yep," I say. "And his girlfriend is living with us."

"Your mom didn't mention that."

"She doesn't know."

The house is dark, but the studio's glowing. We pop in to say hi to Dad and Zara. He looks ridiculously happy to see Meredith again, that I have a friend with me.

Nick sets his work down and comes over to meet her too. She gives him the once-over, then blows him off. It's kind of funny. He looks so disappointed I almost feel sorry for him. Almost.

Before we leave, he calls out to us, "I'll be working late if you guys are looking for something to do later."

He raises his finger a second, to make us wait, darts into the back room, then back out again, carrying something.

"I found this digital projector in the studio, your dad says Mary left it? How about I hook it up and we screen something in here? Ladies' choice."

I shoot him a small smile, he's trying so hard, then we head back to the house.

"Come *on*!" he shouts after us, laughing. "There's *nothing* to do up here!"

We step in the door and I'm reminded of the day Cal first came. Watching him see the place, take it in. Like he was meeting an old friend. I throw on all the lights and stand next to Meredith a minute while she does the same.

"Nothing's changed!" she says, happily.

"Dad's not big on interior decorating."

"Oh, I used to be so jealous of you that your dad was like this," she says, waving her arm around the room.

"Like what?"

"You know, artsy, loose, not concerned with how everything *looks* all the time. I thought if I had this, a real place to come to like this, it'd make everything a lot easier."

"You have the beach house," I say, without thinking. My stomach takes a dive.

She kicks off her shoes, flops on the couch, and wisely changes the subject.

"So . . . I'm seeing someone new . . ."

I am rushed backward and forward through time. She's seeing someone new. Which means high school ended, she went away to college, and she met new people. New friends.

She watches me closely, waits for me to ask.

"Okay, spill." I raise my eyebrows. Like I'm excited to hear everything. This is exactly what I'm not sure I can do. Care. Like I did before. But I can try.

"Oh!" She pops up and grabs her purse. "That reminds me, I didn't tell him I got here. I said I'd let him know." She sends a quick text.

When she's done, she smiles. "And, since you asked, Middlebury's great. Cool people, I love the campus, and finally some new guys, a fresh crop, thank God. After the same Bly boys for twelve years—" She shakes her head, like she's not sure how she made it through.

I feel like an out-of-touch social anthropologist, listening to her. Did I used to talk like this? I can hardly remember what it felt like, what I thought was so exciting or important.

"His name's Matt," she's saying, almost singing his name. "He's my roommate's brother's friend. Third year. Poli-sci. From L.A. He kind of has that surf thing going on."

She savors the details. I would have loved this a year ago. I can almost picture him from the look on her face. I remember it now, how we did this, talked about guys, the way it felt to imagine yourself attached to someone new, to another life in your imagination, feel like someone different, or more than you already were. It's just that the stakes turned out to be higher than we ever dreamed. I sit next to her on the couch.

"I'm glad," I say, sounding like someone my mother's age. But Meredith's from the other side, an emissary from the land of what my life might have been, a road not taken.

"That's all?" She deflates. "Don't you want to see photos?" She waggles her phone at me.

I take it. Look at her pictures. He is cute, exotic, so not New York. Very white teeth. Probably really popular. Kind of reminds me of Nick. I shiver a little.

Meredith pokes around the house while I scroll through her photos. "God, your dad has some *crazy* art." Admiration in her voice.

Life at Middlebury. This is what it looks like. Going away to school. All these shots of her with her arms around people, faces I don't know. She's smiling in every one. Seems like a lot of work. All that smiling.

"So." She plops back down next to me, tugs a lock of my hair. "In case we were still friends, I snuck us a little treat."

I look at her. No idea what she's talking about.

She pulls on her boots, grabs her keys, and runs out to the car. Comes clomping back in with two bottles of champagne. The kind her dad buys by the case. The stock we pilfered at the beach house.

"I thought," she says, "we might celebrate. You know, that everything's okay."

Everything's okay. She wants it to be okay, everything. Maybe it is. I wish it were.

"I'm sorry." I apologize again, like we're sealing a deal. "I—"

What? I'm sorry I'm not the person she wants me to be?

She sets the bottles on the table. Hugs me.

"Me too," she says. "And, it's okay. You're a freak. It's not your fault. They only let you out of The Home as an experiment anyway. We're tracking you with interest."

She stretches out on the couch. Puts her head in my lap. Bites me on the arm. Makes puppy eyes.

"So, you ever going to go to college?" she asks, casually. I can tell by the way she's holding her voice she's been dying to ask and is probably going to report everything I say right back to my mother.

I sigh. I wish I had a clear answer for her.

"Probably," I say. "I guess my dad's been talking to people at RISD. It sounds like they might take me in the fall if I want."

"RISD?!" She bites me again. "Your wish! Wren, that's great! You got your wish! And your mother's coming around?"

My wish.

She has no idea how that sounds. She can't possibly, or she'd never have said it.

The wish that sunk Patrick. Me. Sometimes I wonder how deep underground they buried him, whether he was cremated or if he's stretched out in dress clothes in some bizarrely padded but tasteful satin-lined box. Did his mom buy him new clothes or is he wearing something I knew, buttons I slipped out of their narrow holes? I wonder if I could go and lie on the grass above him. Arrange my body like his. Look at the sky for both of us.

"Earth to Wren," Meredith's saying. The present rings off her like an alarm. "Let's chill this champagne. RISD. So awesome."

I close my eyes. Try to come back.

Be normal.

I follow her to the kitchen, will myself to go on talking. Take a shaky breath. "Either that or I'll go to Berlin—remember all those cool, weird German gifts I used to get on my birthday from Theo and Marta? My dad's friends? They're offering to have me stay with them for a year. Take some classes over there."

But I realize as I say it that it's not going to happen. Berlin. Not yet anyway. It's too much. Too different. I would have leapt at the chance a year ago. I lean against the counter, remember Cal in this same spot, looking so beautiful on New Year's Day. Maybe Theo and Marta will let me come later. After college or something.

I'm holding two squishy, cold, overripe avocados while she rearranges the fridge to make room for the bottles, when my dad and Zara walk in. Dad eyes the bottles, opens his mouth a second, but says nothing. Zara holds his hand tight, like she'd stop him if he were going to object. She keeps him near the door, tells us there's dinner in the fridge. Some frittata thing she made that we can just heat up. They'll leave us to our night, she says, firmly. They need to go to Mercy House anyway, pack a few more things. May or may not be back. I wonder how much of this is cool with my dad. He keeps quiet.

I hand the avocados to Mer and run over to hug him. Hug them both. It's the first time I've hugged Zara, but I know she's looking out for me, and I feel a surge of love for her because of it. They leave us, with promises to call in an hour or two. Check in.

As soon as the car pulls away, Meredith grins at me and says, "Warm bubbly never hurt anyone. Let's pop one of those babies."

She bangs around looking for glasses while I reheat Zara's frittata. Finally she hands me a jelly jar full of champagne. "I couldn't find flutes."

I laugh a second, to her surprise, then she laughs too.

"Here's to your damn health," she says, raising her glass.

We drink.

I make a small salad. Meredith sets the table. Before we sit, I text Cal. Having Meredith here makes me feel weird, like there's a possibility Cal doesn't exist, like he was something I dreamed up.

It makes my heart race to imagine them meeting, but I invite him over. Read through his last few texts to me. He was working on something. I take a deep breath. Maybe it's stuff for school. He's getting ready to make a case for going back to Cornell. Whatever it is, he's been busy for days.

Meredith watches me with curiosity, says nothing.

We move to the table.

"I'm kind of seeing someone up here," I offer, finally.

She grins. "I knew it!" Takes a huge bite of frittata. "God, this is delicious." Looks at me. "See? You're not in such bad shape."

My phone beeps.

It says, CAN'T. BUSY. SORRY.

"Shit." My heart sinks. Not that I can really picture the three of us hanging out, but still.

"Trouble in paradise?"

I shake my head. Disappointed. Try not to let it show.

She eyes me a second, then chooses not to mention the look she just read on my face. Teases me instead, "So you hooked up with a local. . . ."

"Shut up." I fling a cherry tomato at her. "His name's Cal. He and his brother went to Auden. His dad's an architect, did this place."

"Auden," she sighs, weary. "Way to branch out. This world is too damn small."

I lean back in my chair and toss my phone onto the counter. Swallow. Not sure why I feel so nervous again all of a sudden.

"He's doing architecture. At Cornell." Small lie.

Her brow furrows. "So, it's long distance? I don't get it. What's he doing up here?"

"An internship." I'm vague about the details.

"Grad school?" she says, fingering a chain around her neck.

I spot a small diamond hanging from it. "An older man . . . ?"

"Undergrad. And he's only three years older—" I stop. "Like Matt."

Suddenly I don't want to talk about Cal anymore. Like words might wreck it. Meredith will say something. Make me feel weird. Kill how I feel about him. Like talking to her about Cal might pull him, us, into my old world and I won't be able to find my way back out again or something.

She tops off our jelly jars. One bottle down. I can feel it in my face.

"And you didn't think I'd want to hear about him? That hurts, Wells."

"You'll meet him," I say, before I can stop myself. "Tomorrow. He's busy tonight. Working on something. We'll go over there when I get off work."

We're quiet a minute, eating. I forgot how drinking does this, makes me ravenous. Or maybe it's Zara's food. Right now it feels like I need sustenance and by some miracle it's here in front of me.

"Your job," she laughs, looking a little rosy herself. "Where'd you get that one? I don't know how you can sit in that dingy library all day. You have to admit, it's kind of pathetic, Wren."

"Don't bash the job," I say. "I like it. Besides, the dinginess is part of the charm."

"You always had weird taste," she says. She takes another bite, chews slowly, like she's weighing whether or not to say something, then leans over her plate toward me, all drunk serious.

"Your mother told me everything."

Of course. God knows what she means by "everything."

"Oh?"

She lowers her voice, like there's anyone around to hear us. "You know, your—misadventure? She's pretty worried."

I say nothing.

She picks five fat olives from the salad and pokes them onto the tops of her fingers. Wiggles them at me like tentacles or something. Gauging my mood.

I keep eating.

She makes a crazy face, tries to be funny. "It sounded pretty weird—what were you thinking with that whole popsicle episode? God, Mamie, you could be dead right now."

It almost makes me laugh. Something about the right now. Like dead isn't always, never anything again. Like it's a state you'd keep checking on.

Still dead.

Dead right now.

And now. And now.

I can't look at her. Obviously my mother didn't hold back. Why would she? I used to tell Meredith everything.

Shit. Shit.

She gives up, pushes back from the table.

"Time for that other bottle," she says, moving toward the kitchen.

"Mer—"

But I've got nothing. The good drunk feeling is turning into the slow, heavy drunk feeling.

She pops the second cork, letting it fly my direction, and

does a little dance on the way back to the table. Some of the champagne bubbles out and onto the floor.

"God. It's so silent in here. How can you stand it? We have to put on some music."

I want her to leave. I don't want to be here, with her, like this right now, pretending everything's normal, just like it was. She dances to an imagined beat and pours more in my glass.

"Don't worry, I won't tell anyone about it," she offers, cheerfully. Then, "Seriously, Wells." Her face shifts into one of exaggerated concern. "I can see you're not going to talk about it, but you're not planning another stunt like that or anything, are you? I mean, I'm glad you're all right. It's just a little weird, that's all."

"Thanks." I shake my head.

She clears a few of our dishes while I sit and watch the bubbles shimmy to the top of my glass. Little chaotic paths. Or probably not. Probably the opposite of chaos, that bizarre order you find in the natural world, something very specific, very scientific, driving the path of their ascent. Patrick would know. He knew stuff like that. And he thought champagne was ridiculous. Whenever we drank it, he'd snag my glass, raise it to his face, and proclaim *big nose, full body* in this idiotic voice he thought sounded British or French or something. Every time. It's a crime to remember something so stupid about someone who died.

"So, Recluse"—Meredith wallops me on the back with renewed cheer—"the only way we're ever going to get caught up is if you read some of these."

She leans over the couch, her gold necklace trickling out of the V of her sweater, the little diamond dangling bright in the light, grabs my bag, and dumps the two ribbon-wrapped stacks of letters on the table next to me. She has got to be kidding.

She's not.

She's drawing a line, assigning penance, her face stiff with purpose.

I don't like how this feels, but it's important to her. I can see that. She needs me to do it.

I pick up the remaining silverware and napkins on the table and bring them to the sink. I linger before the dishes a minute. She eyes me. The whole mood's shifted, the way it does when you drink. Mercurial. Dangerous.

"You read. I'll call Matt."

She climbs over the back of the couch and lies on her back with her phone. Like we're both about to do something fun. Something we want to do. In a second the house is filled with her flirty voice, laughing a lot. She has a life full of people I don't know, might never know. This guy, for one. Even though I'm the one who walked away, it's hard to hear.

I bring the bundles over to the armchair near the window and stare at the stacks. Slip the ribbon off. She organized them by date and mailed them to her house, some addressed to Mamie WhereTheHellEverYouAre Wells c/o Your Only Remaining Friend Meredith at her address, the inky red postmarks an accusing march through time. So many days between then and now.

I slide my finger under the flaps of a few, only the most recent. I can't go in any farther than that. My heart's pounding so hard it vibrates me a little, fluttering the edge of her pages slightly, like a moth wing. I'm disoriented again. Back there. But here, too.

I let the letter fall into my lap. Meredith talks to Matt forever, hopping up once to top off both our glasses, while I blink, unseeing, at the rest of her words to me. Her phone conversation is full of names I don't know and new inside jokes. Jokes I'm outside. When you don't listen for meaning, speech takes on a rhythm that's not unlike how waves batter the shore. I look out the window. Through my reflection, I can kind of see the snow coming down on the water. From nowhere into nowhere.

"That's all you read?" she asks, finally ending the call and coming over to where I'm sitting.

"I can't do it," I tell her, even though at this minute, I'm terrified to say so. Her anger at me is palpable. I look up. "I can't read them. Go back there."

She's silent a minute. Narrows her eyes. Stands her ground, the brewing fight ugly between us. I wish she'd just say what I can hear screaming around inside her.

But she holds back. Lets out a short, sharp blast of air. Wordless frustration. Nothing more. A hand up to smooth her hair.

We need something to do. I go to the kitchen and grab scissors. Two pairs.

"What're you doing?" she asks carefully, after I come back to the chair and start to cut.

"They're mine, right? For me? I mean, it's up to me what I do with them?"

She nods slowly, watching me unfold, smooth, and refold her words.

"Snowflakes," I say, feeling a little drunk and relieved, like now the night's going somewhere, like I can actually make something nice out of this train wreck we're in.

"Snowflakes." She speaks slowly, looking at me like I'm demented.

"Squares, then triangles," I instruct, pointing to the second pair of scissors on the floor near my foot.

She doesn't move. I look at the half-empty glass in her hand, the empty bottle over by the couch. This can't end well.

I open the letters and flatten them with my palm. There's an order to the folding, a calm plan, basic, easy to follow. Originality comes in later, when you make your cuts. I smooth her sharp words flat, then muffle them in folds. I catch sight of *Patrick* and for a second the scissors are heavy as lead, but I lift them anyway, force open their rusty jaw, cut away the crushing words. Each snip straightens my spine until I'm solid as a tree, upright. I'm in the eye of a paper storm, a blizzard of irretrievable time between us.

"I have no idea who you are, Mamie," she says at last, angrily swiping a tear away from her cheek. It's only when I hear the door open that I look up.

"Where are you going?" I ask, thinking for one crazy second she's heading out for a run herself.

"The studio. That Nick guy said he'd show a movie."

The door slams, loud.

flinch

MORNING'S FAST, bright, and hard. The champagne's a drum in my head, a wake in my stomach. I open one eye.

Dad's wire bird floats on a string in the corner of my room. Twists a little in the hot, dry air when the heat comes on. It's innocent, hanging there. And lucky to be wire. Free of complications like the awful bloody rhythm pulsing in my temples.

I open the other eye. Meredith's on top of me. It's always been like this. Every sleepover, I wake up, a million degrees, her legs slung over mine, pressing me flat to the bed.

She didn't leave. That's good.

I nudge her a little, try to ignore the creeping unease moving over me.

"Bed hog," I try, propping myself up on one elbow.

She doesn't stir. She's sleeping so hard, her mouth's open. I can see all her perfect teeth. I check the time on my phone. If I get up now, I won't be late for work. I lift one of her eyelids with my finger.

"Ugh." She bats my hand away. "Quieter, please." Covers her face with a pillow.

She's speaking to me. A second good sign.

"Some of us have to go to work." I toss back the covers.

"Not me," she says from under the pillow, groping to pull the blankets back up.

I can hear Zara in the kitchen. It's the best sound I've heard in a long time. They must have come back late. Dad can't be up yet. He's never up early. I smell eggs. Oh, Zara.

"I have responsibilities."

I stand up. Hold my head a minute.

"Shut up," she moans. "I'm sleeping."

"Sleep as long as you want. I'll tell Zara not to bother you. Meet you back here around three when I get off?"

She doesn't answer, but if how terrible she looks right now is any predictor, she'll still be here when I get back. I grab a T-shirt, hoodie, and her new, cute jeans off the floor. Bed rent. She's spread eagle under my quilt.

Zara's quiet during breakfast. Slides me the paper. Puts a pile of ham and eggs on my plate. Doesn't ask me a thousand questions. I'm grateful. We eat, then she brings me to the library.

Lucy's gone most of the morning. In and out, mostly out. I check my phone a thousand times. Nothing from Cal. I'm on edge. Jittery. I should have gone for a run. Worked off the hangover, Meredith's arrival. I can't shake the uneasiness.

It's like I'm swaying on a high wire, balancing over two sides of something I can't identify, something important, and the slightest gust of wind or turn of phrase could push me one way or the other.

Anxious. Excited. Old life. Now. Here. Then.

I finish shelving and prep more drop-off orders. Work until there's nothing left for me to do. Then I sit at the big table near the front window and flip through the stack of books Lucy left for me to read. She does that. My personal librarian. Emily Dickinson, Flannery O'Connor, Frank O'Hara, Salinger, Lowell. Lucy Shepherd doesn't talk much, but the books she leaves say plenty.

I pick up *Franny and Zooey*. We read it in tenth grade. Before we started on the Russian novelists. I liked the Glass family, how they swelled and contracted around their kids. And Zooey, especially, so cool in the face of Franny's drama. I fan the pages, try to find a passage I like, then I set it down again. It's hopeless. The words shift and turn. I can't make them mean anything today.

I text Cal. Say I'll be by later.

No reply.

My stomach pitches and plummets, a wild up-and-down slide. I tell myself he's not suddenly blowing me off. Of course not. Why would he be? But he hasn't said a word about whatever it is he's working on. It's probably school. He's getting ready to go back, get out of here.

I would kill for a run.

I look at the clock above the window. Fifty minutes left.

Fifty minutes between me and going back to face Meredith, maybe bringing her to Cal. I look up at the clock again. Still fifty minutes. I can't just slip out. Meredith might find it mockable, but I like this job. Lucy's counting on me to be here.

I stand up and walk around. Circle the stacks. I have to do something with this energy. I pick up O'Hara's *Lunch Poems*. Lucy says he wrote them strolling around the city on his lunch break from his job at MoMA. I recite a few to the empty room.

I toss O'Hara on a table and pick up my pace. Just me and the books. A lot of dead writers. All those left-behind words. I'm circling the library like a crazy person or one of those old people who exercise by walking around shopping malls. I'm sure I look insane. But I have to keep moving. Feels closer to anxiety than excitement.

I try the breathing Dr. Williams talked about. It helps, sort of. I gulp air, hold it, let it go again slowly, and try to think this panic through. Drinking last night. Last night itself. Like old times. Only not at all. Like I'd been snapped back to before anything happened, but not. Makes me dizzy. Or maybe it's the walking in circles.

I miss Meredith all of a sudden. It kind of seems hopeful between us, that confrontation we had, or whatever it was, maybe it's over now. I need it to be over. I hope she and Nick didn't do anything she'll regret, and that she's still asleep in my bed.

It's like she let herself into the box I have myself tucked away in, and now it's catching up to me, all the time I've been gone. All the ways I used to be—laughing until I cried when it was Meredith's behind sticking out of a crowded car that made the subway conductor shout over the speaker system, "Do *not* hold the doors!" Trying, and failing, to con the bartender on the roof deck of the Metropolitan to sell us salty martinis so we could toast ourselves and our excellent city while we pretended to look at whatever sculptures they had up there.

God, we laughed all the time. Did stuff. I used to be a person who did things. Then again, I also used to be able to think about whatever popped into my mind. Without flinching. Or worrying that it was going to be too much.

I think that's it—last night I remembered what it felt like to be kind of normal. Like before. But not now. Not today. Today my heart won't stop racing, and I can't shake the sense that everything's about to come down. I hope, hope, hope we're not still fighting. More deep breathing.

I check my phone again. Still nothing from Cal.

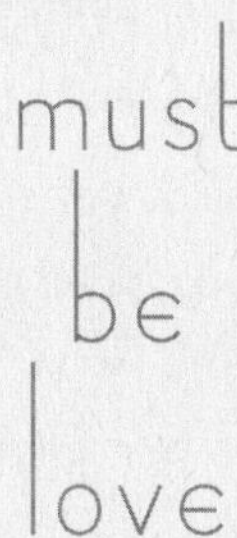

MEREDITH'S STILL IN BED when I get back to the house. She's got a pile of magazines on the floor next to her, but I also spot my copy of Larkin from Cal open on the quilt.

"Lazy."

"Ha, ha," she says, eyeing me somewhat coolly. "Nice jeans."

I can't read her voice, can't tell if she's still mad or not.

"Oh yeah," I say, trying to sound lighthearted, "thanks for these."

She tosses my book toward the foot of the bed.

"Seriously, Wren, you looked like a total hick yesterday with those baggy jeans of yours belted up like that."

It's a dig, but it means she's not going to bring up last night. We're in the clear, for now.

Her eye falls on the pile of clothes stacked against my wall.

"I would have gotten dressed already, but it's not like I was going to put on a pair of your sorry jeans. God, Wren, at least come down for a weekend to do some shopping."

"Come on." I throw a pillow at her. "It's not that bad."

"It's *worse*." She rolls her eyes. "Look in the mirror much? You've lost your touch, Wells." She laughs. "If I'd known how bad it was, I would have brought in supplies. Products, reinforcements from home."

She rolls out of bed. Stretches.

"How was work? Another crazy day at the library?"

Exactly. Gosh, Meredith, work was great, except for the freaking out part, pacing the floor like a demented obsessive.

I don't say it. Make a face instead, like work is so dull.

"You think you're so funny."

"Yes. Well, I am," she says. "And I'm finally ready for a shower."

She pulls a silky little robe from her bag and heads to my bathroom.

"I have to head back tomorrow morning at the latest," she calls out to me. "Okay with you if I stay another night?"

"Of course."

"Let's find something fun to do in this place—if there is such a thing?"

"There isn't."

I'm dying to ask about Nick, what they did, but I don't.

Better to pretend last night didn't happen at all. I look around my room. She left her jelly jar with a sour-smelling inch of flat champagne in it on my shelf. I hold my breath and take it to the kitchen sink.

"Hey, thanks for cleaning up, making the bed," I yell in to her. "When you were so pressed for time, I mean. The place looks great."

Sarcasm. The language of friendship. I force a smile onto my face. Will myself to feel it.

"Say what? Can't hear you," she singsongs back, laughing.

I try Cal. Right to voice mail. His phone's off. Must be. I text him again, even so.

OVER IN A FEW. BRINGING SURPRISE.

That feeling again.

Rise and fall.

I go back into my room. At least I'll look good. Meredith's in town.

After about an hour of goofing around, trying stuff on—*you let him see you in that?*—rejecting it, trying something else, we're out the door. I'm back in my own jeans, but she's loaned me a supersoft, loose cashmere sweater-wrap thing she brought and, after feigning horror and tossing my ancient bra into the kitchen trash—*must be love*—gives me a dove-gray lacy one of hers. I let her straighten and pull my hair into a perfect tousled ponytail and put on a pair of her earrings. I look pretty, but I don't feel exactly like myself. Of course, I didn't before I got dressed, either. And Meredith's happy.

just say it

I SHIFT INTO A LOW GEAR and we four-wheel it up the mud-rutted road to Cal's. I feel like a hard-ass, driving his Jeep, and I'm proud of the woods—how beautiful they are.

She likes the house.

"Hey, it's like your dad's place woke up and took a shower . . ."

I hit her.

The garage is closed. I click it open. Cal's car's tucked neatly in its spot. A jolt of excitement or trepidation or something zips up through my stomach into my throat. Everything's happened since I saw him last. Meredith hauled me out, dragged me back into my life, and I have this terrible feeling if I don't see Cal soon he's going to disappear, fade into memory like a fever dream.

Deep breath at the door. Meredith's with me. To meet him. It's a big step. Too big. One I'm not ready for, but definitely something a normal person would do. Fake it till you make it.

I punch in the code. Wait for the little green eye to blink awake. Open the door.

We step inside. For a minute I'm flooded with relief. It's no dream. His house feels like home. I'm exactly where I want to be.

Meredith lets out a little whistle of appreciation.

"This is more like it." She eyes me with a new respect. "And you come here dressed like you do?" she teases.

"Ha, ha."

I open my mouth to shout to Cal, let him know we're here, when I notice him on the couch, on his back, asleep. Arm over his face. He looks like hell. Sleeping hard.

All kinds of details rush at me at once. The house is too dark, thermostat low. Crutches on the floor next to him along with some dirty dishes and his phone. Pieces of a broken plate by the kitchen. He looks like he's been there a day or more.

"Cal?"

Nothing.

I drop my keys and coat and go over to him.

Meredith's frozen in place.

"Cal?" I say again, quietly.

He doesn't answer.

I kneel near the couch and touch his face. Not sure if I

should wake him. But I have to see if he's okay.

"Cal." I touch his cheek again. His shoulder.

He shifts a little, opens his eyes, and it takes a second before he registers me. Looks like he's swimming up from someplace really deep.

He raises a hand to his face. Pushes his hair back. Tries to sit up a little.

My heart sinks. I lean in close, put my lips near his ear, "How long have you been on this couch?"

His phone's right there on the floor next to him. He just looks at me, like he's not sure how I got here.

"Why didn't you call me? I would have come over," I say.

Now he's awake. Angry. Sits up a little more. I slip a pillow in behind him.

"What are you doing here?" he asks, cold.

It takes me a second to understand the question. His tone.

"What am I doing here?"

"You just let yourself in?"

"Why didn't you call me?" I ask again, starting to feel completely disoriented.

"Battery died."

Looks away from me.

"Battery died . . . ?"

It dawns on me slowly.

"Oh my God, Cal." I start to cry. "You couldn't make it across the room to plug in your phone? Let me help you get to Dr. Williams."

He shakes his head. Annoyed.

"He'll come here, to the house. My dad set it up. He'll come if you call."

He makes another face, like he can't stand what he's saying. Then looks at me, furious, like it's my fault, like I've done something unforgivable.

I'm stunned. Can't move.

Beyond us, out the window, the sky's graying. The fading afternoon light dulling everything.

"Fine," he says, voice tight. "Give me a hand—getting to the bedroom?"

He looks terrible—like he's losing what little's left of his color right before my eyes.

"Oh my God," I say it again. "Of course—why? Why didn't you tell me last night? Why didn't I just come over here yesterday? God, I had the feeling something wasn't right all day." I wipe tears off my cheek with my sleeve. My nose is running now too.

"Shut up," he says, sharp. "And stop crying. I'm fine. Everything's fine. You're making it worse. This has nothing to do with you. I blew it. I'm not supposed to let it come to this. Just help me up, will you?"

He grabs the back of the couch and sits up. I hand him the crutches. But he just looks at me.

It takes me a minute to get it.

They're not enough. He can't do it on his own. For a second, I think I'm going to lose it.

Deep breath.

I wrap my arm around his waist instead. He puts an arm

over my shoulders, leans on me, and we stand up, sit back down fast, try again. It takes a second for him to get his balance.

Meredith clears her throat.

Cal and I both look up in surprise.

"Oh," I say, "I forgot you were here."

"Is everything okay?" she asks in a shocked voice. "Should I call 911?" Her phone's bright in her hand.

I shake my head. Freeze a second. Cal's heavy against me. Then I introduce them like everything's normal.

"Cal, this is Meredith. She came up to see me. I wanted you guys to meet."

"Good timing," Cal says. "My finest hour." He's so pissed off.

Meredith's lips are thin with a forced smile.

"Help me," I hiss at her. He's really leaning on me. I can't do it without her.

She drops her bag and comes over, face frozen in a polite horrified expression.

I wrap her arm around his waist.

"We've got you," I say.

We flank him, help him to the bedroom. He smells sick.

At the door, Cal says quietly, "I've got it from here. Call Dr. Williams."

"Okay. When was the last time you ate?"

He shuts the door in my face.

I can hardly work my phone, I'm so freaked out, I keep hitting the wrong contact. Maybe this is how it went down with his mom. Maybe Cal's MS is like hers after all, maybe he'll end up in a nursing home.

Finally my fingers find Dr. Williams' number, and I get through. They're coming. Will be here in twenty minutes.

Meredith's speechless when I hang up.

Then: "This"—she hustles me by the arm back toward the living room—"is your new boyfriend?"

And: "Have you lost your mind?"

I stare back at her. It's hard to focus on what she's saying. I just want Dr. Williams to get here. Check on Cal. Tell me everything's going to be okay.

"Mamie." She's loud. "What the hell are you thinking?"

I wince. She sounds so bitchy.

"Will you please keep your voice down?"

"I thought you came up here to take care of yourself, to get your shit together," she hisses, not much quieter.

It's fully dark now. I step away from her and start to walk around the room, turning on a few lights. It only helps a little. It's like the cold evening outside the window is tarnishing everything, tugging our light out with it.

She waves her hand toward Cal's room. "This is how you're taking care of yourself? This guy? What the hell is wrong with him?"

She looks like an angry doll. There's an obscene contrast between her beauty and the expression on her face.

"It's not usually like this, this bad. And will you please, please lower your voice?" I plead.

She clatters one of the chairs away from the table and drops into it.

"You're really something, *Wren*," she says. "Really. What was all that stuff you said about not being able to deal with the terrible things in the world? Because this looks like it's about as bad as it gets." Her face is wild with accusation.

I'd like to tell her to get away from his table, get out of his house, but I have no fire in me. I really just want Dr. Williams to get here and check on Cal.

"Seriously, Mamie, this is the last thing you need. I thought you came up here to feel better."

"I did. I am."

She shakes her head like I just don't get it.

"I'm worried about you." But she doesn't sound worried. She sounds mad.

"Well don't be."

I turn away. I can't look at her anymore.

"Does your mother know about this guy? Because I don't think you can see too clearly right now."

"You have no idea—" I start, again. But it's pointless.

"About what? That you're too afraid to come back to your real life?"

She doesn't understand. Won't. How Cal makes it worth it for me to stick around and not just drift away quietly into nothing like I was trying to do.

"You'd rather hide out up here with—" She waves her hand toward Cal's room. "This guy? He looks like a real party."

"Shut up, Meredith," I say in a low voice.

"Oh, I'm sorry. I forgot. You're *fragile*. Am I saying things you don't like? Things you want to cut up into fucking *snowflakes*?"

Angry red circles burn on each of her cheeks.

I open my mouth to defend myself, then close it. This is where I usually shut down. Tell myself it doesn't matter. But it does. Then I open it again.

"Making me read letters I'm not ready to read isn't going to fix anything. You can't just come up here, snap your fingers, and expect me to be the way you want me to be. I'm sorry my reaction to what happened—to Patrick *dying* in a car with me—doesn't fit your expectations. I'm figuring it out. It's not like they gave me a guidebook in the hospital. What else do you want me to say? I didn't know I'd feel like this. I'm sorry I didn't ask your permission before I freaked out."

She puts her face in her hands a minute. Then pulls them away. Looks at me, eyes wet and accusing. "You walked away from us. Not just me. Everyone. Emma. You didn't die in that crash, you know. And you're not the only one who got hurt last year." Her voice breaks, "We all lost Patrick."

There's no air. Darkness stole it with the light, extinguished everything. I'm trapped. Right back where I was when I got here. Caught in this terrible place where there's nothing to say that will make anything different. Better.

Something heavy shifts in me. I take a deep breath, hold it, let it slip out slowly. I can do this. Face these feelings, live through them, like Zara said, even the hard parts. I sink into a chair next to her.

"I know; I know you did; I'm sorry," I say, finally. "But I can't go back to how I was before."

As I say it, I realize it's true. I'm not waiting to return to my old self. It's like the room just got brighter.

Tears stream down her cheeks. She stares at me wide-eyed like she's never seen me before. Finally she stands, pushes away from the table.

"I don't understand you," she says, shaking her head.

She walks to the door, slips into her enormous jacket, picks up her purse and my keys.

"I need to go back."

She holds the keys out, waiting.

I don't move.

She takes one more long look at me like she's trying to figure me out.

"Wren, don't get caught up in someone else's nightmare. You don't need this."

Whatever.

"We're not the same anymore. I don't know who you are."

She's right. I say nothing.

She turns and leaves.

I sit quiet a minute at the table. Shake.

When I'm sure I can stand again, I go back to Cal's room. Knock lightly on the door.

No answer. I knock again.

"Cal? Can I come in?"

Silence. I lean on the frame. Listen. Nothing.

"Can I get you anything? Cal?"

"Get out of here," he says, his voice so close he must be just on the other side. "Your friend's right. Get out of here, will you? Go home. Leave the house unlocked for Dr. Williams."

Fucking Meredith.

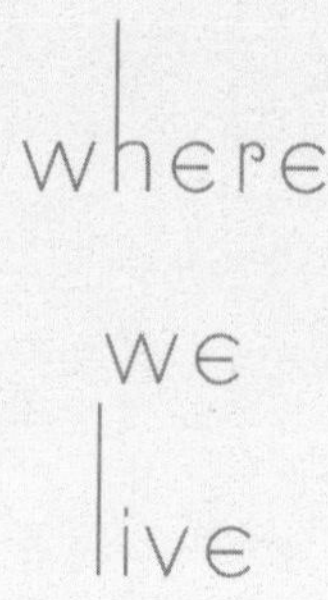

DR. WILLIAMS and a nurse I haven't seen before are at the door less than ten minutes after Meredith leaves.

I lead them back to Cal, then head out to the living room, try a quiet call to the studio. No one answers. So I wait. But I can't sit still. I pull clean sheets out of the linen closet and leave them on the hall table by his bedroom door. Then I go out to the kitchen and wash all the dishes. Check the fridge. It's pretty empty.

After what seems like forever, I hear a shower start.

Dr. Williams sets his bag on the dining room table and joins me in the kitchen.

"We meet again," he says, looking at me kindly. "How are you, Wren?"

"How's Cal?"

"I'd like to admit him, but he wants to stay put," he says. "It's his call. I can arrange to have someone out here tomorrow, but somebody needs to stay with him tonight." He stops a minute, assesses me. "He's pretty adamant that it not be you."

"We didn't fight, if that's what you're thinking," I say. "I just came over and found him like this. And I'm not going anywhere. I don't care what he says. I'm fine here. I'll stay. Sleep on the floor outside his door if I have to."

Dr. Williams nods with a little smile like I've said exactly what he wanted me to.

"I probably shouldn't talk to you about this without his permission," he says, raising a brow at me, "but I know you two are close."

My chest feels too tight and my stomach drops. It's bad news, I know it.

Dr. Williams sees I'm freaking out, because he gives my hand a little squeeze.

"It's okay."

I'm not reassured. Swallow, hard.

"I told Cal the MS is recurring too often. He's going to get progressively worse."

I think I'm going to pass out.

Dr. Williams notices.

"Deep breath." He takes me by the elbow and leads me to the couch.

"Cal didn't like the sound of that much either." Sad smile. "I admit, I said it partly to get his attention. Because, the thing is, it doesn't have to be like this for him."

He walks over to the table and opens his bag. Pulls out a chart. Cal's chart. Flips a few pages.

"There is a new treatment he's been refusing. A few new ones, actually. Possible game-changers. He could research them for himself if it would make him feel better. They're showing great results."

I nod and try to memorize what he's saying. For when I calm down a little and can actually understand it. I think he's telling me Cal's not dying. Or something.

"The new drugs could greatly decrease the number of relapses Cal has. For some people, they go away all together. He doesn't realize it now, but he's in a good position. We're at the front edge of this thing. He's young. Fit. We can do so much more than we could when his mother was ill."

He stops. Looks at me. I nod so he'll go on. I'm more calm.

"Unfortunately he has this idea that taking this step toward treatment somehow means he's sicker than he wants to think he is. Do you understand what I'm saying?"

I nod.

"But, the reality is, without it, he'll get worse. We have a chance here, to modify the course of this thing."

I nod again. The room brightens a little more. Cal has a chance.

"He let me start him on one. We'll go once its done and we're sure he's okay. He's not going to feel great tomorrow, but talk to him, if you can. Make sure he understands how important it is. It's time for him to make a commitment to taking care of himself. My PA will talk to him more about it tomorrow."

"Okay," I say. "I'll convince him."

I'll threaten him if I have to. That is, if he'll even talk to me again after this afternoon.

Dr. Williams leans forward and pats my knee. "Wren, if anyone can get through to him, I have a feeling it's probably you."

He's got to be somebody's nice dad. Either that or a saint. He squeezes my icy hand.

I take a huge breath and feel an odd relief, elation almost, like finally something might be okay. My shoulders are hiked up near my ears. I force them down, try to relax.

Cal's bedroom door opens. The nurse comes out, carrying a bundle of sheets.

"He's showered and in a fresh bed. Probably already asleep," she says to Dr. Williams. Nods at me. I smile back. I'm so thankful to her for helping him. "Where can I set these?"

I point her toward the laundry room.

Dr. Williams turns to me. "I gave him something to help him sleep. He said he hasn't been sleeping through the night. You're sure you can stay?"

"I'm not going anywhere. I'll be here if he needs anything."

"Good." He stands up. "I can tell you're up to this, Wren."

This makes me wonder if he thinks I'm not up to it and is trying to use reverse psychology on me or something.

I'm up to it.

I say it to myself a couple of times. I am. I feel strong all of a sudden. Fierce.

They leave, and I clean the rest of the house like mad, as quietly as I can. I have so much energy I'm almost frantic with it, but instead of letting it tangle me up inside, I let it out, use it, turn it into something good.

Once the kitchen's clean, I pull a few well-splattered and worn cookbooks from a small shelf next to the refrigerator. The fridge is too empty even for stone soup, but after paging through the cookbooks, I find a recipe for spice bread that someone's starred, a woman's handwriting, written *boys' favorite* in the margin. Maybe Cal's mom. I dig around until I find what I need and throw it together. The spices in the heating oven smell purposeful.

From time to time I sneak back to his room and look in. Sleeping.

I'm just about to try home again, tell them what's going on, when a car pulls into the driveway.

Cars.

The Wagoneer. Cal's Jeep.

Dad and Zara.

They come up to the house, arms full, back-lit by the moon. I run out to meet them, ridiculously happy they're here. Dad's carrying some extra clothes for me and Zara's got two heavy-looking grocery bags.

"Dr. Williams and your dad crossed paths in town, and Meredith came to the studio," Zara says when she steps in.

"We fought." I start to cry.

Dad sets everything down. Pulls me into a hug. "How's Cal?"

I shake my head, and suddenly my whole body feels weird, loose, like my bones are more elastic than solid. I can't talk a minute. It's been a rough afternoon.

He lets me out of the hug but keeps an arm wrapped around my shoulders and walks me to the couch.

Zara sets the food out in the kitchen.

"John, this is a nice house," she says, pulling things out of the bags. "We should whip ours into slightly better shape."

My dad makes a harrumphing sound.

Zara brings us all water. Sits on the other side of me. She said "our house." Weird to hear, but it feels like it might be right, okay.

"Dr. Williams came," I say, after a quick sip. "He wants me to help convince Cal to go on some new drug—"

My voice wavers. I look up at them both. A look flies between them. It's a lot of responsibility. I take a big breath. "He thinks it will make him feel better?"

Dad shoots Zara a look and squeezes my shoulders again.

"He'll listen to you, I'm sure," he says, kissing me on the top of the head. He holds me tight until I can get it a little more together.

"Well, Meredith hit the road," Zara says, patting my leg. "We tried to talk her into staying the night and leaving in the morning, but she said she'd stop along the way if she needed to. Said to tell you she'd call you soon."

Unlikely. I close my eyes. Dad keeps squeezing me.

Zara stands again. "I'm going to check on that lovely bread you have going. It smells fantastic, and was, by the way, a thoroughly solid thing to do in the face of a crisis."

I look at my hands in my lap. My cuticles are ragged, but I did something solid. I smile a second. Something solid in the face of a crisis.

"We figured you could use a few things," my dad starts, "if you're going to stay here a day or two?"

I feel an enormous rush of love for both of them. I start to cry again.

"I'm proud of you, Wren," my dad says, choking up a little himself, squeezing me. "You're proving to be a pretty sturdy person."

Damn tears. I say nothing. Don't feel very sturdy.

"So," Zara says, peering in from the kitchen, "if you don't mind, I thought I'd stay too. Tonight. Your dad and I were talking, and we thought it wouldn't be a bad idea if you had someone with you, in case you need anything."

For a split second I'm hurt. They're saying one thing, doing another. They don't trust me to be here, alone, to deal with something hard. But then it dawns on me, maybe I'm not the one they're worried about, maybe they think Cal's really that bad off, that I might need help.

I nod at Zara. I want her to stay. She slips her boots back on and walks out to the truck, comes back in with her overnight bag.

"Come on," I say, slipping out of my dad's warmth, "you can stay in Cal's parents' room."

She sets her things in the room and looks around a

minute, appreciating the larger, nicer version of the same room she stays in when she's at our place. Her place, now, too.

We go back out to my dad. He slips a book from the middle of the stack of clothes he brought.

Larkin.

Winks at me.

"Just in case you can't sleep," he says. He clears his throat again. "I read a few of these," he says, "and I know why you like him. He has the same quarrel with life that you have."

It's a simple statement but may be one of the most true things that's ever passed between my dad and me. I hold the book close.

The three of us make a light dinner from the food Zara brought, then cut into the spice bread. After we're done, I leave Zara and Dad on the couch, talking in low voices, and slip in to Cal's room.

still here

The room's cool and quiet, the moon high at the window, playing off the water, casting a velvet light. Cal opens his eyes a minute when I slip in, and the smallest smile plays at the edge of his mouth, his face less drawn, more relaxed.

"You never do what you're told."

"Too late to start now."

"Your friend was impressed."

"Sorry," I blush.

"Don't be."

He lifts an arm, the blankets, makes a place along the edge of the bed for me to slip in next to him. Warm.

"Are you hungry?" I ask, putting my hand on his heart,

feeling the warm rise and fall of his chest. "We made food. Dad and Zara are here with me."

He shakes his head. "Tired. How long was I out?"

"A couple of hours. Cal, Dr. Williams—"

He lets out a breath, opens his eyes again, takes me in, closes them.

"He talked to you."

"You have to do it, try it. He thinks—"

"I didn't think I needed it."

"You need it." I push up on an elbow so I can look at him. "Try anything he suggests. If you don't, I'm going to start midnight jogging again. Please. You need it."

He looks at me. Reaches up, pulls a lock of my hair hanging down like a bell rope.

"Okay."

"Okay? Just like that? It can't be that easy."

"You're powerfully persuasive."

He runs a warm hand down the side of my neck. A smile climbs into his eyes before they close again.

I lie there a minute and watch him sleep. Trace the length of his nose with my finger. Then I slip out of the bed as softly as possible and make a nest for myself on his couch. Wrap up in a blanket and lie there, quiet in the space between Cal and the wide night sea.

For the first time in a while I think I'm okay. Anchored. Held together. It's a feeling I tiptoe toward, careful, in case it's about to slip away, leave me dissipated in that dark blank place.

It doesn't.

It's still here.

I'm still here.

I open Larkin. Read what I can by moonlight. I skim my favorites, whispering some aloud to myself. Let the rhythm of the language lead me. I stop at "The Trees."

Last year is dead, he says, looking at the lush-topped trees released from winter's death.

Time to begin afresh.

I close the book. Lay it in my lap. Behind me, Cal's steady breath. Through the windows the ocean booms against the cliff.

An echo.

Afresh, afresh, afresh.

acknowledgments

I WROTE THIS BOOK after the sudden death of someone I loved. She was a poet, and on more than one occasion declared, *Larkin's my man.* After her death I turned to him. I'd read Larkin before, but as with all works of art, it bore up differently from a changed perspective. For a time, his poems bridged the otherwise impassable distance between us. If you haven't already read the work of Philip Larkin, his *Collected Poems* is surely on the shelf of your closest bookstore. Larkin draws a fine map and should not be missed.

Once I had a draft, a lot of people stepped in to help me make it into a book. To my friends and family: your love is an incredible verb. To my first readers: Matthea Harvey, Michael Moran, Kathleen Jesme, Stephanie Colgan, Sunita

Apte, Zoë Pellegrino, Cathy Burns, my mother, and my sisters Kelly and Bryn—your enthusiasm and encouragement kept me from stuffing the manuscript under the bed. Kelly, I'm pretty sure I can still hear your typewriter way back in 1982 clickety-clacking my puffy-handwritten words (heart-dotted *i*'s!) from Mead notebooks onto manuscript paper in the off-hours.

I'm grateful to my editor, Alexandra Cooper, for her sharp eye, finely tuned ear, and for seeing Wren so clearly and with such compassion. Working with you has been a joy. Thanks to Amy Rosenbaum, Lizzy Bromley, Justin Chanda, and the rest of the team at Simon & Schuster. To my lovely agent, Sara Crowe: endless gratitude for your cheer, your patience, and your unwavering support.

Finally, thanks to Maeve and Noel for loaning me out to all those people in my imagination and for not complaining about it too much—and Doug—you keep the boat afloat, the larder stocked, the bed soft—how about all the rest of our years?